AWAKENING THE GODS

BOOK 1 OF RISE OF THE CELTIC GODS

KRISTIN GLEESON

An Tig
Beag
Press

Published by An Tig Beag Press
Text Copyright 2021 © Kristin Gleeson
Cover design by JD Smith Designs

ISBN Paperback: 978-0-9956281-6-8

A TREASURE BEYOND WORTH

KRISTIN GLEESON

A twelfth century Irish woman washed ashore in America finds only a stranger to help her survive.

ALONG *the* FAR SHORES

KRISTIN GLEESON

To Bruce, who always heard the music and told the tales

PART I

THE WEST ASLEEP

1

SAOIRSE

I bounced down the road, my feet cooperating for a change, earbuds in, music up, trying to absorb the upbeat vibe. It was an old Planxty track and the mad pace of it was nearly working to help me forget that I was now an unemployed barista with a first class degree in English Lit from Trinity. Who knew that being late five times would end with dismissal? At a glorified cafe. A hot and hip cafe, to be fair, but a cafe nonetheless. You couldn't change that. I made myself concentrate on the neat change up of the music. Very tidy. I smiled. But then out of the corner of my eye, there they were.

Feck.

I blinked and turned my head away. But they were still there, those shadowy little figures whispering, eyes staring. On impulse, I turned to them and glared, made a face but they'd vanished. I peeked down the little laneway at the side of the pub to see if they'd gone there, but it was dark and seemingly empty. I sighed and decided to leave it. Those feckin' creatures were popping up more and more, and for the life of me, I couldn't figure what their purpose was. Imagination it was not, no matter how many times I'd tried to kid myself when it happened as a lonely girl in boarding school, but I knew I couldn't fool myself this time. It wasn't that they were threatening or scary, just feckin' annoying. Like a bunch of gossips talking about me.

I sighed and pushed the door to the pub. I could already hear the music within. The Mangle Pit was my haven, my own little island of joy and escape, where I could forget my rudderless existence and just live in the music.

I walked towards the back, weaving through the crowd of Thursday drinkers, my Doc Martens feeling the familiar stick of spilled beer. Gentrification hadn't caught up with the Mangle Pit. Behind the bar I saw Finbarr and Gregor busy pulling pints, though Gregor glanced up and gave me a flirty wink. I cocked my head and moved along towards the music source. I grinned when I saw all the usual suspects were there playing, plus a few others. I felt a little spark inside when I saw one of them was Luke. He came on occasion but he wasn't a regular. This evening he had chosen to play and I couldn't help the little thrill going through me. It meant an even better time than I'd anticipated. His playing was top shelf, but so were his looks. His blond hair caught the light as he leaned over his uilleann pipes just then and I sighed. Normally I would despise a surfer like him, but you couldn't argue with his musicianship, though if I were to be honest, I knew it wasn't just that. And it wasn't every day a surfer would find a particle of interest in playing trad music.

I closed in on the group, holding my flute case in front of my chest to negotiate the last little huddle. Declan spied me first.

"Saoirse."

He grinned and nodded, still playing his concertina. With his leg he drew up a stool beside him and I took the seat at his side. Around the small tables crowded with glasses, the various musicians winked or nodded to acknowledge my presence. They were winding up the set of jigs they'd been playing as I entered and I quickly shucked my jacket, shoving it underneath my stool, phantom little men forgotten. With a speed driven from much experience I assembled my flute and had it ready for the next set. Cormac led the session with his dancing bow very Slíabh Luachra, and the rest of us followed once he'd set the tune going. For this set he'd chosen a few newish ones and I glanced over to Luke who sat two away, to see if he was okay with them. I knew he would pick it up quick enough, but I just wanted to be sure.

He caught my glance and smiled, his startling blue eyes full of humour as always. I grinned back and nodded because I could already hear his pipes, following Cormac who sat at the other end. Luke was always discreet with his pipes, never doing the overpowering "look at me" playing that some did. Next to him, Eileen sawed away on her own fiddle, her springy curly hair flying all around her. She was nice enough, late twenties, an artist of some sort. Glass? I couldn't remember. Every finger covered in rings, bracelets banging away as she played. God would you ever give those bangles a rest, I thought. But I knew those sentiments were more of a reflection of the way she bantered with Luke every time he came. I turned away and looked at Declan, his pudgy fingers flying along the buttons of his concertina, and I was soon as lost in the music as he was. Cormac was enjoying himself as well, leaning back, eyes closed. He looked a bit like Santa with his full white beard and bushy hair.

Cormac barely paused when the set ended before he launched into the *Postman* set that he knew I loved and he looked across at me and raised his brows. Aw, the dotey creature. I smiled back and lifted my flute to my lips and sailed away on the driving beat that Patrick gave his guitar and we were all going grand.

Behind us, a few whoops cheered us on and feet were tapping as they picked up our energy and spirit. Before I knew myself I'd done it, I looked in the other direction to Luke and saw that he'd switched out the pipes for Mícheal's bouzouki and was picking out a counter tune. Jesus will you look at him, I thought, it kills me. He caught my look and I widened my eyes and he laughed, knowing what I was thinking. Eileen looked almost proud, as though he were her prodigy. I glanced away.

The night sailed on and the music pulled me in, until just before the break, when someone shouted. "Give us a song, Saoirse."

I laughed and shook my head. "Maybe later, lads."

"Go on!"

"You will!"

Cormac gave me a questioning look and I sighed, shrugging. "All right then."

There were a few shouts of appreciation and then shushings all around as I prepared myself to sing. What would it be? Something in English or Irish? I had feck all Irish, much to the disgust of my teachers, but I could sing the words of a song and had a decent idea about what they meant. I decided for English and began *My Lagan Love* on a whim. It was a song I enjoyed, not so much because it was short, though that was a plus for me if my nerves suddenly took hold, but the range also suited my voice.

The pub was silent as I sang, but soon I was lost to my surroundings, getting caught up on the words and the music in my head. My eyes were closed and I could see them there, the pair of lovers meeting up. I finished the song, opened my eyes amid the hush until a shout and whoop broke the silence and clapping ensued. A moment later the talk resumed and the pub was as loud as before. The musicians stood up without a word. Break time. Finbarr nodded over to us and disappeared out the back to fetch the sandwiches for when the musicians returned from the toilet, or smoke, or whatever amusement they decided to pursue.

I moved towards the bathrooms and Cormac caught my arm. "You're in good voice tonight, Saoirse. Lovely song."

I smiled and thanked him and let the warm feeling from his praise spread through me. He was great for encouragement, but his words were always genuine and I appreciated that. When I arrived at the bathrooms the queue was thankfully short. It was only Jilly ahead of me, the English girl who played the concertina, clad in her usual combat trousers and T-shirt. She was about my age and had been in Dublin over a year, waiting tables at a restaurant in Swords.

"Hey," she said.

I nodded. "How's things?"

She shrugs. "Oh, you know."

I nodded.

"You?" she asked.

"I got sacked today, but otherwise, grand." I don't know why the words left my mouth and the regret of them rushed through me an instant later. I barely knew the girl.

"Shit."

"Yeah, but tonight's about the music. I'll think about the rest tomorrow."

She laughed and moved on, the stall free. I sat there and thought about the tomorrow when I would have no job to go to, the "think about the rest tomorrow" girl fizzled out already. Would I ask my father for yet another loan I would never pay back? I could barely afford the hovel I lived in, the rent was due, the lease nearly at an end, and until I got another job I needed something to tide me over. But I hesitated to approach him. He made me feel uncomfortable, always lacking. Though to be fair, it might be all in my head and my own disappointment with myself. The little I knew of my father would probably be seen in his Wikipedia page. A high powered property development mogul who travelled the world. The part that, while he did this,

I'd been in a remote boarding school in Ireland would be omitted from Wikipedia, of course. I could count the Christmases we'd spent together on two fingers.

"Good luck," said Jilly as she passed by, her bathroom visit finished. I nodded and moved into a stall.

A few minutes later, I found myself heading towards the back door, deciding a breath of air amid the fuggish heat of the pub would see me right. Once outside, in the little laneway that acted as the delivery area, I leaned back against the wall and sighed. At the laneway end, near the street, I recognised Cormac laughing loudly among a group of others sucking on fags, their smoke curling up above their heads. Mícheal's skinny frame looked incongruous next to Cormac though he towered over his companion. They were fast friends of the music sort after playing together for years at this pub and others. Their musical chemistry drew many session musicians to share the tunes and the craic. The others in the group I recognised as regulars who came on Thursdays to hear the music. I toyed with the idea of going down to bum a cigarette. It seemed a day for that.

"There you are, Ginger." said a voice behind me.

I turned and saw Luke coming out the service door, the edges of his dark blond hair damp with sweat, a pint of lager in his hand. I struggled not to sigh at the sight of him and what might lie beneath his clothes. His T-shirt, flannel shirt and low-slung jeans gave me only a hint, but every girl and her mother would want to see more.

"Some would call my hair titian," I said.

"Would they now?" He came over to me and touched the long braid that was wrapped around my head. "'The twilight gleam is in her hair'," he quoted. "It's like a crown of flames."

"It's 'in her face', if you're quoting the song I sang."

I studied his expression for signs of mockery. He leaned against the wall, facing me. Even in leaning, his large frame was shouting the lithesome grace I found so attractive. He wasn't my usual type, which was the dark haired, skinny, intense musician, but for him it seemed exceptions were made by all. I looked down at my Doc Martens, purple tights, red corduroy skirt and floral shirt. I wasn't his usual type either, I was certain.

"Good session tonight," he said.

I gave him a wry look. What was he after? "It is that."

"Are you playing gigs anywhere?" he asked.

I gave him a dumbfounded look. "Ah, no, no. Are you, yourself? Sure, you must be."

He shrugged. "I've been tempted a time or two, but resisted in the end." He looked over at me and his mouth lifted on one side. "But I'd be more inclined to if I was playing gigs with you. You've got a great touch on the flute. Good voice, too."

A flush of pleasure bloomed inside me. "Sure, you must be joking. I'm only okay."

"No, there's no joke, I promise you. You've a grand voice and your rolls on the flute are first class. Where did you learn? Were you playing sessions growing up?"

I looked away. "I segued from classical," I said evasively. How to explain my childhood? Learning classical flute in boarding school and then sneaking off to try out the latest tunes I'd loaded on my iPod. It was a chance interview Martin Hayes had given on the telly years ago that had first attracted me. His thoughtful and compelling explanations of his love for traditional music, followed by his haunting and mesmerizing performances had driven me to make these tunes my own. It wasn't until I was at university that I even had the opportunity, or the courage, to play at a session.

"Well, you've a grand style."

"Thanks," I said. "Are you getting up a group, now? Is that it?"

"Maybe. I'm exploring possibilities at the moment."

"And the late nights won't get in the way of the surfing?" I asked in a teasing tone. "Or your day job?"

He raised his brows. "That is a consideration."

Shit. I'd been caught out. He would know he hadn't told me himself that he was a surfer. He took a deep drink of his lager. I eyed it disdainfully. I was a beer, stout or whiskey person myself, or at a pinch maybe tequila. But for his praise of my playing, I could forgive him.

"What do you do, anyway?" I asked.

"Something in design," he said.

"Something in design? Is that like code for it's too embarrassing to say, or too complicated to explain?"

He smiled. "Neither. Too boring. I design logos."

"Oh," I said. What do you say to that? He was right. It was boring.

"What do you do?"

I hardly heard his question because behind him, *they* appeared in all their bold glory. I'd never seen them before when I was talking with someone. Their whispers were audible and I could even make out their eyes this time, they were that close. I glanced nervously at Luke, who stared at me questioningly.

"Are you okay? You've gone pale."

I closed my eyes and straightened. When I opened them they were gone and so was the whispering. There was only a crow perched on the roof above, cawing away like it was cackling with laughter at my reaction.

I sighed and shook my head. "I'm grand."

"Come on you two," said Cormac from the group at the end of the laneway. "It's time."

2

SAOIRSE

I threw the keys on the table and placed the flute case on the floor by the wall. Gentrification hadn't caught up with this flat either. It was on the top floor of a definitely not Georgian old house that had seen better days, and swinging even a mouse would be a challenge. A small table leaned up against the sofa to mark the end of the sitting room and the beginning of the area of a wall of cupboards, sink, fridge and cooker that was the kitchen. A box room off the area stood in for the bedroom and the small toilet and stall shower was crammed in beside it.

Still, it was mine, at least until the end of the month or I could find another job quickly. I'd asked around at the pub briefly to see if they knew if anyone was hiring, but no such luck. It was early days, I told myself. I stepped over to the counter and switched on the kettle. A cup of tea would settle me down after the session.

I thought again of Luke. Would he have kissed me if we hadn't been shooed into the pub? He had certainly given me a few winks and flirtatious little flourishes on the pipes afterwards. And all during his low whistle piece he had looked at me.

I had played a piece on my own low whistle along with Cormac on the fiddle. Afterward Luke had taken my whistle, examined it, blew a few notes and leaned over and told me that he thought something was off with it. I had been surprised. I knew it wasn't perfect, but it had been all I could afford at the time. Seeing my dismay, Luke had squeezed my arm and told me he would take it and fix it sometime. And that had been it. No lingering after the session. He was out the door with a "see you lads" before we'd even begun the last piece. No parting look at me, nothing.

Now I just had to sit down, drink my tea and forget it so I didn't spend all night dissecting every detail of what was clearly just a musical flirtation. Sure, didn't it happen all the time? You get so into the music someone played and their skill that you start with your own bits, back and forth, sly and subtle or bold and brassy, however it took you. A little wink and nod at what was going on and no one hurt.

I was just pouring the tea into my mug when the buzzer went for the door. I pressed the intercom.

"Who is it?"

"Is this Saoirse Doherty?"

"Yes. Why do you want to know?"

"It's the Gardaí."

My heart pounded. What did the police want with me? I ran through all the possibilities. Sure, they couldn't be here for yelling at my boss after he fired me, or any of the minor things I may have done in the past few days. I grabbed my keys and went down to let them in.

When they entered the apartment I felt my nerves heighten even more, no "music for now" in sight, only the "saving the bad for tomorrow", or whatever bollocks I'd said earlier.

"Can we sit down?" The tall dark haired man in his early thirties asked. Beside him was a young woman, her blond hair pinned back under her peaked cap.

It was when I saw her face that I realised this was not anything to do with some imagined misdemeanour. Pity filled her eyes and softened her mouth.

I blinked but gestured to the sagging sofa. "Have a seat."

They sat down almost in unison.

"Tea?" I asked. "I just made some."

The woman glanced over at the man and he shrugged. "Since you've made it."

I took out mugs and filled them quickly, wanting to get this chat over with. Once the tea was brewed, bags sorted, I handed out the mugs and took the chair from the kitchen table and brought it round to sit on. With an expectant look I stared at them.

The man cleared his throat. "I'm Garda Murphy and this is Garda O'Connell. I'm sorry to intrude at this late hour, but I'm afraid I have bad news about your father." He paused.

"My father? What about him?"

He cleared his throat again. "I'm sorry. It seems he's been in a car accident. A serious one."

I stared at Garda Murphy, disbelieving. "Is he all right? Is he in hospital?"

"Uh, no, Miss Doherty. Saoirse. He died."

I sat frozen for a moment, staring at him and all the impossible words that he'd spoken. "Dead? But that's impossible. He's in South Africa. At least I think he is. Let me see." I reached for my phone to look at the most recent message I'd had from him.

"Yes, it was South Africa. That's where the accident occurred."

I stared at my tea, still trying to make sense of the words he'd just said. "How? When?"

"The South African authorities just notified us. Apparently it was a few hours ago. His car went off the road, crashed and went up in flames. If it's any comfort, his death would have been instantaneous."

I looked up then. "Instantaneous?"

Garda O'Connell nodded. "Yes, that's what they said. I took the call. I'm sorry for your loss." She leaned over and squeezed my hand.

"Thanks, thanks. Yes, it's good to know. Thank you for telling me." I uttered all those phrases, my Irish instinct to say those reciprocating phrases said at death, at the wakes and funerals, to replace the keening wails and shrieks.

Other thoughts flooded my mind and it all seemed a bit much. "What shall I do? Do I need to go over there and claim the body? Isn't that what you're supposed to do?"

Garda O'Connell looked at her companion. "Um, well you don't have to do that. It seems there really aren't any remains to speak of."

"Oh." No other words came into my head.

"The South African authorities will be in touch with our embassy and they'll let you know if you are required to do anything. In the meantime you can go ahead and plan his funeral."

"How? I mean there's no body."

Garda O'Connell studied her a moment. "Ask your priest."

I snorted. Priest. My experience at the convent boarding school had left me giving all of that a wave goodbye. "Sorry. I don't really have a priest. Not around here in any case."

"And your father?"

I shrugged. "I don't think so. We never really talked about it."

They both gave me a bewildered look.

"We were never really close," I said. "I was in boarding schools most of the time and he was always off travelling."

Garda Murphy nodded. I caught Garda O'Connell surveying the dingy apartment with a puzzled look. I could just imagine the debate going on in her head as she tried to figure out exactly why I was living in this hovel with a father who obviously had money.

"Call his solicitor, then," said Garda Murphy, his voice a little kinder. "I'm sure he had one. Would you know who it is?"

I nodded, relieved. "Yes, I do. I'll call him, then. Thank you."

The two of them rose and I was glad. I'd had enough. I wanted to be alone.

Garda Murphy took out a business card and handed to me. "If you need anything else from us, feel free to ring me."

I thanked him and ushered them both out.

An hour later I was out of the apartment, striding down the road. I tripped but managed to right myself. No skinned knees tonight, thankfully. It was madness to be out walking at this hour, but I couldn't help it. I needed to move and my few metres of space was not going to satisfy me. There was an all-night gym the next road over, maybe I could go there. I laughed. Who was I kidding? I'd never worked out in my life. I didn't have any gear on and I was a hopeless klutz, bound to do myself an injury.

My steps kept on and I found myself heading towards The Mangle Pit. I'd only got to the end of the next road when I saw them. They were nearly visible this time. One was taller than the rest, dark trousers and dark jackets, in an older style, standing there at the edge of a small laneway. There was no whispering. Just silence. They nodded to me as I met their eyes. I froze.

I STUFFED my earbuds more firmly in place and tried to focus on the music that came from them. It was a sweet recording of Martin Hayes and Dennis Cahill, made before the Gloaming and all of that diversification. Not that I minded the musical collaboration, but there was something fun and pure about the playing of the two of them that I really loved. The phrasing and chemistry, the diddly di di humour of some of it, the magical wonder of other bits that caught me up. But not, it seemed, so much today. Today the door was open, but I couldn't quite get inside.

I looked over at the secretary who worked busily at her desk. She caught my look.

"Not to worry. He won't be long. The phone call was unexpected but it will be brief."

I nodded and forced a smile. I decided to imagine the bow work and how Dennis matched some of the strokes with his own beat. But I still couldn't help but remember the sight of those...men? Yes, men. The night I got the news about my father's death. I'd tried to convince myself for the past week that it was just the result of shock. Nearly had when I'd attended the excuse for a funeral that was held for my father two days ago. It was all a bit rushed. An unfamiliar priest. A few strange people who presented themselves as colleagues of my father. And a few of my own friends. Nina from the cafe and the lads from the session, along with Finbarr and Gregor. Lads minus Luke. He was the invisible man, the phantom musician, appearing only when you least expected, never when you wanted.

I sighed and shifted my weight, determined to shove it behind me, away from that room of music I wanted so much to enter now. Fiddle away those men, dance a jig instead. Blow away the piper, reel and slide and slip jig into the tunes instead. Didly, diddly, dee moves and shifts, a hop and skip. Aah now.

The phone buzzed. The secretary answered and looked at me. It was time. I sighed, feeling the skip, hop and jump. The spin and whirl, fade away into the harsh fluorescent light above.

I rose and slowly walked into the solicitor's office. The only tune playing here, I thought, was money. The kind of money I hadn't encountered since boarding school. The kind of money that I'd only glimpsed on the few occasions I'd been to my father's house. The money tune played out in his suit, his hair, his furniture and his perfectly groomed face and beard. I knew from the outer office that it was a far from seedy firm, but the wide expansive space now—floor length windows overlooking the Liffey and expensive artwork took it up a notch.

"Sit down, Saoirse."

I decided against shaking his hand since none was offered. Right, so. Quick and efficient. Well I wanted this over with as quickly as possible.

"When can I get a set of keys to my father's house?"

"I'm sorry Saoirse. I didn't realise you were under the impression that this would be anything but a quick briefing on the process."

"Process?"

"The process of probating your father's will?"

I pressed my lips together and took a deep breath. "I realise that the will has to go through probate, but I assumed it was just a formality. That I could get the keys to the house. There are probably papers that you need."

"Oh I have access to the house and have retrieved the papers, no need to worry about that."

He smiled. The money smile. The solicitor with money looking after money, and I knew then there was some kind of little twist coming.

"I'm sorry, but there are few matters to clear up and establish before I can allow you access to the house."

"What matters? Is there a problem? Are you suggesting I'm not due to inherit the house?" I sat there, stunned. I knew that we weren't on the best of terms recently, but this seemed too much. Surely just because I'd called him everything I could think of when he refused to let me go to America and be a writer didn't warrant this behaviour.

"I know we weren't on the best of terms recently, but I am his daughter. Surely I can have keys to the house? Please? It's only that it would be handy out. I mean, my lease is up soon on my apartment... and well I can't stay there any longer and..."

The solicitor gave me a sympathetic look. "Oh that is unfortunate, Saoirse, but I'm afraid I can't help you there. There are some complications. Things I need to verify. I'll explain in a minute."

"But, I'm his daughter. He's dead. Surely as next of kin I'd be entitled to know the details."

He shook his head. "Of course."

I looked at him sceptically, knowing without a doubt that ethics were defined very loosely around his office when it suited.

"How long will probate take then?"

He steepled his hands in a studied manner. "It's hard to say."

"Roughly speaking, then."

He shrugged. "A few months. I can't be certain. It could easily be longer."

I rose. "Well that's that then."

"Sit down, Saoirse. There are a few things I need to explain."

"Miss Doherty."

"Pardon?"

"You can call me Miss Doherty."

He gave me an indulgent smile. "Yes, well. That's precisely it, my dear. I have to explain to you at this point that you are in fact not really a Doherty. At least by birth. You were officially adopted by Seamus Doherty at birth. You are in fact..." he leaned forward and picked up a piece of paper. "Oh. Well the details of your birth parents are vague."

I sat down hard. "Magdalen Laundries?" I said, in a feeble attempt at humour. It was all too surreal.

The solicitor frowned. "There's no reason to believe that. Your records just say your parents were Irish. The mother is named, but it's indecipherable."

I nodded. What could I do with that? In some ways, I felt relief that the cold man I'd thought of my father all these years wasn't really my father. It was strange that the grief that I felt was for the mother I'd imagined died giving birth to me. His wife. The fact that she had only been a vague photo at the back of a shelf and entire imaginary landscape in my own mind seemed a minor detail. I blinked back the tears that suddenly filled my eyes.

"What does that mean now? Does it affect the will?" I finally asked.

"Well not ultimately. I have to verify the adoption, the birth, those kinds of things. I'd been under the impression they were all in order, but, well, I just want to be certain. That's all I can say for now, and until then, well, I'm afraid you'll have to wait on the house."

And that was that.

3

SAOIRSE

I stared at the ringing phone. The number that flashed up was unfamiliar. Was it the solicitor, or rather his secretary? I didn't think so. I answered it with trepidation.

"Hello?"

"Saoirse?"

"Yes." I didn't recognise the female voice that spoke. It was deep and soothing and, without meaning to, I relaxed.

"Saoirse, I'm your grandmother."

"I don't have a grandmother," I said, on my guard again. "At least not a living one."

"Ah, but you do," said the woman. "And I'm her."

A dozen thoughts raced through my head. "Sorry now, but is this some sort of joke?"

"Not at all, sweetheart."

"I don't understand."

"I know. I only just heard from your father's solicitor about his death and was able to get your contact information."

"I still don't understand."

"Of course you don't. Would you mind if we just meet up and I can explain it all?"

I thought for a moment. "Are you my grandmother by blood? Was your child my real mother or father? Is that it? My father, well my adoptive father, knew my parents and you?"

"Look, if you just meet with me I'll explain it all then."

I bit my lip. The woman uttered another plea and maybe it was her voice, the curiosity but I couldn't help it in the end.

"Okay."

ROASTED BEANS SCENTED the air and tantalised, a sensation undimmed the recent loss of my job grinding, brewing and serving it. The flavour filled my mouth even before I drank it, the waitress only now putting on the finishing touches. She was good. Her little flourishes a nuanced performance any theatre goer would praise and I couldn't ever hope to achieve. A chorus girl admiring a star. I took up the cup when she'd finished and I'd paid and turned to search the tables until I spied the woman I'd come to meet. It didn't take me long. She was so out of place I could barely suppress the laugh that rose to my throat. There were no wellies in sight, but there was no mistaking where she lived. From her long grey hair that was only just held in place by the braid down her back, to the old mud stained corduroy trousers, worn green cardigan and serviceable shoes, she showed none of the trends on display in the rest of the cafe.

She looked up at that moment and caught my eye. From this distance her large eyes were kind and the smiling mouth wide and generous. I nodded and made my way over to her, a little flutter of nerves rising up.

When I reached the table I saw she was nursing a cup of tea. I unloaded my cloth bag that acted as my purse and carryall onto the chair next to her.

"Hello, Saoirse," she said.

I nodded again." Hello." I noticed she had no food in front of her. "Do you want anything?"

She shook her head. "No, I'm fine. You suit yourself."

I took my seat. The chatter that surrounded us brought the noise level up to just below unbearable. I leaned forward, cupping my mug. "So, you say you're my grandmother."

The woman nodded. "I am. It's a long story. Your real mother died when you were young, your father, my son, gone off who knows where, and before I could come and arrange anything, you were taken and put into care. I didn't know where you were until your adoptive father's solicitor got in touch with me the other day." She beamed at me. "And now I've found you, at last."

I looked at her, dumbfounded. However brief her words, they were filled with so much information it was overwhelming.

"Jesus," was all I could manage. I took a sip of my coffee and it scalded my throat. I coughed and put the mug down and stared at the hot liquid. "Jesus."

She patted my hand. "I know it's a lot to take in, especially with the recent shock of your father's death on top of it. Seamus Doherty's death, I mean. Not your real father."

I raised my head and stared into her grey eyes. They were nothing like my own green ones, but I thought I could trace a bit of a resemblance in the shape of the face. "My real father, is he still alive?"

My grandmother nodded. "Yes, but I haven't seen him in a good while. I'm not certain where he is at the moment."

Questions suddenly crowded my head. "What does he do? Where does he live?"

My grandmother shrugged. "A lot of things. He has his fingers in many pots, so," she said with a cryptic smile. "I haven't a clue where he is at the moment, as I said."

I could hear the hint of a Cork accent that hadn't been so present before. "Many pots? An entrepreneur?" I asked.

She laughed. "You could say that."

I paused a moment to take in what she'd just told me. "Where are you living?" I asked.

"Near Ballyvourney, in Cork. I have a small dairy farm there."

I frowned. "You farm?" I paused and decided to ask the next question that had been in the back of my mind. "Is my grandfather there with you?"

"No husband, no. Just me. I have some labourers who help when I need it."

"Were you ever married?"

"There was never a man in the picture," she said.

I nodded, not wanting to pry any more than that, but I could imagine a single woman, pregnant back then. A difficult thing. I wondered how she'd managed in an Ireland of that time.

"You have no other family besides your son?"

She hesitated. "My family are everywhere, you could say. I've lived so long in on that farm now that I feel like I'm everyone's grandmother."

"But you are my grandmother, right? I mean truthfully."

She squeezed my hand. "I am."

I still had my doubts. It just seemed all a bit too... something. "And what should I call you, then?" I asked lightly. I didn't really think I needed to know because I wasn't certain that we'd ever be meeting again.

"Well, most everyone calls me Anna or Áine. But why don't you call me Nan. That covers it all, I suppose."

"Oh, right. Nan."

She smiled brightly. "Now that we have that out of the way, I want to ask you a question."

"Can I ask you a few more questions myself, first?"

"Of course."

"My mother. What was she like?"

Nan gazed out the window for a moment before she turned back to me. "She was beautiful, like you. But I'm sorry, I can't tell you much more than that."

I nodded slowly. "And my father? What's he like? Besides having a finger in many pots?"

Nan laughed. "Well, he's bigger than life, has all the daring and cunning of the most dangerous warrior and he can charm any woman within seconds."

I gave her a puzzled look. The description was so strange in itself, being at once so impossible yet vague that it gave little that was tangible. But the words she'd used left me even more confused. Who describes a person as a warrior? This wasn't some medieval saga or Fenian cycle. Had she spent too much time watching *Game of Thrones*?

"I mean, what does he look like? Is he dark or fair? Does he look anything like me?"

"There is no doubt that he's your father. He's fair, but not with your hair colour. And such wonderful hair colour it is." She raised her hand and touched the braid that was wound around my head as usual. "You have his height and grace," she added. "But there's plenty of time for that. At least I hope so."

Still vague enough, but I realised that I would have to be satisfied with that for now. I nodded.

"The purpose of this meeting, well besides explaining our relationship, was to ask you if you would consider coming to visit."

"Visit?"

"Yes. It would be a chance to get to know each other. To try and build a relationship. I would love to have my granddaughter in my life."

I felt a pang at her last words. It was all so overwhelming, though. I felt I needed time. But the continued lack of job, the looming eviction from my flat and the mounting bills, meant that time wasn't really on my side. I regarded the woman, my grandmother who sat before me. What harm could it do to visit her for a month or so? If I didn't like it I could return to Dublin, maybe kip on friends' sofas until I got myself sorted. I pushed away the fact that those sofas were few and far between.

"Oh, right." I shrugged. "Grand."

4

SMITHY

Smithy threw his hammer across the yard, cursing loudly. He sighed, dropped the tongs on the bench, flipped up his safety glasses and walked over to retrieve the hammer from the ground, just outside the stone shed, where it had landed. It was a stupid thing to have done in so many ways. The damp hung in the April air like a wet blanket, but he was still hot from the heat of the forge. He lifted a muscular arm and wiped his brow on the sleeve of his T-shirt. Sweat blotted, he went back to his anvil, picked up the tongs that held the red hot blade and tried again. He banged for a short while and tried to get lost in the work. Maybe if he didn't think about trying to get the magic going it would flow from him. But there was nothing. He took a deep breath and cast words to create the spell that would drag it from him. The words came but that was all. He held up the blade. It was well shaped, folded perfectly and would please any craftsman or collector, but nothing more. He could feel no buzz, no hum or spin, none of the elements he would be hard pressed to describe that marked it as a magic blade, regardless of its small size. With resignation he plunged it in the water, knowing he would get no further with it today and if he was to be truthful, any other day. He had to face it once again. He no longer had the magic. No matter what Anu said or anyone else, he didn't have it and never would. He'd lost the magic long ago. He could fight battles and even acknowledged to himself that he wouldn't refuse to fight when the time came, as it was surely coming, but he would be no more than a warrior who would rely on the ordinary capability of weapons, whether he'd fashioned them or not.

Sighing, he put down his tools on the nearby bench, removed his safety glasses and scattered the coals of the furnace so the heat would dissipate. It was no use, really. He looked around the limewashed shed that served as his forge and surveyed the clutter of his tools and failed efforts. He had the makings of enough swords and knives to outfit a small band of warriors. Battalion? Troop? Isn't that what they called it nowadays? He tried to comfort himself with the fact that each sword and knife would serve credibly to anyone who chose to wield one. But of course no one used such weapons now, except actors. He smiled grimly. And re-enactors. He was half tempted to gather up all these failures and bury them in the field. But he knew he wouldn't.

With one last glance around to ensure that everything was safe, Smithy exited the shed, shut the door and clicked the padlock shut. It was late enough. He would fix a bite to eat. When he got inside his small kitchen, a rundown appendage to the original one that now served as a sitting room come most everything else room, he found he wasn't that hungry. He eyed the nearly full bottle of Powers whiskey that beckoned him from the shelf above the cramped table and opted for a bit of the *uisce beatha*. He pulled it down from the shelf, grabbed a glass and sat at the table. He poured a generous amount and drank deeply, the fiery liquid sliding down his throat. An appreciative sigh escaped him. A good choice, so, he thought.

He sat there, slowly enjoying his drink, his mind bent on nothing but savouring its taste. It was an enjoyment that lasted perhaps five or ten minutes before the niggling worry and doubts crept back inside. Feck it, he told himself, angrily. He hadn't come back here all those years ago for this. He got up, shoved the whiskey bottle back on the shelf and went to the fridge to look for something to eat.

SMITHY OPENED the door to the pub and knew at once he'd made the right decision. It was as hot as his forge at the moment, but he didn't mind. The music was loud and someone was off key, but they were all playing with enthusiasm. It wasn't a serious, top drawer session, but a bawdy, brash group who liked their pints and the craic. He headed over to the bar first and ordered a Murphy's. He could nurse that for the better part of the night, a choice made not in part because he'd rode his motorbike down to the village, but also he didn't want to make a fist flying donkey of himself. The mood he'd been in earlier had been warning enough.

Pint in hand, he moved over to the tables where the musicians sat along with the hangers on who maybe enjoyed the banter a little more than the music, but were wholehearted nonetheless in their foot tapping and bouncing. He spied Seanie banging away on his banjo and Eamon on his accordion, the sweat pouring down the both of them as if they were doing the marathon. Others were ranged around playing guitar, flutes, whistles, and fiddles. There were even a few god awful bodhran players, hammering away with gusto on the stretched skins, as if they were preparing for some Indian war. Still, he wasn't here for finesse, he was here to drown out his thoughts.

He took a proffered stool, sat down and pulled out his fiddle.

It was old and battered and had an indifferent tone, but he was accustomed to it and now liked it. It was different, it was comforting in its modern pitch and it wasn't metal. Though he did make whistles on the rare occasion he found himself persuaded by a very talented player who understood the quality of his craft and begged him to make him a low whistle or even a flute, he would never willingly play anything wind or metal. He couldn't explain it to anyone, let alone himself, except for the plain and simple fact that he wouldn't do it.

He rosined his bow, tested the strings, and turned a few pegs, struggling to hear over the din of the music to tune the fiddle. Finally, he tucked the instrument under his chin and ran the bow along the strings. After a few little tweaks he was satisfied. Tuning his ear in again to the music, he recognised the piece and began to play, tapping his foot automatically to keep the time. It was one of the Kerry jig sets played in the style of a Ceilí band. He could hardly hear himself play for the din of the pub and the music, but that was grand. He played along, relaxed, stopping between tunes to chat with Jerh Connell next to him between the sets, each of them shouting towards respective ears.

About an hour later and they were all ready for a break, Smithy included. He laid his fiddle down in its case which rested at his feet and rose. Would he head outside for a smoke? He looked around and decided that was his best bet, for the din was still loud and he would have no decent bit of banter in here. He made his way through the crowd towards the front door and opened it, welcoming the cool air that hit him as he stepped outside. There were already several standing outside, smoking and chatting with glass in hand. He nodded at a few he recognised and moved over towards them. Someone caught his arm and he turned to see old Tom Pat Paddy.

"Smithy," said Tom Pat Paddy.

"How are you keeping, Tom?"

"Grand, grand. Anything strange?"

Smithy shook his head. He had no news that this old farmer would understand. "You? How's Mary? She still going to those yoga classes at the hall?"

Tom scratched his grey stubble and grinned. "That finished. She's moved onto ceramics, so."

"They're doing that now?"

Tom shook his head. "Over to Kenmare, some woman does it. All I know is suddenly we've got more vases than space and never a cut flower in the house."

"Ah, but at least it isn't garden gnomes."

Tom raised his brows. "They might be good for scaring crows, though."

Smithy laughed and pulled out a cigarette, offering the pack first to Tom, though he knew he didn't smoke. The expected refusal given, Smithy pulled out one and lit it. He didn't do it often, but he felt he deserved it tonight after the day he'd had. After the week he'd had. And if he were to be honest, the months, years and decades he'd had, but he was here to forget all that. He took a deep drag of the cigarette and blew out the smoke a moment later.

"I wanted a word with you about something," said Tom, his craggy face a little sheepish. He put his hands in his battered jacket pockets and shuffled nervously. Smithy was instantly curious. This crafty old man was great for an old banter and a good joke, but anything more required a bit of care.

"No bother. What is it?"

"Well, you see now, you know Peadar Sullivan over my way?" He paused, waiting for Smithy's nod and he gave it. "Well he has this cockerel. Have ye heard about his cockerel?"

Smithy narrowed his eyes. "I might have."

"Well if you haven't then you must be the only one. I can hear the feckin' thing crowing morning, noon and night."

Smithy laughed. "Fair point. What about it?"

Tom cleared his voice. "Myself and Seanie," he paused looking around, "we thought we might have a bit of fun, like. You know. Stir it up a bit with him."

"I see," said Smithy in a tone he hoped wasn't too encouraging.

Tom nodded and continued. "It's only a bit of fun, and if you can't do it, well it's no bother."

"What exactly do you want me to do?"

"Make a cockerel. You know, one of those weather vane things. And instead of the arrow below the cockerel, pointing the directions, can you put the arrow through the cockerel?"

"You want me to make a cockerel weathervane."

"Yes. You know, in metal."

"Fashion it in my forge."

Tom nodded. "It's what you do, isn't it? Make things in metal? Like gates and things? Well instead of a gate, this would be a small biteen of a thing, just a little weather vane."

Smithy gave him a look. "I don't ordinarily do these kinds of pieces."

"But it won't be much. I can get you a picture of a weather vane if you like."

Smithy knew that Tom had no idea what went into creating anything at a forge, let alone a weather vane. The question for Smithy was if he would find the job interesting. He wouldn't even dignify this request with the word commission because he knew that Tom had no idea the cost involved with a project like this that he was suggesting for a biteen of "fun". He took a drag on his cigarette and blew out the smoke, thoughtfully.

"And where would you be using this...weather vane?" he asked, not sure he wanted to know. "It wouldn't be for on top of your shed, or your house, would it?"

"Ah, well it may end up there, of course."

"Of course," said Smithy dryly. He sighed. "Right, fine. I'll do it. But I can't promise when it will be finished. I have a few other things on at the moment."

Tom frowned. "Oh, right. No bother. But if you could get to it at your earliest convenience..." he pronounced the last phrase carefully.

Smithy snorted. "Of course. My earliest convenience."

Tom grinned and squeezed Smithy's arm. "Good man yourself."

He nodded to Smithy and rejoined his group over at the edge of the building. Smithy was just turning to go back into the pub when he heard a voice.

"*Dhia's Muire dhuit.*"

Smithy turned and frowned when he spied the dark haired woman. "And exactly which god and Mary do you mean, Maura the Rookery?" he asked in a low mocking tone. Mocking because he knew what a mockery this whole exchange was.

"What do you mean?" asked Maura. The mischievous grin on her face belied the innocence of her question.

"God and Mary be with you, too," he replied, his brows raised.

She laughed. "Ah, don't be like that, Smithy," she said, emphasising his name the way he'd done hers. "It was only a bit of fun. I meant no harm."

"That remains to be seen," said Smithy. "What exactly do you want?"

"Ooooh. Straight to the point. I'm hurt you don't want a bit of a catch up first. It has been a while."

"Not long enough for me."

Maura rolled her eyes and laughed. "You don't mean that, really. I know. Why, you used to thrive on the very meaning of my existence."

Smithy narrowed his eyes. "Stop the banter, Maura, and get on with it. I've no patience for you."

Maura pulled her face into an offended expression. "Well, and I'm only having an innocent conversation. No need for rudeness." She pulled a cigarette out and lit it. The cigarette was one she'd obviously rolled previously and now, smelling it as the smoke wafted from her lips, contained a scent that seemed laden with tar and death. "It's Anu," she said finally after a few drags. "She wants to see you."

Smithy shrugged. "So?"

Maura snorted. "So, she wants to see you."

"Good for her. I don't want to see her."

Maura studied him and then gave a toss of her head. "Well, I've delivered my message. Don't say I didn't warn you. Things are afoot. Wouldn't it be better to find out what they are? They do say forewarned is forearmed."

"And what things are they, Maura? Or are you just trying to stir things up as usual?"

Maura cocked her head. "Well that's for you to decide." She turned around and walked into the night, a trail of smoke in her wake.

5

SAOIRSE

I stepped down from the bus and looked around me. The traffic passed by busily on its way to Kerry, I supposed, since there was little else besides a row of houses, a few shops, a carpark and a post office that gave evidence to a village. Very "Ballyrural", but still there was something about it I found...something.

I pulled my suitcase off to the side and prepared to wait. To my horror whispering greeted my ears but when I turned to look behind me there wasn't anything there. I breathed a sigh of relief. This time obviously, it was just my imagination. I was tense and excited about this journey and what would be at the end of it. Sure, that was it. I hadn't seen or heard from those... men, people, for a week at least and I hoped I would leave them in Dublin.

When I'd travelled down here the train journey had passed by at an alarming rate, my music unable to calm the nervousness I'd felt about this woman who claimed to be my nan, a thought that still felt strange. The "who was she, why now really, who the feck could believe all that'd happened" thoughts streamed through my mind.

Once in Cork, I'd made my way to the bus station, half convinced that I should just turn around and head back to Dublin and the world I knew. But the bus was right there when I arrived and so it seemed fated, destined and all the other "meant to be" sayings, so I climbed on. Soon the bus was lumbering out of the city and onto the main artery, with the cityscape giving away all too quickly to the rural countryside. The thought stream resumed and my implied sophistication of a boarding school life followed by university seemed all too remote in the face of visiting a strange woman at a strange house in a community I'd never been to. Any feelings that it was a happy opportunity that I'd thought in Dublin now felt like a stupid feckin' notion of a right eejit.

"Saoirse."

I turned towards the carpark to see the aforementioned person walking towards me, clad in a bulky wool pullover, wool skirt and wellies. The thick grey braid she wore was in its usual dishevelled state. She gave me a wide smile and a nod. I found myself nodding back, not knowing how to greet this woman who said she was my grandmother. She solved the problem for me by enfolding me in her arms and giving me a solid hug. Tentatively, I lifted my arms and placed them around her, aware of her very capacious breasts that seemed without any kind of support at the moment. The hug was motherly, warm and deeply reassuring.

She pulled back from me and smiled again. "You're almost home, now. Welcome."

"Thanks," I said, words still deserting me.

She took my case, bundled me into the aged SUV she had and we were on our way.

"Is it far?" I asked after a short while, just to make conversation.

"No, not at all. It's just along the road a little."

I nodded, uncertain what to make of that vague measurement. A little could be as long as a piece of string, I somehow felt. That piece of string seemed to endlessly unspool as we followed the road which kept winding along, past cow- and sheep-dotted fields and scattered houses. Finally, we turned right, and the road wound upward, in a series of bends, until it eventually levelled out. To the left sprawled an old stone house with a yard and several stone sheds. In the front stood several very tall fir trees, their boughs covered in clumps of what appeared to be nests.

"What's in those trees?" I asked.

"Crow's nests."

I turned to look again and I could see huge numbers of crows circling and cawing above the trees. A murder of crows, I suddenly thought. I looked away, uneasy.

We made our way along the road that became more a boreen than a road and had shrubby tree filled ditches rising on either side. We passed a few more farm houses before we pulled into a small yard in front of a small white farmhouse, its walls rendered smooth. Beyond the stone wall that marked the end of the yard was a large open field that sloped down to a valley then rose up again to a hill opposite. The sun poured in over the field. It was as though we'd entered a different world after the semi-dark road.

The thought echoed in my head when we got out of the car, the air pungent with slurry spreading and cow dung. I paused a minute, taking it all in. The sense that I had left my own world and entered another remained with me.

After a silent tug on my sleeve, my grandmother ushered me inside. The house was very simple and small with a small entry way that had a door on either side of it. My grandmother entered the door on the left and I followed, towing my case behind me. I stopped almost immediately, too stunned to go much further. It was as if I'd somehow stumbled into a heritage park. Limewashed stone walls, flagstone floor and a huge fireplace, complete with working crane, greeted me. My grandmother headed over there, picked up a poker from the side and gave some of the turf a little shove around, before taking a padded cloth and swinging the arm that held the kettle and pulling it off.

My grandmother nodded to the large settle against the wall opposite. "Take off your jacket and sit yourself down. I'll just make some tea. You must be hungry too, after your journey. I've got some bread and stew here for you."

Wordlessly I walked around the small deal table and two chairs, over to the settle and perched on the end. After a moment I unzipped my grey cord jacket and after a brief glance at my Doc Martens to assure myself I hadn't slipped back in time I looked back over to my grandmother.

She handed me a mug. Modern. Normal. A cuppa anyone would have anywhere in Ireland. I stared down at the tea and took the familiar comfort it offered. I took a large sip. Perfect. Sitting at the table now, my grandmother nursed her own mug. It took me a moment to realise it wasn't tea, but milk.

"Don't you drink tea?" I asked.

"Milk is my drink, she said. "And sometimes water."

I nodded as if I understood but my unease returned unbidden. I tried to shoo it away, but it wouldn't listen. I glanced across at the little doors that closed off the stairs to the rooms above. Who knew what lay beyond those stairs? I could only imagine. And if it came to it, perhaps I didn't want to imagine.

IT WAS LATER, after we consumed a lovely and warming stew that did much in shoving the unease into a dark corner, that my grandmother took me up the stairs to my bedroom. I had to bend my head to go through the door to my room, which was at the other gable end, just off of the little corridor. A bed covered in a knitted blanket and coverlet stood against one wall, with a small rag rug on the floor in front of the bed. Against the chimney wall was a press, wash stand and chair. A single window provided the only light. It appeared the heritage park extended to my bedroom. I sat down on the bed and sighed after my grandmother left, the notion of sleeping becoming a scenario that wasn't particularly appealing. I opted for a book half-read on my tablet. Better to escape into a world I understood and knew wasn't real.

A WATERY SUN greeted me the next morning when I pulled back the curtains from my window and opened it. It was a mild enough day that held promise. Outside, the huge ash tree still lay bare, but I could see the buds of leaves on the branches. The small yard was below and my grandmother's little car was parked there where she'd left it the day before. Through the trees of the ditch that lined the border to the next field I could just about make out some cows. I looked at the sun again and tried to make out the time of day, but it left me clueless except that to guess it was still probably morning. I went over to the little chair I'd put beside my bed the night before and picked up my phone. Nine o'clock. I looked back at the bed, its cosy nest drawing me, and resisted its lure. No, it was best that I make an effort.

A while later I went downstairs and was relieved to see my grandmother seated at the small deal table, a filled bowl in front of her.

"Saoirse, *Dhía dhuit.*"

I nodded. "Good morning."

"Ar chodail tú go maith?"

I reddened. "Uh, sorry, I don't understand. Um, *ní thuigim*?" I thought those were the words for I don't understand.

My grandmother raised her brows. "No?"

I shook my head. "Sorry, my Irish is dismal. I only have *cúpla focail.*"

My grandmother frowned and sighed. "We'll have to do something about that." She paused. "I asked you if you had a good night."

I brightened. "Oh, I did. Grand. Best I've slept in a while."

My grandmother nodded and gave a pleased smile. "Good. Now, will you have some porridge? Or there's some bread. Or both if you prefer. I have some blackcurrant jam and honey as well."

I gave her bowl of what I realised was porridge a dubious look. I hadn't had porridge since boarding school. I saw there was also a plate of bread slices. Beside it were earthenware pots of butter, jam and honey. My stomach grumbled.

"Maybe I'll start with the bread and see how I get on from there," I said.

I helped myself to the bread, grabbed a knife and began to spread honey on it. It spread beautifully and looked heavenly. I loved honey. I took a big bite of the bread. The bread was divine and the honey, well, I'd never tasted honey like it.

"Oh this is fabulous," I said. "Is the honey local?"

My grandmother gave me a wry smile. "Yes, very. It's from here."

"You have hives?" I don't know why I found this so amazing.

"Of course. Many of us have hives around here. I'll show them to you later, if you like. In fact, I was thinking of giving you a small tour of the farm after you've finished eating."

"You don't have to do the milking or anything?"

My grandmother laughed. "No, the milking was done some time ago. It'll be a while before the next one."

"Oh, of course. That was stupid of me. The milking would have been done earlier."

My grandmother shrugged. "Not to worry. You'll soon get to know what goes on around here."

I PEERED inside the milking shed, blinking at the dim light. Light poured in from a small window at the back, but other than the door where I stood there was no other source of light. Still, despite the limited illumination, I saw that there were few stalls, perhaps eight at most. They looked very basic, with little modern equipment in evidence.

"How many dairy cows do you have?"

"Ten," said my grandmother.

I looked at her. "Ten?" That didn't sound like much.

"I have some dry cows as well. About forty in all."

I knew nothing about farming, really, so I just nodded doubtfully.

She smiled at me. "It's enough for me. My needs are simple."

I looked away, uncomfortable because it seemed as though she'd read my thoughts.

"Come," she said, taking my hand. "I'll show you the hives."

I followed her down the ramp and away from the shed, passing by a stone enclosure that I realised was a piggery. Inside was a large pig. Sow? It wasn't until it turned slightly sideways that I saw the teats hanging down and felt a little pride that I had guessed correctly. We crossed the yard. This yard was bigger than the one my room faced, its concrete worn and cracked from age and use. It was immaculate, though. Swept and clear of the farmyard detritus I'd noticed in a few of the farmyards on my journey here. I stepped through a small gate and onto a field, my Doc Martens squelching against the wet grass.

The field dropped away on a slope and at the bottom I could see a row of hives, or what looked to be hives. As we approached them I saw that they weren't the usual kind of hives I'd expected. Instead of boxes, they were the dome shaped old fashioned sort, but instead of straw, or whatever it was that they were usually comprised of, the domes were thatched with grass and underneath, briars, stripped of their thorns, were coiled.

"Isn't that a different way to construct hives?" I said.

My grandmother smiled. "Yes, I made them in more of a traditional manner."

I raised my brows but said nothing because that was precisely what I knew about beekeeping.

My grandmother grinned at me, a look so incongruous it startled a laugh from me. She was so unexpected. As if to prove my thoughts, she turned and began to amble around the hives, murmuring, humming and even singing a little while I watched, fascinated.

A while later, she looked up and straightened. "Now, so. They'll be cutting silage today in the far fields and they'll be needing feeding later, so I must get on. Feel free to wander around, if you like, but don't go into the field next door. The bull's in there and you wouldn't care to meet him, I think."

"I would not," I said and grinned. I glanced around and nodded. I had no intention of clinging to her all the day, just because it was all so new and strange. "I will go for a walk, I think. Just a little one, to get the idea of the area."

"Good notion."

I nodded and paused, uncertain how to bid her farewell. In the end I just turned and headed up the field to the road, conscious of her eyes on me. I reached the road and looked back down the field for my grandmother, to give a wave so she knew where I'd gone, but I could only see the distant shapes of the hives and the ditch and few trees beyond. I shrugged and after a few seconds decided to head down the road, back towards the house with all the crows. I was curious about it.

The cows were still in the field to my right as I passed by and I wondered if they were the dry cows that my grandmother had mentioned earlier. I peered at them closely, but all I could see was that there wasn't an udder in sight. Not a rural bone in my body, really, I thought. Any culchie had long ago been bred out of me.

I heard the crows before I saw them, perched in the branches of the fir trees that towered over the house next to them. Caw and caw again. The sound echoed through my head. I studied them, several perched on the high branches of the fir trees, squawking at each other like gossips. There was a rhythm and beat nearly, so. A just beyond reach tune that seemed to speak to me. I stilled, trying to hear it, but then three of them flew down to the grass at that moment and stalked around, eyeing me balefully. *"Where shall we gang and dine the day?"* I thought, remembering the lyrics from the Scots folk song, *The Twa' Corbies.* I stared at the most aggressive looking one and then I swear it winked at me. I cocked my head, wondering for a moment if I'd imagined it. A dog barked. I looked down and saw it approach and sniff at my feet. He continued to sniff as I made some soft soothing sounds and hoped that it wasn't mistaking me for some errant cow, sheep, or a piece of meat. Some of the farm dogs, I knew from my grandmother, were bred to work the farm and not always given to affectionate and friendly interactions with strangers.

"Don't worry, he's grand," said a voice.

I raised my head and saw a woman heading towards me from the direction of the house and trees, dressed as black as the crows with hair and eyes to match, creating an effect both striking and compelling.

"Thanks," I said, feeling her intense gaze. "I wasn't sure. Is he yours?"

"She. And yes. She belongs here, though she loves to visit the neighbours down the road."

"Do they have dogs?"

"They do, but it's more the scraps that get left out that draws her. She often as not beats the others to the best ones."

I looked down at the dog cautiously. Any dog with that much fight in her needed to be treated warily.

The woman laughed. "Ah, but she's got no harm in her, really. Just when it comes to food."

I gave the woman a weak smile and nodded. "Is this your house?"

"Oh, sorry, now. I'm Maura. And yes, this is my house." Her voice was warm and friendly.

"Saoirse. I'm staying with my grandmother down the road, there. I just arrived yesterday."

"You mean, Anna?"

I nodded.

"Isn't that grand. I'm sure she's delighted to have you. You've not been before, though, have you?"

"No. I'm only new to her, really. I only met her recently."

"Mmm," said Maura. "I had heard something of it."

At that moment a crow landed on her shoulder and cawed softly. I watched her curiously as she turned and smiled at it.

"Sorry," she said. "He's somewhat tamed. He was injured as a chick and I tended him."

"I see. How lovely."

Maura grinned. "It is." She paused. "Look, I'd invite you in for a cup of tea but I'm off out. We'll do it another time, will we?"

"Of course. That would be good."

"In the meantime, if you're out exploring, you would do well to head up the other direction. You'll get some fab views and if you walk far enough you'll see the holy well and St Gobnait's shrine. Eventually you'll come to the village."

"St Gobnait? I don't think I've heard of her."

"If you're to live around here, you must get to know about St Gobnait. She's the local patron saint. Also patron saint of bees."

"Bees? Is that why so many people have hives around here? My grandmother was mentioning it only this morning."

"Did she? Well, it might be the reason. Who's to say?"

"I suppose different things motivate people. Who can resist honey, anyway?"

Maura smiled. "True enough."

I collected myself, knowing that I didn't want to hold her up. I raised my hand. "I'll let you be off then. Thanks for the tip. It's much appreciated. It sounds perfect."

"No bother," she said. "No bother at all."

6

SAOIRSE

I walked down the steep winding road. Trees rose up along with higher ditches, creating a little shelter from the wet misty rain that had managed to soak through my thin dark jacket and the T-shirt underneath to my skin. My Doc Martens had preserved my feet for the most part, though I could now feel a little bit of damp on the toes of the thick tights I wore under my fuchsia plaid skirt. My hair was wet as well, and for once I wished I had the one hoodie I owned.

It had started out fine enough, but it seemed as soon as I swung down from the upper road to the lower one leading towards the village the mist had crept in, getting heavier and heavier, until it had become an outright rain. Very soon too, any shelter from trees or shrub lined ditches had disappeared as the road rose and fell, completely open to the fields around, except for the very low ditches on either side. The limited view I had of the landscape around me was lovely, and I knew on a different day I would have slowed down to appreciate it more. But my sole aim had changed its focus to one of finding a cafe where I could shelter until it improved.

A short while later I saw heritage signs to my left. One had said *tobar* which I knew meant "well" in Irish and another that I felt indicated St Gobnait's shrine and cemetery. I paused, my curiosity aroused. I may as well have a look. Sure, I couldn't get much wetter.

I opted for the well first, since that had the stronger draw for me. I walked up the path and saw a large pollarded tree with loads of clouties and tokens hung on branches and scattered at the tree's foot. Below the tree was the well, its entrance outlined in stone. Above it and beside it were mugs and cups for drinking. Light shone down on the well from the gap in the trees and I could see the glint of coins at its bottom. The silence cloaked me and I withdrew into its world. Apart. Separate.

I squatted beside the well and let the peace settle over me. Music of no distinguishable pattern or rhythm drifted about faintly, difficult to pinpoint. I shut my eyes and tried to let it just be. The tree rustled overhead, shushing the air and adding its own support to the music. I leaned over and scooped up a handful of the water and drank. It was cold and tasted pure. Would I say a prayer? It seemed like I should, but I had not one in my head. I had only a vague memory of my first communion and my confirmation, but it was too hazy to be a statement of any commitment on my part. I saw the rosaries and other religious items strewn around the well. It was a holy place, if only for those items, but it somehow felt more. I scooped another handful of water, drank deeply and then stood. On impulse I crossed myself and then shrugged. But somehow it didn't feel part of this world I'd been in.

Retracing my steps along the path, I reflected on how different it was here to Dublin. But yet here I was. But who was I? Was being a barista my path in life? I baulked at the thought, even though I'd hardly been successful at it. I had no further insights, though.

I went through the metal gate and turned again to look one

last time at the well. It was then I noticed, just beyond the tree by the well, a group of men standing in the shadows. Those men. The "four corbies" I thought wryly. I stopped and gazed at them, feeling suddenly bold. They stared back, no whispers, no gossip exchanged, not even a murmur I couldn't quite hear, just the eyes staring back. They were all about the stance, the look, the stare. No scuttling or shadow seeking, no sudden disappearance.

I moved back from the gate, too unnerved to speak. I turned away and walked quickly away. After several metres I looked back through the trees that surrounded the clearing where the well was situated. I could make out the cloutie filled tree. Behind it, where the men had stood, only the scattered shrubs and trees remained. And their shadows. The men, with their stares, were gone. I didn't know whether to be relieved or not. They hadn't ever seemed threatening. Just unnerving. In so many ways. But this time, strangest of all, they had seemed different. And it wasn't until I remembered their expressions that I realised what it was. Most of them had been happy. One had even grinned.

IT WAS the music that drew me to the little farmyard. I'd decided to have a look at the shrine, even though it was off the main road. My initial thought after the experience at the well was to go to the village, to walk among people, to connect to the reassuring world of café and shop, but yet another impulse changed my mind and took me backtracking a little ways and taking the road to the shrine. It was then, as I passed the stone buildings that surrounded a small farmyard, that I heard the music and then the singing that accompanied it. It was a man's voice, deep and lyrical. I stopped, pausing to see if I recognised the song. I drew closer and the sounds of metal tools greeted me. Curious, I opened the small gate and walked down into the yard, heading towards the outbuilding containing the music. Double doors were flung open to let in the light. I peered in and saw a man working at a bench to the side and a large metal chimney over a raised hearth in its centre. It was a forge. The man looked up at my appearance and stopped singing. The music played on without him on a phone lying on the bench beside him. His emerald green eyes regarded me curiously, his thick black curly hair framed his face and hung loosely at the back to his T-shirt. I noticed his arms and torso, thick and ropey with muscles that gave credence to his trade.

"You're blocking my light," he said.

"Sorry, sorry," I said quickly moving inside the doors.

"Come in, so," the man said dryly.

I flushed. "Sorry, again. Would you prefer it if I left? Only I heard you singing and I was wondering what it was. I'm a musician. Well, of sorts. I only play at sessions and I sing a bit too." I forced myself to stop, cursing the blathering that suddenly spilled forth.

"Do you, so?"

I blinked. "Do I now what?"

"Sing. Play."

"Oh. Yes."

"And what is it you play?" The amusement was clear on his face.

"Flute, mostly. And the low whistle."

His brow raised. "Trad?"

She nodded. "Do you play?"

"Not flute. But I do play some. On the fiddle."

She brightened. "Really? It sounds like you sing as well."

He shrugged. "Thanks."

"Thanks?"

He laughed. "For saying it sounds like I sing."

She reddened again. "You sing well. There's nothing 'sounds' about it."

He looked her up and down. "You're wet through. Do you want to come in for a cup of tea? Dry off a bit?"

"I don't want to interrupt your work."

"Don't worry, you're not. I was just finishing up."

"Grand, so."

He put down his tools, went over the forge and shut the drafts and scattered the coals. I could see the sweat marks on his T-shirt and the damp curls on his forehead. The heat from the forge was strong, its warmth felt good to my chilled body.

"What are you making?" I asked, curiously surveying the metal form on his bench.

"It's a weathervane."

I looked at it closely. I could make out the traditional shape of the cockerel, the directional points, but the cockerel had an arrow going through it.

"Unusual," I said neutrally. "The work is really lovely though." I eyed the finely executed detail on the cockerel and the arrow.

The man snorted. "It's a commission. The design concept is nothing to do with me."

I looked up, a glint in my eye. "You mean you're not delivering any subliminal message here?"

"Not me, no." He shut the box on the tools he'd placed inside. "Right. We'll go into the house. The sitting room should be warm enough and the kettle won't take long to boil." He paused. "Unless you'd prefer a bit of punch? Or straight whiskey?"

As much as the whiskey tempted me, I decided to be cautious. "Cup of tea would be grand."

7

SMITHY

I nside the small kitchen he flicked the kettle on and turned to look at her. She was quirky. He didn't know if it was that, or something else which appealed to him. Piqued his interest. But he found himself smiling at her as she surveyed his little kitchen. Her wet hair, coiled in a braid around her head was certainly not a fashion he often encountered around here. Nor were her clothes.

"I'm Saoirse, by the way," she said, pulling him out of his reverie.

"Oh, Smithy," he said. He reached into the press beside the sink and pulled out two mugs.

"Smithy? That's original."

He heard the dry tone and allowed himself a smile. "It is, isn't it."

"I take it that wasn't your given name."

He shook his head. "My given name is something unpronounceable in Irish."

"Oh," said Saoirse. "I better stick to Smithy, so."

"Everyone does, so don't feel bad."

She studied him a moment. "So are you a Lynch, O'Sullivan or McCarthy, or one of the others?"

He laughed. "One of the others. I'm a Shee."

"Shee? That's one I've not heard. Did the priest run out of ink?"

"What?" he asked, puzzled. And then it hit him. "Oh, Sheehy, you mean. Aren't you the riot." He grinned and shrugged. "Ah, you know yourself. It was desperate times, long ago. Ink was very scarce."

She giggled. "Now who's the riot."

He snorted. He wasn't often accused of being funny, not for years, but for some reason this girleen, for that's what she seemed at first glance, brought it out of him. He poured the boiling water into the two mugs where tea bags were draped.

"Milk, sugar? I'm afraid I've no biscuits. Only bread and butter, if you have a fancy for it."

"Nothing to eat, thanks. Just milk in the tea, please."

When the tea was ready he led her into the main room and offered her a seat by the warm stove that sat in the large fireplace. He took the chair opposite.

"Now, what are you doing out in weather like this, with only the light jacket to protect you?" he asked once they were settled.

"The weather was grand when I left the house."

"You're visiting here from...Dublin?"

She shrugged. "I am. Does that make a difference?"

"Well if you were from a rural area you'd know that the weather can change quickly enough. It can't be that different in Dublin, though."

She considered it. "I guess I could always take shelter somewhere."

"So, you are visiting, then."

She nodded. "My grandmother. She lives up the hill. It's my first time here."

He smiled at her. "You're forgiven, then."

"For not being a local?"

"For that, if you like."

She smiled and took a sip of her tea.

"Would you like a little whiskey in it?"

She paused, considering. "Go on, so."

He rose and left the room, returning a moment later with a bottle of Powers. He gave her a generous tot and did the same in his own mug. He resumed his chair, placing the bottle beside him.

"How long are you visiting?"

"I don't know," she said. "We didn't really set a time. A few months, I suppose. Until my father's estate is settled and I can move into his house."

"Oh, I'm sorry for your loss."

"Thanks, but we weren't close. I hardly saw him."

"That's a shame. Family is important, especially in this area. But you have your grandmother."

She wrinkled her nose. "I do I suppose, though I don't really know her. She wasn't around when I was growing up."

Smithy, looked at her closely. He could see the confusion and the hint of vulnerability there. "Pity. Grandmothers are important."

"I never really had a chance to know any of mine, for various reasons. Were you close with yours?"

Smithy gave a harsh laugh. "It's complicated."

Saoirse looked at him wryly. "Isn't it always?"

He nodded slowly. "I suppose."

She scanned the room, looking at the books that lined one wall and then the little desk and chair and finally the fiddle case that sat beside it. "Is that your fiddle?"

He nodded. "It's old, but I like it."

She rose and went over to it. "Do you mind?"

"Help yourself," he said.

He watched her open the case and examine the violin. Carefully, she lifted it up to her chin, took the bow and stroked it across the strings tentatively. She paused, adjusted her chin and then moved the bow again, this time playing a little melody. She took the fiddle from her chin, looked up at him and shook her head.

"It has a lovely tone to it."

"I didn't realise you played."

"Not really," she said. "I only dabble. Flute is my thing. And low whistles."

She handed the fiddle to him. With only a shade of reluctance he took it and the bow and began a tune. It just came to him, it wasn't planned, but he started it, low and plaintive. He was conscious of Saoirse watching him at first, but then he got lost in the tune and it took him back, long ago. When it was finished he frowned. He hadn't allowed himself to play that music, ever. But here he was, bow moving through the tune in front of this girleen. Someone he hardly knew.

"Beautiful," she whispered. "I've never heard it before. What was it? It's modal, isn't it? Or something like it. Old in any case."

"It is old," he acknowledged. "It's close to how it would have been played, but the fiddle has a modern tuning, so it's not quite accurate."

"Modern tuning? You mean the pitch?"

He smiled. "Something like that."

"Still, it's very beautiful. I'd love to learn it sometime."

"You should come to one of the sessions in the village," he said, putting the fiddle back in the case.

"They have sessions? Where? I'd love to go to one."

"Usually on a Thursday, at the pub in the west end of the village."

"Do you go then?"

He shrugged. "Sometimes. There's another on a Saturday at the other pub. Sometimes I'll go there. That one is fairly loud, raucous and not top shelf, but fun."

She grinned. "Thanks. They both sound good. Maybe sometime, at either one of them, I could have that tune off you. I think I might have some of it already. It's really haunting."

"You might," he said, and decided to leave it at that.

She picked up her mug, drained the last of its contents and rose. "I'd better be off then. Thanks for the hospitality."

Smithy glanced out the window and frowned. "There's still a heavy mist, though it looks like it might be clearing in a bit. Do you want a spin back to your grandmother's?"

"No, no, you're grand. I'll walk. I'll have to get used to hoofing it if I want to go anywhere. I somehow think my grandmother is too busy to ferry me around when the notion takes me. And I can only imagine that I'd be more a hindrance than a help to her around the farm."

Smithy walked her back through the kitchen and to the door. "If you're sure."

"I am," Saoirse said. She gave him a smile that lit up her face and made her hazel eyes look positively green. "See you soon."

"You will," said Smithy.

"At a session."

"At a session," he said.

He watched her as she crossed the yard, slipped through the gate, and made her way back up the road, her lilting fluid walk capturing his gaze until she disappeared from sight. With a sigh, he turned back into his kitchen and shut the door. He still wasn't certain what had happened. All he knew is that it left him uneasy, in both a good way and a bad way.

SMITHY WAS restless after Saoirse had gone. Eventually, he gave up trying to read a book and ventured back out to the forge. There was still some heat in the coals, it would take some time to work them back up to the temperature he needed to make something. But still, he couldn't resist it, if only for a little task, a little experiment that suddenly struck him. It was the curve of a hilt. He could see it in his mind, suddenly and its graceful shape wouldn't leave him, the moment he thought of it. He looked around on his bench, rifling through half completed swords that he'd discarded earlier, until he found the one he'd remembered might suit this design, this approach, best. He laid it aside until he was ready for it. With the key he'd retrieved from its hiding place, he opened the locked box on top of the bench and withdrew some of the precious silver metal and began to prepare to work it.

The work began methodically, his skill and experience driving him, and at first it was just a process, a little trial to see if he could fashion the image that had come to him. But that changed. He couldn't say specifically when, only that the tune in his head, the one that he'd played earlier, the one that represented an entirely different time, a different life, was playing louder and louder, the sorrow of it pushing him, the pain of it, and, he realised, the joy of it. It was when the joy entered his heart that another tune hummed under it, which flowed and vibrated through his body and down his arm. It took him over and entered the metal, twirling, twisting with that joy. It weaved its own joy, joining his and a web of metal, slinky and curling.

It was only later, when it was attached to the hilt, became the hilt, that he realised what had happened. But he was too astonished to put words to it. And it would be tempting fate. And sure, it was only a hilt. The sword was just a sword.

8

SAOIRSE

I gripped the door rest as Maura swung left off the main road. The road gradually descended then wove up and down and a sharp left, then a sharp right. I thought painfully of my flute and whistle cases in the back, sliding along the seat. I should have put them on the car floor. But Maura had been in a hurry and hardly had given me time to think when she'd rung me on my phone and asked me if I wanted to join her at a session at a nearby village. I'd only seen Maura once after our initial encounter, when she was walking by and I was emerging from the milking shed one morning. We'd exchanged pleasantries and phone numbers then, but not much more, so the invitation to the session, when it had come, was a surprise.

"Thanks for ringing me," I said, trying to distract myself from the increasingly bumpy excuse for a road. "Did you know I played trad music?"

"Ah, maybe so," said Maura cryptically. She turned and grinned, her jet black hair hanging straight and almost Goth-like from her head. She didn't wear the makeup but everything else about Maura suggested Goth. Though, to be fair, there was nothing fake about her hair. Which, with her very pale skin, gave an otherworldly appearance that was almost fae.

"Oh, did my grandmother tell you, then?"

"Mmmmhn."

"Do you farm as well?"

Maura let out a raucous laugh. "Jaysus, no. Not at all. Your grandmother is enough of a woman of the land for the two of us."

I smiled. "Have you known her long, then?"

"Yes, a long time. All my life, you could say."

"She seems a good woman," I said. "Though we're only just getting to know each other."

The words were true enough. Something about my grandmother made me feel as though I'd known her a very long time, but sometimes it was as though I would never know her. It had been over a week since I'd arrived, but other than the mundane daily things I'd seen her do, there was little more I could say about her. Any questions I'd asked about my parents she deflected. I put it down to her grief and sensitivity about the whole subject, but it still would have been nice to know something about my parents. Something to give me a picture of who they were. It wasn't as though knowing about them would change how I defined myself, not really. Or would it? Defining myself had sometimes seemed elusive. I would call myself a musician. Yes. But did it give me a direction, a way forward? I already knew I wasn't a barista. Or any kind of wait staff. What did my degree give in the way of hints? Not much, I decided, except my naive dream of writing. I'd brought my notebook with me from Dublin and had even jotted a few musings down that might at some point make a poem. Or perhaps a song. I'd dabbled in both poetry and song writing at university, but had produced nothing of consequence in my clever, but not too clever attempts.

"You're very quiet," said Maura.

"Oh, sorry. Mind gone wandering."

We'd just crested a ridge and I looked at the vista in front of me. The light was beginning to fade, but in the approach to summer and the solstice, the day ended late. The streaks of sunset stretched out across the landscape, casting the rolling hills in an almost peach light. In the distance I could see a small lake shimmering. It was so settling, so peaceful. Except to the right, towards the west, where I could see wind turbines, dotted across the landscape, rising like triffids, still and threatening.

"Jesus, aren't they just awful?" I said before I could think. "Those turbines look like an army invading."

Maura gave me a quick glance, frowning. "They do, all right."

"Is it a big thing around here, then?"

"Wind turbines?"

"Yes. They just look so awful, feckin' up the landscape like that." I sighed. "I suppose I sound like a typical Dublin visitor— 'don't mess up my view' while I suck up all the power they provide."

Maura laughed. "Ah, no, you're grand. It's a not a pretty sight, I grant you. And many would echo the sentiment. It's supposed to be environmental and all that craic, but, I don't know. I've heard that they use more energy to produce those huge things, pouring the concrete, creating the roads to them, then they'll ever generate."

"Just more fat businessmen getting fatter," I muttered. "Subsidised by the government."

"And a few farmers getting fat, too. Well, maybe not as much as the businessmen. And many around here have struggled terribly in the past. They feel it's their time, I suppose."

"It's so feckin' frustrating," I said. "I mean I support renewable energy and all that..."

I let my sentence trickle off in the midst of traversing a very bumpy stretch of road that stole my words.

"Sorry, this back road is used by log lorries and they just tear it up."

The road, which was barely wide enough for one car, was twisting and turning. On either side was bog land with a few sheep grazing the sparse grass. It was definitely a time out of time place, with no house or dwelling of any kind in sight.

"Is this road used much at all?" I asked after we drove over a load of sheep droppings.

"Not much," she said. "But it's the quickest way to the village. Cuts the journey by half. Besides, at this time of evening we won't see many, if any, cars."

I shuddered to think what would happen if we did right now. We'd have to reverse at least a 100 metres, if not more. But there was nothing ahead, as far as I could see, I suddenly found the whole situation funny. Maura was already proving to be the key to adventure.

We hit a straight patch of road and then dropped down a bit. I looked over to the right and a short distance away, at small copse of sparse trees, I saw a group of men standing around. I stared and looked closely. It was the men. The Twa' Corbies. Standing there, in their dark clothes, talking to someone. A man, tall, gesturing firmly. I tried to make out the man who held their attention. One of the corbies handed him a small bag and the imposing man took it, tucking it into his jacket. He turned and began walking to the road. It was then I noticed a motorbike parked at the edge of the copse in a little gravel clearing. The figure took the helmet that rested there and put it on his dark head. But it didn't matter now. I'd recognised him as soon as he'd turned from the men. I'd know him anywhere. It was Smithy.

THE PUB, when we entered, was noisy and busy. There was no music yet, but I could see a few musicians gathering in the corner near the front. Behind the bar there was an older woman with curly fair hair caught back by a tie at her neck. She looked up when we entered and her mouth tightened, then forced itself into a pleasant smile.

Maura grinned and nodded at her. We went over to the corner and put our instruments down by a padded bench that leaned against the wall. I looked dubiously at the bodhran Maura had brought and hoped that she had some notion how to play it. The three musicians greeted Maura.

"How are you, lads?" she said.

"Grand, so," said a young red faced fair lad. He was fiddling with the concertina on his lap, unfastening the straps that held it closed.

"Who's your friend there, Maura?" asked a large older woman with brilliant purple hair that hung thick and straight to her shoulders. She wore a flannel shirt, jeans and lace up boots. She was tuning a fiddle.

Maura nudged me. "Ah, this is Saoirse. She's staying up the road to me, so be kind to her." She turned to me. "Saoirse, that young lad who loves to squeeze things hard is Cían, our whiz on the concertina, Catherine there is an enthusiastic fiddle player and this here," she indicated the thin wiry man with shaggy auburn hair plucking a few notes on a guitar, "is the beautiful Finn."

Finn looked up at me with his large blue eyes and high cheek bones and gave a brief nod before returning his gaze to the guitar. I could see why Maura called him beautiful, though I would call him more ephemeral, elusive? Or maybe timeless? It was difficult to explain or describe.

I nodded to all of them and removed my jacket, placing it on the empty seat at the bench.

"Drinks first," said Maura. "What are you all having?"

Catherine shook her head. "I'm fine, Maura. I have one."

Cían declined too, his pint of lager nearly full on the table in front of him.

"I'll have a pint of Beamish, thanks Maura," said Finn, looking up briefly again. His mouth curved into a smile and then Maura's earlier descriptor came true. There was a definite beauty to his face.

Maura pulled on my arm and I turned to follow her up to the bar, weaving through the people. It was a fair sized pub and, judging from the crowd, maybe the only one in the village. There was no theme, no trace of anything but the usual dark stools and tables, the long bar with the drink and optics lined up behind and the pumps in front. No fancy ales promoted on slates or beer mats. There was a fridge with a few bottles of what seemed to be fancier fare. I sized up the few options at the pumps and tried to decide.

The woman behind the bar came up to them.

"Hanny. Didn't expect to see me tonight, did you?" said Maura.

"Ah now, Maura. You know you're welcome whenever you do turn up," Hanny said. "Now what will you be having?"

Maura ordered her drink and Finn's, turned to me and asked what I wanted. I surprised myself and ordered a Bulmer's Cider, something I never drank. Maura raised a brow, as though she was as surprised at my choice as I was. I ignored her and studied Hanny while she filled the glasses.

When we returned to the table the others were chatting quietly. Maura handed Finn his drink and set the sparkling water down in front of her place. I slid into the bench that I had marked for my perch and reached down to begin the process of unpacking and assembling my wooden flute. I'd had it for years and liked the way it felt in my hands and the tone it had was good, considering it had come to me via an online ad in a music magazine. I blew a few notes once I was ready to test it out and was happy with the response. Catherine took that as her cue and set off on a familiar reel that I was soon able to join. Cían followed suit and Finn added his guitar, slowing down Catherine's near manic pace with his strumming. Maura had the bodhran up and, striking it confidently with the tipper, matched Finn in a more subtle manner than I would have given her credit for. She was good. No bin lid banging sound for her. I watched her for a few moments then switched my assessing gaze to Finn, appreciating his fine fingers that strummed the guitar with graceful confidence. I wondered for a moment what it would be like to hear him on his own, playing a lyrical tune, rather than supporting someone else's melody.

The door opened. I didn't glance up at first, too intent on the music and the musicians. I felt a presence near and saw an instrument case placed on the bench to my right side out of the corner of my eye, but my raised elbow blocked the view. It was only later, when I glanced up at the bar and saw the familiar head through the numerous people that crowded the room that I realised who owned the instrument by my side. Smithy. And he was staring right at me, his gaze filled with surprise and something else.

It unnerved me for some reason, though I knew I shouldn't be surprised that he'd turned up. After all, I'd only just seen him a short distance from here earlier on. But the very thought of that recent memory of him in the middle of some kind of exchange with those men only added to my anxiety.

The tune ended and Smithy approached. I felt myself tense.

"Saoirse," Smithy said, placing his Guinness on the table and taking the seat beside me. "Good to see you. I didn't know you'd be here tonight."

I gave him a nervous smile. His words were pleasant but his tone was hesitant, uncertain. He studied me carefully.

"Your hair."

I looked at him, puzzled. "My hair?"

"It's ...not the colour I thought it was," he mumbled.

"No?" I was still puzzled. "What colour did you think it was?"

"Uh, brown?"

I laughed. I don't think I'd ever been mistaken for a brunette. "No, it's not brown," I said wryly.

"No," Smithy said flatly.

"Titian," I said, continuing the light tone in the face of his cautious expression. "I think that's the word you're looking for,"

He nodded slowly. "I guess because your hair was wet, I thought it was brown."

I considered this unlikely, but maybe, given the gloom and the wet hair it might be remotely possible. I nodded agreeably. "Probably."

He shifted a little and began to busy himself with his fiddle case, removing the instrument and the bow to start the tuning process. As he proceeded I realised he'd distanced himself a bit from me. For some reason he was as wary of me as I was of him. Did he know that I'd seen him earlier, talking with the men?

"We don't see you here that often," said Maura, a slight challenge in her voice. "What brings you out this way?"

Finn raised his brow and exchanged glances with Catherine and Cían.

Smithy smiled at Maura blandly. "Last time I was here for a session, Maura the Rookery, I don't remember you being here. Or the time before, for that matter. Anything in particular bring you out here?"

Maura laughed, delightedly. "Ah, Smithy, Smithy," she said,

emphasising his name with the same strength as he'd given hers. "I've brought Saoirse, of course. Show her a bit of the local music. She's visiting. But then I think you already know that."

I reddened at the mention of my name. There was clearly something going on between the two of them, but I couldn't make up my mind if it was complete hostility or a dark kind of teasing.

"You've a fine flute there," said Finn, directing his words to me. "And you play well. We're happy to have you. Do you have any tunes you'd like to play? We'll do our best to pick it up, so."

"I'm sure you know all the tunes I do," I said. I was grateful for Finn's deflection. The tension had lessened considerably now. "But here's one that I play often up in Dublin and I'm sure you know."

I launched into *Jenny Picking Cockles*. It was lively and set even the hardest person's foot tapping. I'd chosen it because of that and because it was well known. We played along, lively and in rhythm. Smithy joined us after a short while, his fiddle tuned up. I could hear this confident bow strokes, and noted his subtle note changes, his fingers flying and sliding. He was a cut above Catherine, there was no doubt about it, her scraping and attack with the bow almost an assault on the poor instrument. It was difficult to watch.

I turned away from her slightly and caught Maura's grin, as though she could read my mind. I shifted my gaze, unwilling to get the giggles, and focused on Finn. He caught my glance and his face assumed an innocent look, his mouth set firm. His guitar strum suddenly increased in volume and I knew he'd picked up on the humour between Maura and myself. I felt the giggle rise up again, becoming a snort. I would have to take the flute away from my mouth before I strangled the note or myself. A kick against my shins startled me out of it and the giggle receded. It took me a moment to realise that Smithy had been the one to administer the kick. I glanced at him, angling the flute slightly and he widened his eyes at me and then made them cross-eyed. It caught me by surprise and stirred the giggles to such enormous proportions that I took the flute away and began to cough. The others continued playing. I took a sip of my Bulmer's and glanced at Catherine, praying she hadn't noticed but she played on, oblivious, her bow still attacking the fiddle as though some assailant had just tried to grab her.

I joined the group again when they bridged onto another tune. It was less well known, at least to me. I'd played it once or twice, but after a few bars I was able to catch it and raised the flute to my lips. I watched with interest as Catherine sat it out, obviously finding it unfamiliar and beyond her ability to pick up at this point. I suddenly wondered if there was more to Finn's request for me to start a tune than pure politeness. The tune continued and it caught me up. We were flying it. The instruments and musicians in sync as we entered a different world where the only thing possible was to hear, feel and live the music.

When it ended I felt almost deflated. Dropped from the sky, fallen off a winged horse. That was as close as I could come to describing it. I looked around, blinking. The others seemed just as dazed as I was. Except for Catherine. She looked puzzled, irritated.

"Will we take a break?" asked Finn.

It seemed at once a terrible idea and the best idea. I wanted to carry on, find that place once again. But I also wanted to savour it. Recover from it. Give myself some time to reconnect to the pub, the people around me. After a while I managed to get myself up and off to the loo, but the music still sang through my body.

9

SMITHY

Smithy returned from the bar and took his seat. Saoirse still hadn't come back by the time he'd been served and returned to his place. He took a deep drink from the glass. He never had a second pint when he was on the motorbike, he didn't like to appear to be going over the limit. But tonight he'd made an exception. Though whether it was down to the set they'd just played or the shock of seeing Saoirse, or rather Saoirse's hair, he couldn't pinpoint it. Earlier, he'd tried to brush it off. So her hair was ginger. Or titian, as she described it. It wasn't even the exact shade. It didn't match Bríd's hair colour, not really. Was it the coronet hair style? Bríd had worn her hair in that mode as often as she'd worn it flowing freely. A surge of grief overtook him and he nearly retched with the force of it. He pushed it down with a deliberation and frowned. Where had that come from? He'd not had such a violent reaction in a long, long time.

Finn took his place to Smithy's immediate right. "How's things?" he asked. "You still riding the bike?"

Smithy smiled wryly, glad for the distraction. "Just because you haven't the skill for the roads around here, that's no reason to cast aspersions on my vehicle of choice."

"Ah, you're only turning green there, Smithy. You know my Miata is a classy car, sure to turn any girl's head. Whereas your bike...well, maybe a certain kind of...chick? Isn't that the term?"

"That's the difference though, Finn me lad, I don't need the Miata or the bike to turn a lady's head. I can do that on my own."

Finn burst out laughing. "The state of ye, Smithy. The state of ye. Turn a lady's head? I love the phrase. Sure, you need more than a classy car to turn a ladies head."

Smithy looked down at his ripped jeans, rumpled T-shirt that had a trace of black grease on it. "What? They love it!"

"Oh and I can see them all queuing up for you." Finn shook his head. "Sad, sad, sad."

Smithy shrugged. He took little notice of Finn's ribbing normally. But somehow tonight he'd felt a tiny sting at the last comment. He rarely took anyone home with him. And he couldn't remember when he had what would be called a girl-friend. What was the point?

"Why so glum, Smithy?" asked Maura as she slid onto her stool.

"This is my face, Maura," he said, turning to her. "If you read glum there, it might be because it's what you're feeling."

"Me? Glum? Ah, no." Maura gave a peal of laughter. "I'm having great fun tonight."

"I am as well," said Saoirse.

She squeezed past Smithy and resumed the seat next to him. Her legs had bumped his in the process and he nearly flinched at the touch. There was something about her that unnerved him and yet drew him to her. He didn't know why. Before he could stop himself he put his hand on her shoulder.

"What are you drinking?"

She turned to look at him, her hazel eyes pinning him into

paralysis. The eyes were different, he told himself. The hair was a different shade too. She was smaller, slimmer, almost lanky. There was no comparison. The smile she gave him was a near grin and he caught his breath.

"Thanks, Smithy. I'll have a Bulmer's."

He nodded and asked the others for their orders. At the bar he gave the drinks order and made himself do some deep breathing. He'd just been carried away by the brief bout of grief. All the pressure he'd felt from the work at the forge, trying to get the blades and hilts to do his bidding, probably added weight to the disturbance of his usual placid demeanour.

When he returned with the drinks, ferrying them in stages, he felt calmer and resumed his seat with a smile for all. He caught Maura looking at him speculatively. She was up to something, he could tell. She had been for a little while, now that he thought about it. It wasn't just at Anu's behest that she'd met up with him. And tonight was no accident, he was sure of it. She'd not paid him this much attention for a long time. Not since time beyond thinking about. Maura the Rookery. He nearly laughed at the thought of it. Crows all right. Carrion. Just picking over the bones of trouble she stirred. He sighed. He'd find out soon enough, he supposed.

"Saoirse, play us a tune on the low whistle there I see you hiding at your feet," said Finn.

Saoirse narrowed her eyes, but they were full of humour. "And how do you know that it's a low whistle I have at my feet? It could be something else altogether."

Finn's eyes slid over to Maura. "A certain bird told me."

Saoirse laughed. "A certain bird next to you by any chance?"

He shrugged. "It doesn't matter who. Just give us a tune?"

"No, you're grand. I'm not worth all that fuss."

"Let us be the judge of that," said Catherine. Her voice was strident and deep throated.

"And I'm sure the judgement will be overwhelming," said Finn. "Besides, we'll join you if we can."

Saoirse gave a weak smile and leaned over to pick up the soft case that held the low whistle. Watching her, Smithy hoped that she'd picked up Finn's hint to pick an obscure tune or Catherine was sure to join in and drown her out. He knew Catherine meant well and she was enthusiastic, but it was difficult sometimes to fully appreciate this intimate session when she contributed her talents.

Saoirse struck up her slow tune. It was a haunting air, one that was vaguely familiar to him, the notes striking something at the edge of his mind. It pulled at him deep in his psyche and for a moment he allowed access to that part of him. The tingle was there, that fullness of body. Before he knew what he was doing he raised the fiddle to his chin and stroked the bow across it slowly and softly. He played along with her, a supporting note, a slightly counter note. The air held him in its grip and he knew he dared not look at Saoirse for fear what he could see there. It was then that he realised that the whistle itself couldn't support the tune. Not in the way it should be, so that the air filtered in through your heart and opened up your soul, becoming your very own *anam cara* that would see you to the world beyond. Suddenly, for this very air he wanted to re-tune his fiddle to the old way. The real way, and play it like it was meant to be played.

The air was coming to a close, he could feel it, so he wound down his playing, became fainter and then disappearing altogether just before Saoirse stopped. There was a hush across the pub of the most reverent kind. The moment passed and shouts of appreciation rang out.

"Not worth all the fuss is it?" said Finn. "*Tá se go hailinn,* Saoirse. Truly."

The others murmured their assent, but Smithy had no words to utter. Not yet. He was struggling with the turmoil that threatened to overflow inside him. He forced himself to nod and breathe slowly.

"Thanks for the accompaniment," Saoirse said softly next to him. "It was perfect."

Smithy managed another nod and muttered words that he hardly knew he was speaking, so that he barely heard when Cían asked her where she got the air from.

"Oh, uh, it's mine," she answered.

"Yours?" said Catherine. "You mean you composed it yourself?"

Saoirse shrugged and nodded, clearly embarrassed. "Yeah. Last year."

The discussion went on about the tune for a little while, but Smithy heard none of it. The details, whatever they were, became too much extra weight to the already heavy burden pushing on his chest. How could she have done that herself? Surely she'd picked it up from a few strands here and there that he knew had made their way down through the centuries when one of them had slipped in a bit here and there. Like Lugh. He was one for something like that. And the gods knew he'd done it a few times. It couldn't be helped, it was too much a part of them to discard. Not if they wanted to play music. And without the music there was little else to keep him sane in these times. Especially with the magic gone from him. He pushed down the niggling hope that had rekindled just now, when he'd been playing that air with Saoirse.

He was jostled out of his thoughts when Catherine struck up a jig on her fiddle. It was *The Banshee's Wail Over the Mangle Pit,* Catherine's version of an obscure tune. He suppressed a snort and just raised his fiddle and glanced over at Finn. The guitar was already in his hands and the strum begun, a little lyrical picking to fill it in as well. Finn caught his glance and cocked his head. It was his version of "the poor cratur, she knows nothing". Maura was tapping on the bodhran and Cían's fingers flew over the buttons of his concertina. They blended well and nearly masked Catherine's fiddle, forcing a sound that was acceptable and good. Saoirse joined them finally, her low whistle packed away and the flute out once again.

The tune became lilting and so full of life they were nearly all tapping their feet, feeling the joy of it. Smithy became immersed in it, his previous worries forgotten, shoved aside because they were too difficult to contemplate. The tune blossomed and became something else, moved on by a perfect instinctive bridge of key change and finesse. When the set finished, Smithy felt a sense of completeness and joy he hadn't experienced in a long while.

The tunes moved on and Smithy was happy to follow, desperate to maintain that joy and thrill of the music. Finn gave him a shove under the table to acknowledge the pureness of the session, the rare synchronicity of this night with these musicians. He glanced over at Catherine and he could see that even she was feeling it. Her bowing was more subtle and the rhythm and notes finding their right place.

After a few more sets Finn called a halt for a short break. Smithy nearly protested, so concerned that they might lose this close intuitive playing they'd had now, but he said nothing because he knew by the look on Cían and Catherine, that some of them needed to come up for air. Once again he recognised how Finn read the group's energy so well.

He decided to go outside. He was feeling hot for many reasons, not least of which was the pub was heaving. He nodded to the others and made his way outside and leaned up against the wall. The road in front was quiet, but several people gathered in bunches along the pub's walls in front of the few picnic tables that held the pub's spillover in the fine daytime weather.

A few of them nodded to him, but sensing his need for a bit of solitude they let him be.

It was a small village with a few shops along the one side of the crossroads that led to the church. Across from the shops were homes with curtains pulled against the night. Sleepy old village, he thought fondly as the murmuring voices from the nearby group nearly lulled him to sleep. He closed his eyes and breathed deeply.

"They're a great group of players."

Smithy opened his eyes and looked at Saoirse. "They are that."

"Do you play here often?"

He nearly laughed at what almost sounded like a clichéd pick up line. "I play on and off. When the feeling strikes me."

"I'd come here all the time if it was always like that playing with them. It's like nothing I've ever experienced."

He studied her a moment, weighing her sincere tone and the joy in her face. "Tonight is rare. I haven't often experienced it like this, either."

"Really?"

He nodded. "Really."

"What do you think made it so tonight? Musicianship?"

He considered what he should say. "In part. Sometimes, though, there can be an intuitive communication born from musicians who are sympathetic in their approach to music."

She waited for him to say more, but he left it at that. How could he explain what he knew in his heart to be true when he wouldn't even acknowledge it himself?

"It was more than that," she said softly. "You felt it, I know. While we were playing that air. It was there so strongly. It was as if you knew the music before I even played it. I never felt like that before playing the air. The music became part of me in a way I can't explain. As though I was the music and nothing more. It was magic."

He started at that last word, even though he knew she was saying it only in a trivial trendy manner. But it made him want to cry out, even so and he had to clench his hands to stop himself from uttering the cry. Deep breaths, deep breaths, he told himself.

"Your low whistle is fine enough, but the air would sound better if you had a slightly different tuning to it," he said finally in desperation. "There's a few notes that don't quite ring right." It was almost true but it was the best he could do to explain what he meant without saying more than he wanted to.

"Really?" she said. "I hadn't noticed. But then I don't have your ear, obviously."

"Obviously? Why obviously?"

She shrugged. "I'm not the class of musician you are."

"You are. I just know, because I make flutes and whistles on occasion."

"Do you, so?"

He nodded and before he could rein in his mouth he said, "I'll make you a low whistle that will suit that air, if you like."

Her face lit up and any regret at his foolhardy offer vanished. Even in the dim light of the few street lamps he could see the fine bones sculpting her face.

"Would you do that? Ah, now, that's too much."

"No, no. It's no bother. I'd enjoy it."

She gave him a shy smile. "If that's the case then, I would love that."

He nodded his affirmation and took a deep breath. He was lost now, he knew it, deep inside. But he was determined to enjoy these moments, whatever was behind it. For something was in the air and it was more than magic.

10

SAOIRSE

Sinead's chatter filled the car as we turned off the main road onto a rough back road. She's lovely, I thought. So full of enthusiasm and anxious to share her love for the local history and land. I tried to concentrate, but it's too early for me and the coffee hasn't really seeped into my blood. Sinead talked on as Maura sat silent beside her, head turned towards the window, looking out at the passing scenery. In the passenger seat next to Sinead was another woman, Ingrid, who was from the Netherlands or Germany, I still hadn't made up my mind which.

"Have you done this yourself before, Maura?" I asked when there is a lull in Sinead's conversation.

She turned to look at me. "Not like this, no. But trust me, you'll enjoy yourself."

I looked at her dubiously. When I'd seen the mountains in the distance they seemed harmless enough, but now, as we approached, I wasn't so certain.

"Relax, there are plenty of people climbing the Paps today," said Sinead. "And many do it every year."

I nodded, reassured a little. When Maura had first suggested this trek up the Paps, I hadn't hesitated. It wasn't just the chance to walk the landscape on what promised to be a glorious day, but the chance to participate in a local tradition, or rather ritual, added extra qualities I couldn't explain even to myself.

The Paps. It was a strange name for a set of mountains, at least that was what I thought until Sinead had explained that paps were another word for breasts. I could see it then, the two mounds rising up from the ground rounded in just such a manner a woman with generous curves might have. Voluptuosity? Voluptuousness? The terms turned around in my head, their sound as rolling as the mountains we were about to climb.

"Will she mind?" I suddenly asked. I was being facetious but then felt silly.

"Will who mind?" said Maura.

"The woman with the paps?"

Sinead turned and gave me a puzzled look. Next to me Maura laughed.

"Ah, I'm sure she'll be grand," said Maura. "She probably loves people walking all over her breasts."

"She's a goddess," said Sinead severely to Maura. "Anu. The mother goddess." She glanced over at me. "I'm sure she is happy to have us there, as long as we approach it in a respectful if not reverential manner."

"What goddess?" I asked, curious. I looked out of the window up to the mountains that rose on my left. The other one was slightly behind it. I could see something perched on top, like a nipple.

"Anu," said Sinead. "She was the goddess of the Tuatha de Danann, which means 'the people of Anu. You know all that, from university?"

"Oh, right," I said.

Something stirred vaguely in my memory. I supposed I learned it, not in university though. Maybe somewhere else. Too many boarding schools, too many teachers and I never really started paying attention until secondary school. And then for some reason I excelled. It was as if a switch had been turned on and suddenly I was very curious and able to soak it all up. The trauma of being shoved around and feeling adrift finally focused into discovering things.

"Were the Tuatha de Danann around here then?" I asked.

"Well," said Sinead. "There's lots of legends about where they were. The other gods and goddesses associated with her and Daghda take place all over Ireland, but with the core of them at Tara, of course."

Beside me Maura gave a soft snicker. "What? You disagree?"

"Me?" said Maura. "Not a bit of it. It just seems odd hearing about it. It's been a while."

"They're just tales," I said. "But they're interesting and in some ways are metaphoric I guess."

Maura raised her brows. "Metaphoric is it?"

I shrugged.

"You're right, Saoirse," said Sinead. "The Paps of Anu are the ancient idea of Mother Earth and how we related to the feminine energy of the Earth, It's no harm to think of it that way, and if everyone did, we might not be so quick to pillage the Earth for her resources until she's so depleted she can no longer support life."

Maura rolled her eyes. "Ah she's not doing so badly, all the same."

The Dutch woman (or maybe German) turned to Maura. "You cannot say that. We are poisoning the planet with our pollution of the air, the ground and the oceans."

Maura sighed. "I wasn't saying that nothing was going on. I just was pointing out that Mother Earth wasn't dead yet."

"But not for want of trying on our part," said Sinead. "We

must now take responsibility for our past actions and stop those who are trying to make it worse."

Maura shrugged. "I'm not condoning it."

"We must do more," said Ingrid. "Don't you agree, Saoirse?"

Her manner and voice were so full of certainty. If she would have it so, it would be so. "Of course," I said. Who could disagree with that?

"Have you read the applications for planning permission for the new transmission station and wind turbines that Balor Energies Group are submitting? Supposedly offshore but I'd say it'll creep inshore if given half a chance. It's a disgrace, like that company. You can be certain something else is behind it as well. They're the same company who are trying to get approval for fracking up in Galway. And they want to build a refinery in Cork. The company's safety record is a disgrace."

I listened to Sinead's passionate words and for a moment admired that she could feel that way about these issues. I knew they were important and I should be doing my part, but honestly, it seemed more than I could manage at this point in my life. I didn't even have a job. I was living with a grandmother with whom I had little more than a nodding acquaintance. How could I take on these worldly issues when I could barely solve my own?

"Have you signed a petition about the company?" I said. It was the only thing that occurred to me at the moment.

"Oh, I've signed the petitions. There's plenty of those, so. And what good are they? No, it's time for greater action."

"Protest?" said Maura.

I detected a sardonic tone to her voice and I almost nudged her with it. Instead I gave her a glare. She looked back at me with a "what did I say?" innocence.

"Radical protest," said Sinead. "We need to do something that will get everyone's attention. Focus on Balor Energies and show that company as the poison chalice they are, with their iPads for schools and green spaces for inner cities."

"Have you anything planned?" I asked.

"Nothing certain," said Sinead. She glanced across at Ingrid and then turned to me. "But you'll know when the time comes."

THE PATH WAS smooth enough at first and the sun felt good as it began to peek out from the horizon. The other walkers were sparse, but behind me I could see that they were some winding their way to the starting point. Immediately in front of me was Sinead, strands of her curly blond hair escaping the tie at the back of her head. She wore all the walking gear but it seemed more functional than high tech display on her. Some pieces were faded and her shoes looked as though they had seen more than a few outings on them. Ingrid, up ahead of her, looked a little more just out of the North Face shop. She was lanky and seemed to take one step to my two, so I couldn't dispute her experience, either.

Behind me was Maura. I was surprised she'd made little concession to the fact that we were undertaking what I judged to be a difficult climb through sections of boggy land under a sky that welcomed the first day of summer. She wore her usual black shirt, jacket and jeans with black lace up boots. Her hair flew around her wildly in the breeze. I'd worn jeans, but had borrowed my grandmother's jacket in case of one of the sudden misty rains that could descend on the mountains developed. My hair was in its usual crown.

"There's more people than I imagined," I said. "Are there this many every year?"

"It's a religious ritual as well as a tradition," said Sinead.

"Some will be coming from Gougane Beara as a pilgrimage of sort. And there's a mass held up on the top of the first one."

"Why May 1, Sinead?" I asked. "I know that they're climbing as part of a tradition and it's Bealtaine and all that."

"I don't know. Maybe it's because Bealtaine is the fire festival for the beginning of summer. Fertility and all that. We're climbing the fertile Mother Earth."

I fell silent thinking about this. Somehow it resonated with me. Since when had I become so "at one" with the soil? I tried to push the weird feelings aside and looked over at Maura, who was smirking at Sinead.

"You have a different theory?" I asked quietly.

This time I really wanted to know how she felt and not provoke a flippant answer as I had earlier. She gave me a curious look, shrugged and shook her head.

We all continued our climb in relative silence. The wind was picking up a bit as we rose higher. At first, it was a gentle incline, following the straggling line of people on the climb, some in clusters, and others on their own. The ground wasn't too boggy, since the spring hadn't been as wet as usual. The ground began a sharper rise and I found myself panting a bit as I tried to maintain my previous pace. Maura passed me, not breaking her stride. Sinead allowed her to move ahead and came to check that I was okay. I realised then I wasn't as fit as the other three, but that was no surprise, given that my exercise had mostly been confined to walking around Dublin.

Eventually, we reached the top. Maura and Ingrid were already sitting on a bit of tarp, drinking from their water bottles when I came up to them, panting. I stood for a few minutes, waiting for my breathing to slow and looked around me. People were gathered in clusters, drinking water, eating snacks or just sitting. Some people were praying, fingering their rosaries or closing their eyes in contemplation. I moved to the centre and could see the large pile of rocks that formed a cairn, with a kind of stone pillar altar-type stone in front of it. I looked into the distance, moving towards the edge to get an unobstructed view. The landscape stretched out towards Kerry and it was clear enough that I could even detect the silver glint of the sea. I stared at it, my eyes focused on the distant shore. We were up so high that flying birds were level and I felt like it wasn't just the edge of this mountain I stood on, but the edge of time, the edge of a world. I inhaled deeply and tried to preserve the feeling. Eventually, I turned around slowly and something caught my eye at the cairn. I blinked, uncertain if I was just imagining it. My grandmother, her hair unbound, dressed in a flowing gown and her arms raised up to the sky.

I blinked again, still disbelieving my eyes. But a group of people blocked my view and when it cleared and I could make my way towards the cairn, there was no sign of her. Coins, tied bits of cloth and other offerings were scattered there, but nothing that confirmed what I had thought I'd seen.

I went back to the group and took a seat on the tarp. Sinead offered me a sandwich but I declined. I'd brought an apple and a granola bar, thinking that would be enough. I wasn't until I'd eaten it all that I'd realised how foolish I'd been not to have taken up her offer. Maura gave me a knowing grin and pulled out a small brown roll and offered it to me. I took it gratefully.

"Are you enjoying yourself?" she asked.

I nodded. "This is all new to me really."

"Hill walking?"

"All of it. Hill walking, the area. I haven't really travelled as such. My holidays were mostly spent either in Dublin, or at my boarding school in Galway." I looked at her relaxed pose, the sun glinting in her dark eyes. A stiff breeze blew her hair about in a Medusa-like manner. "You're obviously experienced. I suppose you've done this for years."

"Oh, you'd be right about that," she said. "More years than you can count."

I laughed. "These two mountains or many places?"

"You could say that I've probably been to the tops of most hills and mountains in Ireland."

I stared at her. "That's quite an accomplishment."

She looked over at me and laughed. "Not really. I've had the time."

I looked past her, through the clustered groups near the cairn, towards the other edge of the mountain and back towards a small group by the cairn where it parted a little. I saw someone kneeling by the cairn, his familiar profile to me. His hands were on the ground among the small rocks piled there.

"Look," I said. "Isn't that Smithy, there?"

Maura turned around and stared in the direction I pointed. "Where? I don't see him."

I pointed again, but someone moved and blocked my view. I rose and said, "I'll go see."

I made my way towards the cairn and the cluster of people. When I got there the head I thought was Smithy's was gone. I looked around to see if I could spot him somewhere else, but there was no sign of him. I glanced down at the cluster of small rocks and large to see what he was doing there. The rocks were disturbed in several sections. I tried to locate the one I thought it might have been and knelt down. I lifted up the rocks and saw what looked like cattle horns. The earth around it was damp and was faintly stained red. Blood?

Puzzled, I stood and went back over to Maura.

"Did you find him?"

"No."

"Who are you looking for?" asked Sinead looking over at me.

"I thought I saw Smithy," I said. "But I guess I was mistaken. I also thought I saw my grandmother, earlier. But it was probably someone else. It was strange. Her hair was wild and loose and she wore a long flowing gown. Her arms were raised to the sky as though she was playing some goddess in a film, welcoming the dawn. And that is definitely not my grandmother."

Sinead laughed. "Well, I wouldn't put it past someone doing that, but certainly not your grandmother, however eccentric she might be."

Maura made a noise in her throat, gave me a wide eyed look and turned away. But not before I could see the laughter. But it was the brief glimpse of panic she'd shown initially that had me the most puzzled.

11

SMITHY

Smithy rolled his shoulders and flexed his arms in an effort to loosen his body for the task ahead. Part of him was excited about it. He felt an energy that he hadn't experienced in such a long while he'd almost forgotten what it was like. He breathed deeply. He mustn't count on it too much. Pin too much hope on what he was about to undertake. It was only a low whistle. Nothing important.

He entered the shed and tried to shake off the unsettled feeling that still clung to him from the day before when he'd seen Saoirse up there on the mountain. He'd not expected her to be there, though it shouldn't have been a complete surprise that she might want to join all those who made the climb on May 1. Still, it had been unnerving to see her just when he was performing the small ritual that had been his part in the day's events since he could remember. The climbers and religious observers had grown over the years, but he'd still managed his part, as had the others over the years. In some ways it was easier to do it unobserved when so many people were there. Anu was the only one who still wore a glamour so that she remained hidden from the view of mortals. Still he didn't think Saoirse had seen him, and if she did, she probably would think nothing of it.

That's what he'd told himself since he'd returned yesterday. He'd said nothing to Anu or anyone else, because what was there to say? And though he still fulfilled this annual ritual obligation, he wanted as little to do or say to the others as possible. Except perhaps, Oghma, whose musical talent and banter were irresistible. Someone of many words and all of them good. He could even tolerate Maura, though to be fair, she'd not been too bad the other night at the session. And though he couldn't figure what game she was after playing, he couldn't deny that he was glad she'd brought Saoirse with her.

Saoirse. There he was again, bringing his thoughts back to her. He couldn't refute his attraction to her, though she was young. Too young, he told himself. Too young in too many ways. Or was it her youth that appealed to him? The innocence of her, she with her Doc Martens and quirky dress and the eyes that had seen nothing. The music? Yes the music was part of it and how it felt when they played together. He closed his eyes again and remembered the pure union of the music. It was beyond craic, good time, or anything like it. It had been as if the music transcended and fused them at the same time.

He sighed. Enough of this. Time to transcend in a different way. He moved over to the work table and took up his tools. Deep breaths, he thought. He closed his eyes and tried to summon the magic. The air hummed and he opened his mind and his body to it. It'd been so long he could barely remember what it felt like. What the summoning consisted of when it reached out, when it made contact and when it channelled the response to fill his body.

He waited, but there was only silence. Had he done something wrong? He squeezed his eyes shut and tried to recapture his earlier excitement about making the whistle, the certainty that the magic would come, because how could it not with such a feeling, such a notion that what he was about to make would have all the qualities and more of the most perfect low whistle in this world, or even the Otherworld? He tried to remember what it had been like when he'd last made a whistle for the Sídhe. It was Lugh, wasn't it? Who else would demand nothing but the most perfect low whistle and who else would be capable of playing the most perfect low whistle to show it at its best? Saoirse was the only one he knew who might come close to it.

And back again to Saoirse. He stared at the metal pipe in front of him and tried to recall how it was he made Lugh's whistle. It was in a time so long ago he couldn't even categorise it in his mind now. Another reason to stay focused on Lugh and not Saoirse. Saoirse could only ever be a brief period in his life. An enjoyable interlude, he corrected. It wouldn't do to get involved with a mortal. Didn't they always say that? Music, and that was it. Music, and maybe a little flirtation inside and outside the music.

He continued on that line of thought and absentmindedly picked up the metal tube and his little hacksaw and began his work. He thought of the tunes they could play together with the whistle, tunes that would be more than tunes. Tunes and airs that could express a bit of fun and something more. A kiss. A caress. Through the title of the tune, the words of the air he could touch her cheek, run his thumb along her lips, kiss her brow, kiss the dip between her neck and collar bone. Light kisses. Light as a butterfly.

Through the airs and tunes he would pull out the pins that held her hair in place and unwind the braid. Slowly, he would loosen the braid so that it unfurled into the long flowing tresses around her. Tresses of flame gold. Isn't that how it was expressed in all the airs? *Taimse im choladh s'na duistear me.* Don't disturb me indeed as I dream of the loveliest woman ever, he thought.

Her face filled his mind, the curves of her body, the swell of her breasts, the swale of her waist and rise of her hips and thighs. It was erotic and at the same time it was something else. An energy flowed through him and he allowed it to come, feeling both aroused and exalted at the same time. He looked down at his hands and they seemed apart from him, working independently of his conscious thoughts. His thoughts were still taken up with Saoirse, her body and the music that she played. Music that hummed around him and played his lips, his neck and his chest both inside and out. They were kisses, as light as the butterfly kisses he'd rained down on her. The kisses deepened, lingered on his body. Her lips, they were on his, brushing and then pressing. Her arms slid around him and he put his hand on her breast. They embraced each other their clothes gone, discarded, and they met each other skin to skin. Their heat was irrepressible and as he entered her, it became a flame that consumed them both, now finally united. Now finally one. And when he spilled his seed in her it was the release of thousands of years of yearning and love pouring forth, filling the one and only being that could ever receive it from him in this union of perfection.

He opened his eyes, panting. He hadn't realised he'd closed them. He'd realised nothing of what was around him. He'd only known what was going on inside of him. His hands shook and he blinked, his breath still coming in short bursts. He squeezed his hands and released them, forced himself to inhale deeply. What had happened? He felt exhausted and exhilarated at the same time. But also peaceful, loose limbed, almost blessed by Anu herself. He shook his head. It was the strangest, most erotic experience he'd ever felt. But it was also something more. Magic.

He looked down on the work bench. The metal glinted in the overhead light that shone down on it, as if it were basking in the spotlight. The metal that was now fashioned into a low whistle. He stared at it. Magic? He shook his head, trying to clear his thoughts and make sense of what had just happened. He couldn't explain it, and if he was honest, he didn't want to explain it, because it would mean digging deep and exploring things he just didn't want to explore. Things he couldn't explore. Not now, not ever. But this was the first time that he'd ever really thought it might be possible to move beyond the pain, or at least ease it for a time.

And who was he to question how or why that might be? Or what or even who was the cause. Who? Would he even acknowledge that it could be a who? The whistle stared up at him in a challenge. He picked it up tentatively and put it to his lips and blew in it, half afraid of the sound that would be emitted. The note that sounded was clear, resonant. And perfect. He blew another one and another and put them together in a tune. The tune was charming. It charmed him, rang through him and played his body like he was the instrument. He took the whistle away from his lips and breathed. Had he created this?

He tried again, this time letting the notes come. It was a tune, or was it an air, threading its way through the room and wrapping itself around him like some woman's body entwining her limbs with his. He felt the air weave its way down inside him and he was there, again feeling Saoirse against him, feeling himself inside her.

He pulled the whistle from his lips once again and gave a strangled laugh that turned to a groan. A phallic object made real, he thought. Would it have the same effect on anyone else? Would it have the same effect on Saoirse?

HE SAT THERE, staring into the fire. On his lap rested the whistle. He'd carried it around for four days, afraid to let it out of his sight. Was it because he feared losing it? Misplacing it in the large expanse of his house? Hah. He knew the reason had more to do with his own wariness about what he'd created. Created with magic. His magic. Magic born of the gods knew what kind of longing or lust. Lust. Surely it was just lust that had led him to create something so...so, what? So wondrous? So addictive? He couldn't argue with the addiction part. He'd found himself playing the whistle too often for comfort. Initially it was to see if the qualities he'd experienced, yes, qualities seemed a good, neutral term, if these qualities were just a one-time occurrence or if it was something permanently part of the whistle. Something indelible, integral, unmoveable. And each time he tried it, the tune, the air, or whatever music it happened to create, wove its web around him and penetrated his body and his mind in the most euphoric manner. Orgasmic, he thought. Truly. Literally. Addictively. And Saoirse, the living embodiment of this perfect music and perfect union. Holy Mother of God, he thought, sardonically, a phrase that he'd picked up over the years in the most satirical manner possible. But now, he half felt he should be invoking Anu, thanking her, cursing her for waking him up. Or at least this part of him. Holy Mother of all.

And now for the dilemma of whether to give it to Saoirse. Could he even manage to face Saoirse at this point? After all he'd thought, dreamed and experienced this week involving her? There was a session tonight down in the village. It was possible she wouldn't even turn up for it. It wasn't the Saturday night one that he'd said he went to often. It was the Friday night one, at the pub at the edge of the village. O'Sullivan's. The session that was more traditional, less raucous, but very good. He could take the low whistle down there and see if it had the same effect on everyone else as it had on him. And maybe, down in the pub, it wouldn't have the same effect on him. He could play away fine, no bother. That he didn't usually play the whistle might cause a little bit of a stir but would it be worth it to see the result? He took a deep breath. No. No, it wouldn't be worth it. And a little part of him didn't want to share this whistle, or the experience of it. Would he give it to Saoirse though? Could he bear her playing it anywhere but with him? He suddenly disliked the notion of that very much. But would he want her to play it? He found he did. And he also found that since his head was surely all over the place the best decision at this point would be to leave the whistle behind and save it for another time. If that time ever came. For now, it was the fiddle.

He picked up the case, opened it and withdrew the fiddle. A few tweaks with the pegs and he was away. The bow flew across the strings and he allowed himself to get carried away by a familiar tune, the rise and fall of the slip jig, merry and winsome. It was a jig from the Otherworld, fashioned out of the web and warp of the air. It skipped and jumped along and lifted his heart. He hadn't played that in a long time. Or had he ever played it before? The Otherworld tunes came and went as they pleased and he wouldn't pin it down. It hated that he knew and let it come visit at will and skip off when it wanted to. It was enjoying the skipping, for it wove around him and then in him for a good while, until his doubts and tension eased away and he skipped and jumped alongside it. And then, finally, with a last little lilt, it hopped off, back where it came from. He blinked and kissed the air, thankful that some part of the magic still liked him.

12

SMITHY

He had the fiddle case in his hand, weighty enough, as he stood before the door to the pub. Even through the door he could hear the milling throng and just imagine the hot fug of the air inside. He strained for the sound of the music, and there it was—the fiddle, the concertina and flutes winding down a tune. He could tell nothing from the sound of the flutes to know if one of them was Saoirse, but he thought not. And he didn't know whether that knowledge made him feel disappointed or relieved.

The door burst open and a couple spilled out on to him, pushing him back a few steps.

"Sorry, sorry," said the young lad, his companion nodding in agreement. He held the door open for Smithy. "You're going in, yeah?"

"Yeah," Smithy said. "Thanks."

He strode through the door like he'd meant it, like the two lads had collided into him and prevented him from his original purpose. He saw a few familiar faces and nodded to them, studying the crowd as though he wasn't avoiding looking over at the section where the session attendees usually gathered. It wasn't an easy strategy, since the section wasn't too far back from the entrance, but he felt up to the job with the amount of people gathered, glasses lifted and conversation flowing.

"Smithy!" came a cry from the section his eyes had avoided, and the strategy collapsed for the useless bit of junk it was. Any soldier would have known that. He sighed and inwardly acknowledged his pathetic failure for what it was—a half wish only, to be unseen yet seen, and made his way over the tables, a smile plastered on his face. He gave nods to each one of them. It was a way to progressively discover who was here and who wasn't.

"How's things, how're you keeping" as well as direct names were given to Liam, Gearóid, Daragh, Aoife and Eilís. No Saoirse or even Maura, though he wasn't certain if Maura had ever bothered to come to this session. He'd never seen her. He found a stool and pulled it up beside Aoife, who was busy tipping the moisture out of her flute. Daragh was on Smithy's other side, fiddling with the tuning on a guitar that was so sensitive to the humidity changes he nearly had to tune during any given set.

"Not seen you for a while there, Smithy," said Daragh.

"Yeah, busy with work,"

"All that smithcraft," said Aoife, pronouncing the last word with slow emphasis.

She flipped her mid length fair hair over her shoulder and crossed her legs. It was nearly flirtatious and Smithy looked at her uneasily. Aoife was probably in her mid to late twenties, and grand enough, but Smithy never really saw anything but a good musician who sometimes had good banter. Daragh, on the other hand was interesting. He had pale eyes and face full of earnest concentration in whatever he did and always he did it well. He was a luthier of sorts and Smithy liked that and the conversations that interest prompted. Daragh's guitar was one of his own and he treasured it like Smithy imagined he would his three-year-old son.

"Yeah, smithcraft," said Smithy. "As the name says."

"Not a joke, no," said Aoife and she grinned.

Smithy gave a small smile. "No."

He reached down for his fiddle case and began the job of unpacking it, conscious of Aoife's regard.

"Hey now, Smithy," said Gearóid as he fiddled with the buttons on his concertina. "Have you any new tunes for us this evening? That last one was cracking."

Smithy shrugged. "Don't know. We'll see."

"Ah, surely you have a tune for us," said Aoife. She nudged Smithy with her elbow. "You know I love learning a new tune from you."

"I know that?" asked Smithy. Her tone was playful, but he couldn't help the edge that had come to his. "Of course I do."

She laughed, refusing the edge and re-directing it towards her own agenda. "You're a dote, Smithy. Of course you have one. No need to be coy."

"Smithy has no coy about him, do you me lad?" said Liam. He gave them both an amused look and waggled his bushy white brows suggestively.

"And none about you, you old lecher," said Smithy. He forced a laugh and then began the business of tuning his fiddle. The concentration of it, the single-minded dedication to its perfection would surely be evident to all who watched him. And then, by the grace of the land and all that's holy, someone would strike up a tune and they could get on with the business of playing the music.

Someone took pity on him, because he'd hardly finished the tuning when they took off with a favourite set of polkas with a precision and lilt that eased his tension. He felt it enough that it took him away and even allowed him to wink at Eilís, who was doing her own little flourish on her fiddle. She gave a grin that lit up her round flushed face and her stout foot beat out the rhythm even stronger. He heard a few whoops from the crowd and some had stopped their talk and bobbed their heads instead, beating out time instead of words. This was the feel of it, the craic of it all and his tension eased even further. Thoughts and decisions were put to the side, or even far back in his mind where all the other ones kept company and told jokes at his expense. Ah the pure joy of it, the pure drop of it, he thought as the music flowed and the set moved on. He caught the eyes of some friends and gathered up his nods, thumbs ups and even a few winks until he saw her face and the rest of her hovering uncertainly at the edge of the group. The door, he'd forgotten the door. How stupid to face the door when you could play the music and scan the crowd and know that you had them all in the palm of your hand. Until she stood hovering there uncertainly, so there was no avoiding, no denying she'd come. Saoirse. Saoirse with her hair loose and wild about her, framing her fine-boned face.

She saw Smithy and her face lit up and that lit him up. Suddenly, he was glad for the heat and the fug that made him as red as he ever could be, so there was no evidence of the effect she had on him. His face must have shown something of the joy that rang through him, because she moved forward and the music stopped. Or rather the set finished, but for him it was as though the music itself recognised this was a moment that should be marked as she moved towards him and greeted him.

"Smithy, hey."

He nodded and found a foolish grin had slapped itself across his face.

"Who's your friend there, Smithy?" asked Liam.

His brow set off on another waggle and Smithy tried to get hold of himself.

"This is Saoirse. She's a musician," Smithy managed to say.

"We can see the case, Smithy," said Gearóid, his voice amused.

"What is it you play?" Liam asked Saoirse.

"And are you any good?" asked Aoife and then she laughed. Like wasn't it all a joke, but Smithy felt the darkness of it and suppressed the urge to kick her.

"Don't mind her," said Smithy, forcing a light tone. "She plays no favourites, she's rude to everyone."

"Come sit down and join us, so," said Gearóid. "There's another stool there behind Smithy. Smithy, Aoife, make a space for the newcomer."

Aoife threw him a glance but shifted her stool and Smithy watched as Saoirse dragged the one behind him up alongside him. She nodded to Aoife, her manner polite, but her arms were close to her side like she wanted to contain herself, or even put herself into the smallest space possible. But the space was there and it overlapped his, to his utter joy and consternation.

He smiled and nodded at her, trying to give her the encouragement he knew she needed in this strange pub among musicians unknown to her.

"They're all grand," said Smithy in a whisper to her. "You're well up to their standard and more. Get yourself set up and you'll see."

"Thanks," she said.

She smiled again, her hazel eyes wide and filled with gratitude. She took off her jacket and shook out her hair and Smithy was nearly undone all over again. He looked away, and Aoife caught his glance, her face filled with puzzlement and a mixture of other emotions Smithy didn't even want to contemplate. He took a deep breath and started to twist the pegs of his fiddle. Anything to distract him. Distraction was his current strategy, and it was as effective as a cobweb against a storm. He plucked a string and turned the peg. Pluck, twist, pluck, twist. He mimed the words in his head and couldn't help but think of others that rhymed. Her scent drifted over and he tried to analyse it, since the distraction approach was obviously abandoned before it had ever really begun, being the failure it was always meant to be. Jasmine? No, she wasn't one of those types. He thought on. Not musk or flowers, but something else and oh, the dead purity of it. The singularity of her scent and he thought, no. It's the numbers game, so. He started counting prime numbers and as the numbers rose in his mind, so did other parts of his body.

"Let's have another tune, then," said Smithy in desperation.

"Why don't you give us one, Smithy," said Gearóid.

"Oh, yes," said Aoife.

"Yeah," Liam said. "You know how Aoife just loves it when you give her a tune." He laughed with his mouth open and Smithy nearly counted all the teeth he'd dearly loved to knock out at that moment.

"Ah, no," said Smithy. "There's nothing that's come to me now. We should play one we all know. Give Saoirse a feel for the group and then she can join in."

"Oh, yeah, of course," said Liam.

With a word to Gearóid the two of them were off and the others following. Smithy pulled his bow across the strings, joining in with a gusto built of the relief of the music and the pace of the tune. Beside him he could hear Saoirse joining in and then Aoife who managed somehow to get the notes angry and aggressive. Oh, for feck's sake, thought Smithy. Will she just leave it alone and enjoy the music. The frustration and annoyance were good and he held on to it for a short while before the music and the playing took him over, and it wasn't the strident notes of Aoife's flute that wound their way inside him, but the lyrical clear tones of Saoirse's playing. It joined his fiddle and they danced around together, exchanging bows, circling and swinging like the partners they always were and were always meant to be. It was a tryst of the most flirtatious and bewitching kind. A tryst that you never wanted to end but knew that time and circumstance would part you all too soon.

Smithy let it happen. At least that's what he told himself, though he knew deep down inside there was no choice on his part, ever. It was as inevitable as any two things or happenings could be and he could only wonder and hope that it might be even a fraction the same for her. He daren't look at her to check, the disappointment would be something to unbearable on any day or circumstance, he just blindly stared across the pub, his bowing fluid, the music alive.

The music wound down, as it would of course, but the dancing and weaving rhythm in his body still moved and twined inside him, coursing like two hares in the madness of March. He took the fiddle from his chin and stared at his feet, trying to breathe. But the breath of him was gone. It was the hand on his arm that brought him to himself.

"Are you okay?" asked Saoirse, her eyes wide, filled with concern and something else.

It was the something else that caused him to look away again.

"I'm grand. Nothing to worry about. " He made himself look at her and smile.

"That was great craic," said Saoirse, her smile widening. Her eyes were sparkling and full of excitement. "Don't you think? I've never experienced anything like it. Like Inchigeela, only better. You were on fire. It was as though our instruments had a mind of their own."

"Yeah," said Smithy. He nodded weakly. "Something like that."

"Smithy is a real talent," said Aoife.

She reached around Saoirse and squeezed his arm. It lingered there for a moment and Smithy wanted to shake it off.

"Come on then Eilís, give us a song," said Liam.

"Oh, yes," said Aoife. "You must give us a song."

"*Does Your Mother Know You're Out,*" said Gearóid. "Give us that one."

"You want that song?" said Eilís. She shook her head and laughed. "Really?"

"It's a great song," said Gearóid.

"It is," said Daragh. "My own lad is learning it."

"Your lad?" said Eilís. "I can't see that. Who's making him, you?"

Daragh laughed. "No, you're wrong there. It's school."

"No, that can't be right," said Eilís.

"It's just a song," said Aoife.

"It's local," said Daragh. "That's the reason and nothing more."

"Come on, now," said Gearóid. "You sing it well."

Eilís shrugged. She closed her eyes a moment to find the note. Once found, she opened her eyes and began the song. It was a lively one, full of humour and innuendo. The pub crowd quieted and listened to it, roaring approval when required and a few whoops to back it up.

Smithy enjoyed it too. It gave him space to breathe, time to collect his wits and rein in his body which was having too much to say up to this point. He could still feel Saoirse's presence beside him, and her scent had taken up residence inside him. She held her flute in her lap and her hands played absently with the levers and the more he tried not to think about her fingers, her hands and the flute that she held, busily tapping and fiddling, the more it invaded his consciousness, the traitorous beast that it was. She licked her lips and the fingers kept tapping. She brushed her hair back from her right shoulder. The hair brushed his arm in the process and though he had the cloth of his shirt between his skin and her hair, it was as though every strand was touching him directly.

The song ended, but not the pure agony of his longing. He blinked and looked at the door, willing himself to get up and go outside, have a cigarette that he never smoked and do something to escape all this. All this that he knew was bad. All this that he'd never felt before but was certain wouldn't end well, because you could never risk something this intense with a mortal. Isn't that what Smithy knew? Isn't that what he'd seen others try, only to have it result in a grief that was deep and terrible? He sighed. To have lived this long and only now want it, when he knew all its pitfalls. His pure love for Bríd, the knowledge that he didn't deserve her, let alone anyone else, had protected him in the past, why not now?

He looked at Saoirse as if trying to puzzle out what it was that had made it happen now, even when he knew, deep down inside what it was. The flame coloured hair, not exactly like Bríd's, but close enough. The eye colour was close with its hazel colour, though the shade was darker. Her frame was more slender, less full breasted than Bríd's. She was tall, but not quite as tall. Her facial features were sharper, the nose wasn't quite the same. But all in all it was close enough, he supposed.

Saoirse, catching his glance, smiled at him again, her eyes soft.

"Thanks," she mouthed.

"For what?"

"For suggesting this. For being so good about it when I came."

He nodded, not knowing what else to say. His own stupidity was the reason he'd found himself in this state. Nothing else. He sighed.

The song finished to the clapping all round and a few shouts of praise. Eilís nodded and smiled and Gearóid beamed like a Fear an Tí who knows his crowd, because it was his idea to sing the song.

When the clapping died away and the chat resumed, Saoirse leaned across towards Eilís.

"What a song," she said. "I'd love to learn it. The humour in it. Perfect. I'd love to sing it up in Dublin sometime."

Smithy heard Dublin. He heard the 'going back' inference of the speech and again he reminded himself of the sheer stupidity of doing anything with what he was feeling. A feeling that he was about to halt with the getting up. With the walking outside. With the breathing deep and chatting and maybe even that never before cigarette. His feet started to get to grips with the floor. Sure, he could do this.

"Saoirse, you sing as well?" said Liam. "We'd love to hear you. Come, now give us an air, while the crowd is here and the feeling with us."

"No, I don't think so," she said, shyly. "You don't want to hear my songs. Yours are all so pure and local. I'm only a singer off of what I hear on the recording or YouTube, like."

"You're fine, you are," said Liam. "Sing what you will, it's grand."

"Yes," said Eilís. "Don't mind me. I've been hearing and singing these songs for longer than you've been alive. It'd be nice to hear you, whatever you have to sing."

Smithy halted, torn between what he knew to be best and his absolute desire to hear her, even though he was more than certain it would tear at his soul.

"Yes," said Aoife, tightly. "You must sing. Go on away, now."

Saoirse glanced at Aoife and her eyes sharpened. Smithy could see the look and understood it meant she would sing, now.

She looked to the distance to find the note in her head and

before Smithy could even prepare himself, put up the guard that must be erected if only for himself and his sanity, she began to sing. He sighed with the first note and as the song unfurled in its aching beauty he went inside himself, to join the music as the haunting melody of *An Binsin Luachra* wrapped itself around him. He sank into the rhythmic sea of it and even before he knew what he was about, he lifted the fiddle and pulled the bow softly across the strings, weaving the supporting web that carried the melody along—whisper thin, but with a tensile strength.

By the time the song finished Smithy knew he was lost. He lowered his fiddle and saw that Liam had played the flute as well. The pub was silent, marking the moment with the reverence it deserved and Smithy shook his head. Saoirse tugged his sleeve.

"Thank you," she said.

"It's me who should be thanking you," he said. "All of us should be thanking you."

The words came out of him, but he really wasn't noticing. She stared at him, her eyes wide, a small curve on her mouth as though she'd just discovered something that she'd not expected.

"You've no need to be shy about your singing," said Eilís.

"You don't at all," said Liam. "No, you were grand. You are definitely invited again."

They all laughed. Not Smithy though, whose own thoughts would second and third the idea that she might be here again and leave aside the inference that she would return to Dublin. But his heart and soul were otherwise occupied in a war with his mind that kept warning him to get up and take himself outside.

"Thank you. Thanks," said Saoirse. She smiled widely, her eyes alight as she looked at Smithy. Smithy's feet decided to plant themselves but his eyes hadn't left her face. This was a war his brain wouldn't win.

He nodded at her.

Liam chatted to Gearóid and before another word could be spoken by Smithy or his brain, the two were off on a jig and Smithy found himself lifting his fiddle to his chin. Saoirse followed suit with her flute and their eyes were still locked while the music bounced back and forth between them. It was just the two of them, the resumption of the circling, dancing, weaving thing they had going before. He loved it and felt its joy wash through him and knew whatever he did, he couldn't stop what was drawing him on.

The music finished, their dance continued. The fiddle was down on his lap, but the tune continued and soared on its own, he could hear it as clear as any bell that you cared to ring.

Saoirse held her flute tightly and then came to herself, looked down and placed it on her lap. She glanced over at him, the notion first in her eyes and then it slid down through her face to her mouth. Smithy could see it, could hear it before it ever made it out of her lips, shaped words that echoed and lingered.

"Smithy, have you thought any more about the whistle? Do you think you'll make it?"

The words, sure, weren't they already lodged in his heart, wedded and matched to the others that were there, waiting for them, the missing ones, the ones that would take them onward?

"Yeah, I have. It's there waiting for you back at the house."

"Can I come and pick it up?"

"You can of course. Will you come tonight?"

The smile was slow, tentative. "I will."

13

SAOIRSE

I was a mess, and I knew it. He could have asked me to do anything at that moment and I'd have done it. The music, if that was what it was, kept dancing around me, inside me, in a manner I'd never before experienced. I knew he felt it too, the way his eyes held mine, like he could see deep into my soul, or some such flight of fancy. This was no poem, though, for me to parse and tweak to get its best effect. This was bare and bold and true and I didn't know what to do with it.

He guided me through the thinning crowd to the back door and outside, his hand resting lightly on my back. We'd barely given the session time to finish before we were up and out of our seats like jackrabbits. Smithy made no excuse, just nodded to the others, gestured me to move in front of him, and he was off, no backward glance.

Myself, I caught a dark look from Aoife, the jealous cow, and allowed a moment for the satisfaction of it to join the other emotions that were holding court inside of me. But it didn't come, because there was no room, to be honest, there was no room at all, except for the sheer and utter strength of his pull on me, the desire and lust that swam in my body that took shape as music and spirals of dust. Smithy. I said his name in my head and the flash—or was it flush of desire—swept through me as I followed his muscled large frame out into the night.

"I'll take you there on my motorbike," he said. "Are you all right with that?"

"I am," I said. "No worries."

We drew alongside the bike and he unstrapped the helmet that was hanging from the seat and handed it to me.

"You'd best be the one to wear this," he said. "It's not far, though, so we should be fine."

He swung his leg over the bike and rocked it off its centre stand while I strapped the helmet to my head. With a quick kick he started the bike, the move made with practised ease and I loved it. I loved his quiet confidence, the arms stretched out to the handle bars, the spread of his legs along the bike. I loved it all and climbed up behind him. I had my flute tucked between us and his fiddle slung on my back. My short skirt parted and I moved forward to grip my thighs around his and put my arms on his waist. My own intake of breath met his and I wondered how much of this whistle I might actually see and play tonight.

THE RIDE to his house was short. Too short in some ways because I loved the sensation of nestling up against him, feeling the flex of his thigh muscles when he changed gear, or leaning into him and with him when he turned a corner. The bliss of it.

But we arrived and Smithy drew the bike into the small yard and parked it in a little shed next to the forge. I dismounted, shook out my hair and handed him the helmet. He nodded his thanks and once he'd dismounted, rested it on the bike. We'd been silent all this time, but our bodies were still speaking, as was every other bit of us. Our instruments were still playing those tunes and twining themselves around us in so many ways.

He grabbed my hand, weaving his fingers in mine and led me into the house. We went through the kitchen to the sitting room. He took my flute from me and placed it on the floor. His own fiddle he put in its usual corner and returned to me. He caught up both of my hands and kissed them, one after the other.

"Will I show you the whistle later?" he asked softly, his eyes capturing mine.

I nodded and moved towards him. Gently, I pressed up against him, raised my lips to his and kissed him. And he kissed me. Kissed me into next week, kissed me to the moon and back, with his subtle brushing and then deeper, full lipped and sensuous. My body rang out just at the first touch. His hands cupped my face, brushed down along my breastbone softly. I broke away for the barest moment necessary to take off my jacket and his too. It didn't seem enough and soon I was lifting his T-shirt and he was pulling at the buttons of my blouse.

Somehow they were removed, both the shirt and the sheer blouse. We stood there, me in my thin strapped shirt, bra, skirt and Doc Martens and he in his jeans and boots, and our hands paused, our eyes locked. He leaned down and kissed my neck, brushed kisses along my jaw, and down. I sighed with pure pleasure. It was so much, too much, a cup, no, a chalice, that overflowed. Just from the kiss of him and I was sinking into his touch.

He led me away then, into his bedroom and turned on a dim lamp on the table nearby.

"I want to see you, your beauty," he said. "Do you mind?"

"No," I said. "I want to see yours as well."

We undressed each other, the process a song, an air, a waltz that kept us dancing and entwining each other. He pulled my shirt and skirt over my head, pausing to caress my shoulder and my hip. And then a kiss here, a kiss there. He kicked off his boots and I unbuttoned his jeans and pulled them over his thighs, his calves. His jeans removed, he pulled me to him, the thin material of his boxers and my underwear the only thing between us. I ran my hands over his arms, his back. I kissed his chest and placed my hand over his erection. A groan and a sigh greeted the touch.

He pulled away and led me to the bed. With a few swift movements that left me Cinderella like, his hands were on my shoes and then my bare feet and legs as he removed my high stocking socks. He ran his hands along my legs, upward and my underwear was gone, slipped away to find the shoes and socks.

We lay there, together and soon to be one, our bodies finding their pace, their heat and the perfect place to meet. He moved along my body, kissing, tasting inside and out and we disappeared in a twist of stars, a brace of moons circling, twinkling until we were the dust of those stars scattered in the heavens. We'd entered those heavens together and like all the ancient stars, exploded and died over and over as we shot across the universe.

I FELT his kiss at the back of my neck. He'd brushed aside my hair just enough to give him space, his fingers whisper light across my back. I smiled and sighed at the bliss of it. I leaned into the kiss and he drew me closer still against him, raining kisses now along my shoulder while he tangled his hand in my hair. He'd wound my hair around his hand and dragged the hand through the strands many times in the night, kissing it and marvelling at it, as much as he kissed and marvelled at the rest of me.

He hadn't been the only one worshipping last night. It was a night made perfect by each and every time we worshipped and consumed each other. It was a night like no other, that much I knew, and I could only hope he felt the same. We worshipped again now, each finding the other's altar and laying us bare to the desires of our souls and hearts. At least that's how I saw it, how I felt it.

This time, when we'd finished, when we pulled away with our sighs and lingering lips, Smithy ran a finger along my face.

"I'll make us a tea, then shall I? A bit of breakfast?"

"You mean it's morning? It's not a trick of the light?" I said lightly.

"Sadly, it's well into the morning. And I should get you back. Your grandmother will worry, will she not?"

I shrugged. "I feel like Cinderella, about to turn into a pumpkin. She'll be grand. I'll text her and say I'm with a friend."

He grinned. "A friend, is it?"

"A very special friend."

"Well at least I'm special," he said.

"You are special," I said, suddenly serious. I kissed him, put my hand to his face. "So very special."

His eyes were lit, an emerald green that sparkled like a true gem. He was true, all right. He was my true.

He gave me a peck on the cheek and got out of bed. I watched him, delighting in his body, one that any artist would be unable to resist. He shoved on his jeans and left the room, while his image, his presence lingered around me and in me. I leaned over and pulled out the small notebook that always resided in the pocket of whatever I was wearing. The skirt, as it happened to be last night. I looked around the room and saw a biro on the small chest next to the bed and took it up. Deftly I noted the words, the images that came in my head, inspired by the perfection that was him and the night and music that was.

Maybe it was because of the music still playing its notes inside me that it poured forth, spilling out of my heart and the body that had danced the dance since the moment I'd walked in and saw Smithy sitting in the session, fiddle in hand. The sheer talent of him, the body that was him and the soul that played the music. I wanted it all, I needed it all and for some reason, I felt that if I could capture half of the need and desire on paper, it might not escape me.

"What are you up to?" said Smithy, returning, bearing a tray of mugs and a plate heaped with toast.

"Ah, look at you," I said. "You're too good."

He smiled. "Anything for my lady."

"I'm your lady now, am I?"

"You are of course. And I'm your special friend."

"No, you're my man."

"My lord?" he said, his voice teasing.

"My lord, my man."

"My lady, my woman."

He placed the tray on the bed, leaned over and gave me a long lingering kiss. My desire, only somewhat abated, rose again and I reached up to touch his chest, the notebook still in my hand. He pulled away and took the notebook from me.

"What's this, then? Keeping notes? Writing your dark desires in your diary?"

I laughed. "I am of course. You've awakened them all."

He looked up from the notebook. "Them all? Dark desires?"

"What else?"

He lifted my hand to his lips and kissed them, his eyes darkening. "I'm sure I could awaken a few more, soon enough."

"Oh, do please."

He placed my hand on my abdomen, let his hand linger and trace a line over my nipple.

"Soon," he said. "Soon. Breakfast first."

I laughed, the joy of the promise so unexpected and completely wanted.

He handed me a mug and offered a bit of toast. I took one slice and he took another, settling back on the bed beside me.

"I find it difficult to concentrate on my toast, my lady, with your lovely breasts on display," he said."

"Shall I cover my modesty?" I tugged up the sheet. Just as swiftly he tugged it back down.

"No modesty required. I shall look at your notebook and discover what dark desires I could visit upon you."

I laughed, if only to cover my nervousness. Part of me trusted him to treat me well, but honestly, for what he read in there. No one had seen my scribblings and except for the few poems that had either made it into songs, or were published in one of the university rags out of the notebook, no one even knew of my efforts.

The silence, while he read, stretched on for a while, the time longer than I was comfortable with, because I reached over and started to take it away, gather it back inside me and my own thoughts of the ways life had imprinted itself and quizzed its way through the years.

He looked up and kept a firm grip on it. "You wrote these?"

I nodded, my look tentative.

"Saoirse, these are really good. Are you published? You are, I'm sure. Of course you are."

He handed the notebook back to me. "What a woman you are. The music, the poetry." He shook his head. "You honour me, my lady."

There, the hint of a smile. I could hang on to that, ride it out and get back to the desire and play that was our dance.

"Of course, I do. Doesn't any lady honour her lord?" I took a bit of my toast and chewed it in an obvious manner.

He laughed and ran a hand over my hair, trailing it down. "Such beauty, too."

"You're a lucky lad, aren't you then?"

"I am, so."

He took the mug and toast from me and set it on the plate which he put on the tray. He placed his own things there and shoved the tray aside and pulled me to him.

"Now, those dark desires. They must be tended to."

HE UNWRAPPED THE CLOTH, slowly, as if it were a moment of reverence. In a way it was, at least for me. My anticipation and urge to play this whistle, crafted by such a man as Smithy, fed into the reverence and the music that still danced and weaved its way around inside me, heightened everything around this moment.

He pulled out the whistle and I saw it gleam in his hands. Even then, in his hand, it seemed alive, something more than a perfect low whistle. It was something I had no words for.

Without knowing, I reached over for the whistle and took it from him. It felt cool and hot at the same time, alive and not. I ran my fingers along its length, getting acquainted with its shape and learning who and what it was.

Smithy watched me closely, saying nothing, but his eyes were speaking all sorts and they hummed in the air along with the music already in our bodies. This was all part of it, I suddenly knew, this was the completion of the dance, our dance, our hearts, this music. I looked up at him and lifted the whistle to my lips and began to play. I started with a simple tune, unwilling to test any of us so quickly, trying to prepare all parts of myself and Smithy for what we both knew was to come.

Without any discussion or word, Smithy moved over to his fiddle and removed it from its case. I played on, the simple tune, an air that everyone knew and would play given half the chance, while the whistle and I waited for him. We waited and knew the moment he moved the bow across the strings, no tuning required, for this was a moment that was already perfectly tuned. Our bodies were tuned, our hearts and souls. The whistle bound us firmly, moving on to the real tune, the tune that was us. Smithy's fiddle found its place with the whistle and they entered the union that was always meant to be and he entered me.

We played on and on, not needing to stop because there was no end to this piece, this air, this tune, because it was ours and ours alone.

It was only when the light was dimming that I realised so much time had passed and in that time we had moved around each other, changing places back and forth, until we'd found our seats on the chairs next to each other.

I lowered the flute and he took the fiddle from his chin, each a motion so choreographed we knew the thought had been shared.

He looked at me. "Well, my lady, you'd better text your grandmother and tell her you're having dinner and staying the night with your special friend."

"Of course, my lord. I will do as you say. "

I picked up my phone and noticed a text message. It was the solicitor's office.

Matter cleared up. Collect house keys at earliest convenience.

I shrugged the message away. It had little meaning for me now. I was starting to find my home here and this time it was a real home.

14

SMITHY

Smithy shut the door quietly to the house and made his way across the yard to the forge. His arms were singing, his body was singing. He was singing. He could barely remember the feeling and how there was nothing like it. But then there hadn't ever been anything like the last day and two nights. How could he match what was matchless? Was it the magic that sang through him mixed with her, Saoirse, into a blend that was matchless and priceless and filled him with all that could be and ever was? It was everything he thought it was with Bríd and ever could be with her, and here, in this little out of the way place, he had found an echo of all of it with a mortal. Any question or thought that didn't rejoice with him at this moment he set aside, pushed to the outer realms of his thoughts and body to take up residence in the "Take Yourself Off" land.

For now, he resisted the pull back to his bed where she lay, with her glorious soft skin, beautiful hair and musical dance. He would work the forge instead and bring forth the buzzing, the singing into a form that was calling him now.

He entered the forge and let the light pour forth. Over the bench, light emptied in from the Velux window he'd put in the roof and revealed the tools on the bench. Swiftly, he lit the forge, using a touch of magic. He could do that now. Everything else he did as he would have in any age or world. He turned to the bench where the steel bar rested. It was the one from the Watchers, the men he'd bargained with back in the fairy hills outside of Inchigeela. They'd brought it for him from the Otherworld, never averse to a little deal here or there, as they moved between worlds and kept watch on those that were marked. Why they were watching in this area, he didn't care to know. He'd paid them enough of his own precious hoard of silver to ensure it wasn't him. He was going nowhere. This work, this sword in the making, was all for him, and no one else. This magic was too fragile and unknown to be anything else. And he was done with it all. Every last bit of any rising, any further attempt to bring down Balor, to wipe out him and his evil eye. Before, it had brought him nothing but pain and destruction, as well as death. Bríd was gone, and with it, her love. The only thing that was left of their love was his guilt.

Those thoughts he threw into the "Take Yourself Off" Land, to join the rest of that unruly gang that threatened the joy and music of right now. He put on his gloves, and with his tongs, took up the piece of steel with its thread of silver magic in it, shoving it into the forge. The hiss of the fire on metal sounded loud and found its own music. Smithy smiled. He could hear the magic playing and finding the dance. The sizzle and spin, the roar of the flame in answer.

He withdrew the metal when it was ready and took up his hammer to begin the fashioning. Hammer, shape, hammer, shape, ringing the changes. The metal glowed and moved and then it began, the humming and fizzing through his body, weaving around him, in him and through him. The blade began to sing, running the melody of fire and metal. He nearly roared with the pleasure of it, the feel of its response, its jubilant shape.

He felt an extra boost of the energy, the power shaping and singing its music and dancing its dance. It was a few moments before he realised that Saoirse stood next to him, clad only in his T-shirt, her hand resting on his shoulder, her eyes filled with admiration and wonder.

That touch filled him more and more as it linked with his music and the dance grew more potent. The magic roared and grew, encasing them with its heady power. Smithy let it happen, watched the sword blade shape and grow and become.

And when it was ready, when all its shape was found, he plunged it into the water, quenching the fire and imprinting the form. He chose water, not oil, so sure was he of the firing and the blade's response to the power within it. A sword blade added to the world. Magic.

Smithy carefully lowered his tongs, removed his gloves and stared at the blade. Saoirse put her arm around him.

"I've never seen anything like it," she said. "It was like magic."

He turned and kissed her head, slipping his arm around her shoulders. He could feel the warmth of her, the skin of her through the T-shirt.

He sighed. "It was."

She looked up at him and smiled. "You are so talented, my handsome man."

"In what way, my lady?"

She gave him a little shove. "In that way too. But I meant your smith work. I can see why they call you Smithy. It's clearly more than a job to you."

He laughed. "It's definitely more than a job."

"Will you show me how?" she asked. "Maybe something small? I'd like to try it."

He looked at her sceptically. "It can be tiring. I do the hammering manually and that takes strength in the arms."

"But you'll help me, won't you? I just want to get a sense of it myself. Please?"

He couldn't say no, of course he couldn't. It was a given, even aside from the fact or the feeling that he really wanted to try and create something with her. To see if the pure magic of their coming together in music and making love would spill over into the forging of metal.

He drew her close to him and gave her a kiss on the lips. "Go dress yourself properly, then."

She hugged him briefly and then was away. He watched her leave, taking in the long legs and the way his T-shirt found all the right curves of her body and rested there.

"Oho, hey, hey," said a voice from outside. One of the Watchers popped its head at the door.

"What are you doing here?" said Smithy irately. "Did I not tell you to never come here, directly to my house?"

"Ah, now, don't be like that," said the Watcher and he stepped inside.

Behind him came the other three, all short, dark haired and dressed the same. Brothers? Probably, he couldn't remember. So much of that world was foreign to him now. Almost as if he'd never lived there. As if that life was someone else's. Almost.

"Have you need of more fairy blade steel?"

Smithy frowned. "Fairy blade steel? The filming for *Darby O'Gill and The Little People* finished decades ago, lads. Just so you know."

"Oh the humour of him," said Your One, the first one in.

"Humours of Smithy," said Your One, the second one in.

They all laughed. Not Smithy.

"Just go, lads. I've nothing needed."

"But we wanted to see," said Your One, the third one in.

The three others nodded.

"There's nothing to see," said Smithy. "Nothing at all." He

kept his eyes away from the blade on the bench where the sun, curse it, was shining down in its glory, rimming the new blade in light.

"Oh, but there is," said Your One, the first one in. "We can smell the magic."

"We can smell it in the blade," said Your One, the second one in.

"We can smell it on you," said Your One, the third one in.

Smithy looked at Your One, the fourth one in. "Nothing to say?" he said.

Your One, the fourth one, shrugged.

Smithy rolled his eyes. "Nothing to see here lads, really there isn't. Yes, I used the metal and tried my hand. But that's all it was. And all it has been, you know that."

They all looked at one another and began to laugh.

"Ah, Smithy, aren't you the devil," said Your One, the first one.

And just like that, they left. Your Ones. The Watchers. Just like that and every other time.

But it wasn't just like every other time, Smithy knew it and he felt uneasy.

SAOIRSE RETURNED SOON after the Watchers departed. She had on her boots, sock stockings and skirt, but she still wore his T-shirt and he found that he was glad of it. At the sight of her smile and the light in her eyes when she entered, the uneasy feelings were successfully pushed aside. She came to his side and slipped her arm around his waist.

"Well, are you going to help me set the world afire and forge a whole new experience?"

"And what else would I do?"

She squeezed his waist. "Then set to, my lord."

He felt the little thrill that she'd carried the playful banter from the day before through to now. Sure, that meant something? Something added to all the other things that were piled up now, piled so high he couldn't see in front of himself or behind.

He scooped up a clump of her hair, still hanging loose. "We should tie this back, first. Though your hair might be the colour of flames, I would hate for it to become a head of flames."

Laughing, she started to gather it together, but he put a hand to stop her. "Let me. Please."

She gave no reply, just nodded. Smithy brushed the hair off her shoulders and collected up all of it in his hands, smoothing it carefully as he went. It was so soft, thick and silken to the touch. He wanted to bury his face in it, smell its sweet scent, but he made himself section it off and begin to plait it, weaving slowly, loving how the locks twined and slipped through his fingers. When he was done, he tucked the plait inside her T-shirt and patted her back.

"There now, hazard removed."

"Thank you. I feel safer now."

"I should hope so, my lady."

"My brave and handsome knight."

"Handsome?" he asked, his tone teasing.

"Of course. I would have no other kind of knight."

He laughed at those words from this strange girl. What girl in this age, these times, spoke like this? Not the kind of banter he was used to hearing. Not that he was complaining, not at all.

He moved over to the small press near the bench and retrieved a pair of safety glasses.

"More hazard avoidance," he said, handing them to her. "We can't have any harm come to your lovely eyes."

"Lovely?"

"Of course. I would have no other kind for my lady."

She laughed this time and he drew her over to the bench and began to tell her about smith work. She listened attentively, nodding and asking intelligent questions. Soon, it became more than just a cursory demonstration in which he would include her in only the most basic parts, but a real lesson with a prospective craftsperson. She was quick, she was a natural, even as she gripped the tongs and heated a small piece of ordinary steel, readying it for shaping. He hadn't thought to make a blade with her, not in the beginning. He had decided to try something simple, just a shape beaten from a thin piece of metal, but he found himself explaining the process of making a blade. Maybe it was from her questions, or her quick understanding, but that's where it led and he could only follow.

When the shaping began and she lifted the hammer, Smithy could see the absolute focus in her eyes and the true aim of her hammer. He saw the muscles tighten, even as he issued the instructions in a soft voice, repeating his earlier explanations. His voice coaxed and supported. As he stood close behind her, watching and supervising, he began to feel the hum rise inside of him. He closed his hand around hers that held the tongs when he thought there was a slight shake and the hum rose to a roar. The roar exploded as he grasped her other hand, giving it his strength and support as they hammered the blade into shape. The roaring sparked and lit into stars that coursed and danced inside him, outside him and around them both. He'd never felt this, not ever in this world. She pressed against him and the feel of her back against his chest, her buttocks against his groin set him afire and the sparks flew off him and circled her.

"My god, Smithy," Saoirse whispered softly.

But Smithy couldn't speak. The magic was in him. The magic was around him, it was filling the room and creating something out of the blade in front of him. No need for the magic-filled metal. They had created it on their own. The blade itself was pure magic.

With few words, he helped her plunge it in the water to temper it and worked with her through the next steps. There was nothing he could say, for no words came to his mind that she would understand, accept or need. That she felt something of what had happened couldn't be denied. But he could offer nothing to her should she ask, because, above all, he had no understanding of it himself. This strange mortal girl had found ways to unlock so much of him and who he was, without even knowing it. If indeed it had been her, but before that thought was given full voice he knew there was no doubt. There was something special about her and though he knew it should make him cautious, he could only surrender to her and how completely undone he felt.

When the blade was finished and laid gleaming on the bench, Saoirse turned from admiring their handiwork and looked at him. She reached her hand up and stroked his face, her hazel eyes holding his. They'd gone greener now in the sun that poured from the roof light, and he caught his breath with the sight of them. His skin was hot, racing still with the sparks that lingered and circled his body. Saoirse closed the distance and kissed him slowly, deeply. He responded at the instant of her touch, all of the magic and fire pouring into the kiss and spreading out. And the magic and fire raged between them, binding them, fusing them into one. And all Smithy could think was how glorious it felt as, clothes removed and they lay naked on the shed floor, the two became one.

HE HAD one more night with her. The two of them couldn't break away, couldn't part. Not just yet. So another text was sent and her grandmother's reply was more humorous than annoyed so they could relax and Smithy could woo his lady the rest of the evening. They made time for a little music, some conversation and food, but the rest was spent together body as well as soul, as if any time apart was time lost.

So, when the morning came and Smithy reluctantly admitted to himself that his work was looming and she said she had to get fresh clothes on, the two agreed that they would part, but only for now. Only for now and the now would become then, the then that would have them back together again.

Oh, this mortal girl, Smithy thought as he cleared away the breakfast things, how she weaved me in her lovely web. And I'm a willing captive. He gave a mental snort at his soppy self. A fool for love, yes indeed. Wasn't that the song?

"I'm ready," said Saoirse, coming into the kitchen. She had her flute case in her hand and the whistle tucked safely in her soft leather jacket.

Smithy sighed at the sight of her. She was beautiful, so innocent and untouched. Well almost, he thought wickedly. He'd touched her most thoroughly over the past few days.

He leaned over and kissed her. "Right, so. I'll take you back on the bike."

"Ah, you don't have to," she said. "I can walk. It's only a fine mist out there."

"Don't be silly. It will be quicker and save your clothes."

She grinned. "You just want me gripping you tightly for a little while longer."

He gave her a mock pout. "You found me out, so you have."

She nudged him gently and they both laughed. Smithy pulled on his own jacket, took her hand and led her out of the house to the small shed where the bike was parked. He handed her a spare helmet and put on his own. When it was secured he rocked the bike off its stand and rolled it out of the shed. Saoirse followed and waited while he started it and then climbed on behind him. He felt her push up close behind him, her legs gripping close to his, her hands tight around his waist. It felt good, almost too good and he tried not to think of her breasts up against him.

They rode the bike up the back road towards her grandmother's house. Saoirse pointed when to turn and he followed her directions without any thought but the feel of her and how soon he could make the few days pass until she would come again for another few days. Maybe he could persuade her to stay longer. Forever. The thought didn't send the panic through him that in any other instant it would and he let it settle on him. Forever. Well, her forever, let's face it, thought Smithy. Not his forever. But that would do.

Saoirse tapped his arm and pointed. "In there," she shouted.

He pulled the bike up suddenly, too shocked to do anything else. The bike stalled.

Saoirse pulled off her helmet. "No, it's grand, you can pull into the yard there."

"You live here?" asked Smithy, his voice choked. He could barely get the words out.

"Well, yes. At least this is my grandmother's house." She dismounted from the bike and went to face him.

"No," said Smithy. "No, it can't be."

"What?"

A figure emerged from the side of the house. Smithy nodded to the figure.

"You don't mean...is she your grandmother?"

"Goibhniu," said Saoirse's grandmother.

Smithy turned to look at her. He removed his helmet, if only to give his rage, his horror, his feeling of betrayal, room.

"What have you done?" he roared. "What the fuck is going on? Whatever it is, I'm having no part of it.

"She's here to help you," said Saoirse's grandmother. "Admit it, it's true. Have you not felt it, seen it?"

"She's gone," he yelled.

"You know that's not true," she said. "Deep down you know that. And haven't these past few days confirmed it?"

"I told you no," said Smithy. "I can't do it. End of story. The magic is gone. Bríd is gone. And I'm partly to blame. Nothing can change that. Do you hear me? Nothing."

"You know that's not true either. Any of it. You can and will do it. She's not gone, she's here. And you are not to blame."

Saoirse grabbed Smithy's arm. "What's going on? What are you talking about? Who's Goibhniu? Who's Bríd?"

Smithy stared at her, assessing her, but his mind screamed, his soul agonised. No, he couldn't do it. He couldn't revisit that pain or risk more.

"Get your grandmother to tell you." He said, his voice dripping with sarcasm. He gave Saoirse a dark look, started the motorbike and drove off.

15

SAOIRSE

I stared after Smithy as he retreated up the road on his motorbike, still shocked by the exchange I'd just witnessed. What had happened? I just didn't understand it. All the joy, the emotion, and yes, the love I'd felt developing over the last few days wilted under the onslaught of his recent actions. Assault. That's what it had felt like, in truth. Slaughter, a cutting down. A slashing, burning of everything inside me that had blossomed. I was numb.

I turned slowly to my grandmother. "What did he mean? Why did he say all those things?" I fought the tears that threatened suddenly to overwhelm me. "He acted as if he hated you." I swallowed. "And hated me."

"He doesn't hate you," my grandmother said. "In fact, it's quite the opposite. He loves you. Too much, maybe, but that's how it's meant to be."

My head snapped up at her words. "What do you mean by that? Stop being so cryptic. What is going on? Who's Goibhniu? Who's Bríd?"

My grandmother gestured to me. "Come inside. It's wet

enough standing here. We'll have a cup of tea and you can ask your questions then."

I knew she was right and reluctantly I followed her inside. I wouldn't let my questioning rest for long. I was determined to get some answers from her. I swallowed the pain that rose, the music inside me now drifted into a mournful air, the dance solemn, yearning for a partner that had gone quiet. Had left. A flare of anger took me by surprise. I'd done nothing. Nothing to bring on the onslaught of vitriol and rage that Smithy had directed towards my grandmother. And me.

I sat at the table and waited for the tea. There were no words spoken while I waited, as if she knew I would have batted aside anything trivial or mundane spoken with the anger it deserved. And it was anger that settled on me now. Settled from above and rose from below. It would consume me soon, I knew, but I wanted answers first. For now, I suppressed it all.

My grandmother, mugs in hand, took a seat opposite me and pushed one of the mugs towards me. I took it, cradled it in my hands and organised my thoughts.

"Now, can you please tell me what's going on? Who is Goibhniu? Who is Bríd?"

She smiled at me warmly. "Smithy is Goibhniu."

"Smithy? What do you mean? That's his name?" Puzzled, I considered it. "Why is that so upsetting? Doesn't he want anyone to know? I mean it's not a conventional name, it's more like something from the ancient myths..." my voice trailed off. I looked at my grandmother darkly. "What's going on? You're not telling me that...that Smithy is Goibhniu? The Goibhniu? Goibhniu, the Smith God?" I stared at her confused and horrified. "But that's absurd. That must be a joke. A joke he doesn't like. Is that it?" Even as I said those words, which were more about convincing myself than confirming what had happened, I looked at her face and I knew. I knew it from the music inside me that lifted at his name. His real name. The dance that played at the sound of Goibhniu. The name echoed inside me, calling me. Calling him.

"Oh, my god, it's true."

I gave a little hysterical laugh at the words I'd just spoken. My god. I'd even called him a god. Another little hysterical laugh escaped me. My grandmother reached over and put her hand over mine. I looked up at her, saw the expression of concern, understanding and something else. Relief mixed with joy. Joy? For feck's sake.

"If he is Goibhniu...then who are you?" I asked slowly, partly afraid of her answer. I suddenly had a thought. "Anu," I said softly. "You're Anu."

My grandmother, or the person who told me she was my grandmother, nodded.

A small gasp of hysteria escaped from me. "Of course you are."

I shook my head, my hand on my mouth. As if my hands could keep in all the thoughts so they wouldn't spill into words.

Anu put her hands on top of mine and this time she squeezed. "I am your grandmother. Whatever else I am, I am your grandmother."

I pulled my hands away from hers. "You're everyone's grandmother," I said, sardonically. "Isn't that right? Are you not the ultimate in grandmothers? The Earth Mother?"

She smiled sadly. "I am most of all, your grandmother."

"Why? Because I'm here with you? Because I'm an orphan and you took pity on me?"

"Because you are my granddaughter. You are Bríd."

I sniffed. "Yes, of course. Bríd. The other mystery in this little puzzle. The fact is that I'm not Bríd, I'm Saoirse. No, wait. My communion name was Bridget. But that's as close to Bríd as you'll get concerning me." I pointed to myself. "Not a goddess. Sorry."

"You are. You just aren't aware of it. At least not fully. You may have had inklings up until now."

I narrowed my eyes. "Inklings?"

"Think about it, Bríd."

"Saoirse," I said, stubbornly. But her words struck something deep within me. I withdrew my hands and bunched them in my lap. But I shook my head. "Sorry, nothing."

She sighed. My grandmother. Anu. Whoever she was. She sighed and sorrow rose filled her eyes.

"Bringing me to life?"

"It's a long tale, Bríd. And I will tell you if you will listen." Her voice was gentle, kind.

"Tell me then," I said sharply.

She looked down at her hands. "Do you know something of the tales of our people?"

"Tales of your people? Do you mean the myth cycles? The stuff Lady Gregory and others wrote down? Those tales?"

"Our people, Bríd. But yes, those tales."

I shrugged. "Some."

She sat back, settling in a bit. "Have patience then, while I tell it in my own way."

She took a deep breath. "In the time before time, peoples led by Nemed came to settle in this land and became known as the Nemedians. They arrived from a land inhabited by the Fomorians, or at least that's what they are known as in the tale. A deceitful and cruel people who were overlords to the Nemedians. Later, the Fomorians left their homelands and came here as well to settle. The Nemedians defeated them eventually, but they would not stay subdued. And finally, they succeeded against the Nemedians and exacted tribute. The Nemedians were furious and they sought help from others across the sea from their land. Powerful warriors, strong in magic. They came and the fleet anchored off shore. Spells were cast by both sides. The Nemedians were victorious in the end in that battle, but Conann, the Fomorian king, remained in his tower. More Fomorians arrived and battles ensued. Suddenly, a huge wave engulfed the land. Only thirty Nemedians survived and a boatload of Fomorians. Following this, the Nemedians lived in constant fear of the Fomorians. Eventually the Nemedians left, some returning to their original homeland.

"A long time later another group of Nemedians came to Ireland, the Fir Bolg. They arrived and they prospered. The land was divided into kingships and the five provinces. The ones we know today.

"Another group of Nemed's descendants came too, eventually. The people of Anu. My people. Our people. The people the tales call the Tuatha de Danann. They were powerful and skilled in all the magic arts and they brought with them their magic treasures, the Lía Fail stone, what eventually came to be called the Spear of Lugh, the deadly Sword of Nuada who was the king at the time, and Daghda's cauldron. The original peoples numbered among them my children, Daghda included."

I started to voice a question, but she held up a hand to silence me. "You promised patience," she said. She cleared her throat and resumed her tale.

"They took refuge in the land that is today called Scotland. It was a bleak and harsh land, so the Tuatha de Danann left and came to Ireland, a land they believed was rightfully theirs. They landed and even burned their boats so any option to retreat from the current rulers, the Fir Bolg, was removed. They conjured up a darkness to help them move around the country unnoticed and surprised the Fir Bolg in Connacht. There were several battles. In the final battle, the first battle of Magh Tuireadh, the Fir Bolg were defeated and those remaining fled to the remote islands around the land. During that battle, King Nuada lost an arm. Since no king who isn't physically whole is permitted to rule, the kingship was given to Eochid Bres, the handsome son of Elotha, a Tuatha de Danann and a man who was a Fomorian chief whom Bres knew nothing about. The condition for Bres's acceptance was that he would step down when he no longer pleased the people. Bres seemed a good choice and as part of this faith, Bríd was given to him as a wife.

"But Bres began to favour the Fomorians, who pushed him to oppress the de Danann, force them to pay tribute and perform difficult and menial tasks. The de Danann reminded him of his pledge that he would quit if he no longer pleased the people and Bres begged to be allowed seven years grace, which they granted. But instead of using the time to prove his worth, Bres gathered Fomorian warriors to his side and crushed the Tuatha de Danann. It was then he learned his true identity from his mother, who took him to the Fomorian lands and introduced him to his father. His father sent him to the ferocious warrior, Balor, King of the Isle and Indech, King of the Fomorians. Together, they gathered an army.

"In the meantime, Nuada's arm had been festering and he sent for Miach, the son of Diancecht, the one whose power was medicine, and told him to arrange for his old arm to be retrieved. Miach put it in place and chanted and in three days it was completely healed, but with a casing of silver. Diancecht was so jealous of his son's power he eventually he killed him, but Nuada's arm remained healed and he claimed himself ready to fight to reclaim his throne.

"He picked Lugh, a warrior of unsurpassed skill, magic and

talent, to head up his army. Goibhniu, whose magic was over smithcraft, was instructed to fashion and repair weapons along with Credne. Goibhniu's weapons were known to all for their ability to make any warrior undefeated.

"Lugh, Daghda and Ogma went to the three war goddesses to ask how to best plan the battle. Daghda knew Morrigan, one of the war goddesses and had an arrangement to meet with her every Samhain. So later, after the plans were formed, and he'd managed to secure an agreement with the Fomorians to delay the battle a while longer, he met with Morrigan and convinced her to fight on their side.

"It came time for the battle that would decide the fate of everyone. Daghda and the others decided that Lugh was too valuable to be risked in the individual battles of the champions and they kept him at the back, guarded by nine warriors. It was the eve of Samhain when the individual battles began and it ran for several days, with champions fighting tirelessly, one to one. In order that the warriors remained fit and well enough to resume battle the next day, the Tuatha de Danann had them bathe in the waters of the Well of Slane, where Diancecht and his remaining two sons had cast healing spells. Desperate to know the secret of the De Danann warriors' invincibility, the Fomorians sent a spy, Ruadan, who saw Diancecht and his sons cast spells on the well. He also watched Goibhniu lead the smiths in fashioning enchanted swords.

"Enraged, Ruadan attacked Goibhniu and wounded him with his spear. Goibhniu plucked the spear from his body and threw it at Ruadan, sending him staggering back to die among his people, but not before he told the Fomorians about the well. Later, the Fomorians filled the well with stones, rendering it useless.

"The armies drew together in pitched battle, Lugh escaped his guards and buckled on the breast plate of Manannan, whose power extended over the seas, and who was Lugh's foster father. The armour was so powerful that whoever wore it was safe from all battle wounds. He also donned a bronze helmet and swung his glistening blue black shield onto his back and attached the smooth sharp sword of Goibhniu to his side. He took up his long poisonous spear in his right hand, got into a chariot and drove into battle. Lugh, the son of Cían, son of Diancecht. Lugh, son of Eithne, the daughter of King Balor. But a Tuatha de Danann fully in heart and spirit, no matter his mother's blood.

"During the battle, Lugh saw Balor, the King of the Isles, his own grandfather, kill Nuada. Furious, Lugh fought his way through to confront Balor. But all had heard of Balor and his power. The magic poison that had been poured in his eye. A poison so deadly that anyone whom Balor chose to look upon with that eye would fall dead. But Lugh knew to be wary and with his shield held up to protect him, he approached Balor, took up a sling at his waist and cast a stone that passed right through Balor's eye out through the back of his head. The poison unleashed and killed all the Fomorians around him.

"Emboldened by Balor's death and Lugh's bravery, the other Tuatha de Danann fought with a renewed ferocity and at Morrigan's urging, along with the other war goddesses that joined her, they drove the Fomorians into the sea. Bres fled with them. When they'd gone, Morrigan climbed the nearest mountain and chanted a paean of victory to the land and its inhabitants."

Her words trailed off and I waited for more. That couldn't be all of the tale. And it was a tale, because what else could it be? Fragments of it stirred in my memory from a book maybe, but this was the first time I'd heard all of the tale. Or this much of the tale, because it seemed to me there were pieces missing.

"Bríd. What happened to her?"

My grandmother—or at least the woman in front of me—

closed her eyes a moment, pain and sorrow passing over her face.

"What?" I said. "You told me she married Bres. Well, did she go with him to the Fomorians lands? Did she flee Ireland with him?"

"No. No, she was left there, abandoned, when Bres went off to the Fomorians. And it was then that Tuirenn, the King of Ben Eadair found her and took her off. Raped her. She became pregnant..." her voice cracked and with effort she added "And died giving birth to his three sons."

I sat there, stunned at what I heard. I certainly hadn't expected that ending. "She died? But how could that happen? What about the magical well, the Well of Slane? Or wasn't she fit for it, being a woman?"

The woman before me frowned. "Women were warriors too. They had as much right to that well. No, it wasn't a case of her being unworthy. It was a case of the King of Eadoir and retrieving her body from him. He wouldn't give us her body. He wouldn't tell us where she was buried, if she was buried. He told us nothing. Not even after Goibhniu pleaded and offered him anything in return for her body."

She'd caught my attention fully with Goibhniu. "And how exactly does Goibhniu fit in with Bríd? You made no mention of those two being involved."

"They were. They were two halves of a whole. Because my lovely Bríd had and has the power of magic over smithcraft, among other things."

I ignored the present tense she'd slipped in. "So they share some of the same powers, is that all?"

She looked at me hard then. "No, that's not all, is it? You know that as certainly as Goibhniu knows. Your energy together creates such a strong magic that it can forge the most power-filled objects imaginable."

I looked away from her piercing eyes, remembering what it had been like with Smithy yesterday and shifted uncomfortably. I forced a shrug. "They made a good team."

"They loved each other. Beyond reason. They were as one, male and female perfectly balanced, whole."

"Then why did she marry Bres?"

It was her turn to look away. "It was a matter of politics. One that left us little choice when he asked to have her as his wife."

I snorted. "Yet again. A woman used as a bargaining tool. Didn't Goibhniu have anything to say about it?"

"Yes, yes he did. But we set aside his arguments, his persuasions. I set them aside. I told Bríd she must make this choice for the good of her people, for the good of the land."

"That didn't really work out for you in the end, did it?"

"No," she said quietly. "It did not."

"Poor Goibhniu. He must have been heartbroken," I said before I could think and nearly clapped my hand over my mouth. Stupid woman, I chided myself. Would you just get a rein on your tongue before you sink deeper.

"Beyond words," said the woman in front of me. "So much so, that when the battle was won he left and we saw nothing of him until the Gaels came."

"The Gaels?" I said. "Oh, right. The Gaels. The whole 'Beyond the Ninth Wave' and your man, Amergin coming to Ireland. "

"Invading Ireland."

"Well isn't that what you did? What they all did?"

She raised her brows and then eventually nodded, conceding the point.

"So Goibhniu joined you in the fight."

"It wasn't quite that. But yes, he stood with us, but apart, in some ways. And when they made their final landing and the negotiations were complete he came with us to the mounds, the forts designated for us. At least initially. I'm not sure where he went after that. Until recently. When the Watchers told me he'd come this side, to this world."

I looked at her, trying to thread my way through her recent words and the mythic tales I knew. "You're talking about the fairy mounds that you were banished to?"

"That's how they put it in these times, but yes. Our forts. We became known as the Sídhe."

A memory flashed of the quick banter I'd exchanged with Smithy when I'd first met him. "Sídhe, not Shee. Oh, feck's sake. The man was playing with me."

"What? I don't understand."

"Smithy. When I asked him his surname. He said "Sídhe. Only I thought he was saying S-h-e-e, as in truncated Sheehy or Sheehan." I laughed but then cut it short. "The fecker."

The woman in front of me smiled fondly. "Yes, that's Goibhniu. Ready with a good retort and a sly joke."

I shook my head. "No, no. That's just playing with me. Not believing it. Not for a minute."

She reached over and patted my hand again, gently. I moved away and sat back.

"So Goibhniu retreated somewhere, but you don't know where and it wasn't until recently that he surfaced?"

"Yes. Well recent in my view. Perhaps not so recent in yours. Say about twenty years ago. He moved to where you found him and set himself up as a smith."

"But why here? Didn't he know that you were nearby?"

"No, not at first." She laughed a little. "No, choosing that area was another of his sly jokes. St Gobnait? He'd had a place there before. And others after him, dedicating it to him and his powers over the forge."

It took me a moment of piecing together the fragments of

the local saint's story to understand exactly what she meant by his sly joke. "Oh," I said finally. "Oh, right."

She nodded. "I thought when I'd heard that he was there, he understood. He'd heard the call to rise. He'd awakened and crossed over from the Otherworld to join us. But he wouldn't talk to me when I asked. He told Morrigan no, time and time again. He told others he was done. But I needed him. We needed him. He was key in our ability to defeat Balor one more time."

"Wait. What? Balor? Balor's back in the picture? Didn't he die?" I shook my head and gave myself a mental slap. What was I doing? Why did I say those bizarre things and infer I was giving credence to her tale. Tale. It's a tale, Saoirse, a tale to entertain you, I told myself. I crossed my arms over my chest and gave her a cynical look.

"Balor's eye was healed, but it took a long time. His poison had spread to his body, but he spent time and found a person of great power who helped him harness that poison, to gather it up and use it. When he'd fully recovered, his fury was endless, boundless, and he swore revenge on us, and most of all his grandson, Lugh. But while he searched for his grandson he began to wreak havoc on the land. All the land, not just Ireland, but the land everywhere. And he didn't stop at the land, he began poisoning the oceans, filling them with every toxin he could harness from every source, especially the deadly power of his own poison."

I nodded. "Balor. Poison. So now is the time for all good men to rise up." I thought of the rebel song. "The West Awake."

"The West Awake," she murmured.

"So why do you need Smithy? I mean Goibhniu," I said, hastily correcting myself.

"Because he must forge the weapons that will defeat Balor. No one else can do that."

"So what's the problem?" I suddenly thought of all the

discarded blades and weapons that were hanging on the wall of his forge.

"He won't even talk to me. To us. He doesn't know how much we need him. Every time Morrigan or I have tried to contact him and explain, he cuts us off. He rejects us."

"Are you certain that he doesn't know how much you need him?" I asked cautiously.

She studied me carefully. "Why, what do you know, what did you see when you were there with him the last few days?"

I blushed, unsure what it was that I was thinking, or if I even wanted to give voice to any of it.

She leaned forward. "Please. You have to tell me."

I wasn't certain if it was her tone, her words, or the combination of the two, but I suddenly found myself saying, "In his forge, there were lots of blades lying around, incomplete. Some complete ones were hanging on the wall, though," I added hastily. "And I mean, he made a blade when I was there and later, we made one together. They seemed fine. Perfect."

She looked at me thoughtfully. A moment later she smiled, her face filled with joy. "Really? Oh, Bríd, that's wonderful news."

"Whoa," I said. "Not Bríd, remember? Saoirse. I'm Saoirse."

She became still and slowly shook her head. "No, Bríd, there is no Saoirse. Saoirse was an invention, a glamour to put on you to protect you from Balor."

"Balor? Why would I need protection from him?"

"So he wouldn't go after you, hold you hostage. Because of your power, because of me, because of Goibhniu and everyone else who cares for you and loves you."

"But you said Bríd was dead." My voice was flat, severe, reminding her of the details of her own tale and to prove her story false.

"You were. But I brought you back."

I laughed then. Long and hard. "Let me guess. The Well of Slane. But, sorry, I'm forgetting, the Fomorians filled it with stones. Oh, and let's not forget that no one knew where I was buried?"

"Yes. All of that is true. And what is also true is that it has taken us this long to find out where they'd put you. A tomb, only recently excavated. Perfectly preserved. It took a bit of doing to get you from them."

"Let me guess, you used magic?" It was sarcasm now, colouring my words. Not the wittiest approach.

"Yes. Of a sort. A glamour. Morrigan did it. She loves those kinds of things. She is a shapeshifter, after all. She posed as an expert. And with a van and some convincing explanations she spirited you away."

"*Spirited* me away? Really?" I didn't know if she realised the word choice.

She nodded. "And then we managed to get you up to the Well of Slane, and with the help of Diancecht and his son, we immersed you in the waters."

"And I miraculously came back to life?"

"Well it wasn't instant, but eventually, yes. And as I said before, I cleansed your mind, to protect you. Placed a glamour on you so that you looked different and younger. I arranged for you to be put in a boarding school and given experiences so that you could safely blend in with people, until the time was right."

"And now the time is right?"

"Yes."

"So, what do expect for me to do?"

"To help Goibhniu, to help us secure the magic treasures so that we can fight Balor on all levels."

I looked at her steadily. The tale had unfolded, and like any good seanchie she'd told it well. It had held my interest. It had all the qualities. Love, war, death, sorrow. She scored on all points. Ah, so she had.

I rose. "Right, so. Thanks for that."

"What? Where are you going?"

"To pack. I think it's time to return to Dublin. My father's will should be sorted enough that I should be able to move into the house."

16

SAOIRSE

I t was easy enough to gather my clothes, shoes and other items and stuff them in my backpack. It was easy enough to leave the bedroom and go downstairs. The ease lessened and disappeared altogether when I reached the kitchen and found Anu waiting there.

"Ah, Bríd, now. Won't you give it some time? Let it settle on you. At least stay the night."

"Saoirse. I'm Saoirse. Not Bríd, or anyone else. I am not a goddess, or whatever you say I am and I have no power. I think, in view of that, it's best I leave. I want no part in your fantasies, your conspiracy theories, or what you think is going on."

"Don't leave now, please. At least have something to eat, first."

"No, thank you," I said forcing the politeness. "I'd just as soon be on my way now."

I walked across the kitchen towards the door.

"At least let me take you to the train station. Or even the village where you can take the bus into the city. There should be one along in about a half hour."

"No, no, you're fine. I've ordered a taxi," I said, lying. I had no idea how to find a taxi here. "I'll meet him down the bottom of the road. He should be there by then."

"Bríd," said Anu, her voice loud and firm. "That's unnecessary. You can ring now and cancel. Let me take you."

"No." I reached for the door handle and looked at her. "Thank you for your hospitality."

I left then and it wasn't easy.

I WALKED DOWN to the main road, trying to get my thoughts in order and at the same time get those thoughts out of my head. I put my earbuds in and began to listen to music on my phone, waiting for the lilting tones of Fidil 3 to get me out of my head and the reminders of the craziness I'd just encountered. I wouldn't even dream of thinking of the hurt and betrayal that threatened to overwhelm me and push out all of the crazy scenes afterward. They were all crazy here, I told myself. Crazy, crazy. Smithy just as much. Who could act that way? Why had he rejected me? It seemed too bizarre to think that it was for the reasons Anu gave. Or whatever her name was. Anna. Smithy had seemed so sane, so down to earth. His craft and his music, no one who could play that well and create such beautiful objects could enter into Anna's crazy ideas.

"Saoirse!"

I looked up, startled. I'd been so wrapped up in my own thoughts I didn't realise I was passing Maura's house.

I gave her a wan smile. "Hello, how are you?"

"More importantly, how are you?" She nodded to my backpack. "You can't be leaving us, can you? It's too soon."

"I'm afraid so. It's time for me to go."

"Ah, no, stay. You've been great to have around."

"Thanks, Maura. It's nice of you to say so, but I still have to go."

"What's happened? What's made you leave?"

There was a gleam in her eyes, and the way she looked at me it was as though she understood everything. But there wasn't any remote possibility that was true. Quirky as she was, I can only imagine what she would make of all that had happened in the past few hours.

"It's not Smithy, is it?"

I stared at her. "Smithy? Why would you ask that?"

She gave me a playful smile. "Well...a little birdie told me that you and he...became closely acquainted."

I snorted. "You need to tell your little birdie that it's wrong and should keep his beak out of things."

She laughed. "Like that is it? Well, give him a few days. He'll snap out of it. He can be a temperamental old bastard."

I shook my head. "I appreciate the concern, but there's no need for it. It's fine. Nothing happened and I won't change my mind. I have to get back up to Dublin."

"Oh, why's that?"

I sighed. "I have some matters to sort out. To do with my father's death," It was as good excuse as any.

"Matters to sort out," Maura echoed. "I suppose you do have matters to sort out." She gave me a sly grin. "Maybe more than you expect."

I gave her a puzzled look then pasted a smile on my face. "Thanks for everything, Maura. I enjoyed meeting you and the time we spent together. Don't make yourself a stranger if you're ever in Dublin. You can always find me at the session in the Mangle Pit in Stonybatter."

"Oh, don't you worry. I won't be a stranger."

I nodded. "Well I have to get on. There's a taxi waiting for me at the bottom of the road."

"Taxi? Where did you get a taxi at this time of day? Do you even know who drives a taxi around here?"

I reddened, caught out. Maura laughed.

"Just wait a moment. I'll give you a spin. Don't argue and I won't either. We can even maintain a silent truce."

I sighed and waited, knowing that she made more sense than I would arguing against it. When I finally climbed into the car she only had a slightly amused expression on her face to show. I held my peace and the rest of my words on the journey down. The music was no longer remotely able to distract my thoughts. For some reason they returned to Smithy. Maybe it was Maura's remarks calling up my emotions as though conjured by a demon. A demon that agitated and shook them, made the anger and then sheer rage come to the fore at the unjust and cruel manner he'd treated me. I felt used. Not just in body, but in every other way too. I would let the anger boil, I would let it help me get on that bus and take that train back to Dublin.

PART II

THE WEST AWAKES

17

SAOIRSE

I put the key in the lock and listened to the mechanism turn. It was a satisfying feeling and I treasured it in a world that had lately given me so few satisfactions. I entered the house, went through to the lounge and put my bag on the floor. It was a mid-sized three bedroom Georgian house with high ceilings and plaster detailing. The decor was modern enough, though I wasn't sure what the kitchen was like. Old fashioned, if I remembered right from the last time I was here.

"This is amazing," said Jilly, following behind me. "I had no idea you were so well off."

"I hardly know the place," I said. "I think I've been here only a handful of times. It doesn't feel like mine. It never has."

Jilly looked at me incredulously. "You've only been here a handful of times?"

I shrugged. "I spent most of my time at boarding school. My father travelled a lot of the time."

"What did he do?"

"Something in business. International developments or something along those lines. We never really talked about it. We never really talked."

"Oh, I'm sorry, Saoirse," said Jilly. She came up and rubbed my shoulder. "That must have been hard."

I shrugged again. "I didn't really know anything else. And we didn't have much in common. He with his business and me with my music and English. He never really approved of the things I chose to do. Well, at least the few times he bothered to express an opinion."

"Well now you have this house and whatever else he's left you. That's not half bad to make up for all the previous years. No worries about rent anymore."

"Just the bills," I muttered.

I know I should have been glad, overjoyed that the probate had gone far enough that I was allowed to have the keys to the house so soon from the solicitor. And that, despite the adoption, it seemed as if I was entitled to it. As much as I was grateful to Jilly for putting me up for a few days, not to mention storing the things that I'd retrieved from what was no longer my flat, I would be glad to have my own place again.

She nudged me. "You'll be fine. I'm sure they'll sort the rest of the will soon and you'll have money to pay those bills. Besides, you can always let out the other two rooms. They'll go for a price, no doubt about that."

I nodded, though I knew that it would be a while before I'd look for housemates. For as long as I was able, I would live on my own, enjoy the ease and comfort of only having to deal with my own idiosyncrasies and habits. And I needed this time on my own to find a way back to my old self, away from Smithy, away from all the craziness that had happened in Cork.

The pain felt so fresh. I had to remind myself it had been only a week since I'd left. It was bound to be raw. I'd barely had time to catch my breath. The thoughts and images of him and our time together were still crowding my mind almost interminably. And it wasn't as if I hadn't fought it. I'd watched films on my tablet, I'd gone on walks and out for drinks with Jilly when she'd come home from work. I even went out looking for work, but had lost heart after half a day because I couldn't focus.

In the end I decided the best thing was to face it head on. To gather up the images and memories and go through them one by one and refute each in turn. Get out the ice cream, the cake or whatever else you were meant to do to get over an event. A person.

"Come on," said Jilly. "Let's get the rest of your things from the car and then we'll make a cup of tea. And after that I'll help you unpack and settle in. How's that sound?"

I nodded. "Good. Fine." Because that's what it had to be. That's what I would make it be.

I STARED out the window and watched Jilly's car pull away, the taillights disappearing in the gathering dusk. She'd stayed longer than I expected and been more of a friend than I would have thought for someone who hardly knew me before I'd rung her up and asked if I could stay with her until I got the keys to the house. She'd been both surprised and happy that I had thought of her and I wondered what she'd initially thought about the fact that I had no other person to ask but her. My circle of friends had whittled down considerably after I'd left Trinity, and virtually disappeared once I got a job and they got, well, careers. Whether it was at a literary firm in London or writing for various magazines and even teaching, it took up their time and moved them into a new social realm in which I had no part.

Why hadn't I found a career? It was something I'd hadn't fully questioned because my father and others made me feel so defensive about it. I had done well in my degree. Excellently in fact. Praise from my teachers. Encouragements to pursue different literary paths. But I had done nothing. Was it because I got more out of writing my poetry and playing music than I did the thought of spending endless time in an office, or in a classroom? Or writing journal articles, or writing for newspapers or even attempting a novel? Maybe I could write a novel now, I thought sourly. Recast that tale Anu told me.

I pushed the thought away and scanned the road outside. The sun had gone and it was approaching dusk. I knew I should try and get something sorted for dinner, but at the moment, I had no great desire to. I watched a few people walk down the road, returning commuters, mothers with a child clutched in each hand. Or were they nannies? You wouldn't know in this area of Dublin.

I sighed and was just about to turn away when I caught sight of something out of the corner of my eye, emerging from the shadows. It was them. The feckin' Twa' Corbies. They were moving towards the house. This house. A moment later, a large crow landed beside them and began to caw loudly. Startled, they moved back, staring at it. They looked at each other, turned around and retreated. The crow flew off.

I watched the exchange, stunned and confused. These men, who I'd seen on and off throughout my life and whose appearance no one else seemed to take note of, leaving me to believe I somehow imagined them each time, had just been confronted by a large crow. Unless that was part of my imagination too, I thought sardonically. Or not. Because someone else had seen these men, I realised. Smithy.

I pulled away from the window, angry that my thoughts had returned to him, even when I didn't want them to. Even when I was reflecting on something that I had no intention of connecting with him. Why had he seen them? In fact, what was he doing talking to them? Having a conversation with them? I'd never come close enough, or seen them long enough to speak, let alone have a conversation with them.

I shook the uneasy feelings from me. I didn't want to pursue any path that was connected to Smithy, and most especially not that path. It prompted too many questions and uneasy theories. I'd had enough of that. I wanted my old life back. Even if it was working in a glorified coffee shop, living from month to month, at least I got to enjoy playing at the sessions, exchanging the banter there and at the coffee shop. I could count on that. It provided no strange circumstances. It was safe.

But I hadn't gone to a session since I'd returned. I hadn't seriously looked for work in a coffee shop and now I had this house. It was a house that would generate bills, though, and I had no real income at the moment. The solicitor had promised to release some funds for me, but I had no idea when that would be. So there was the plan, presented to me. A plan that would see off those silly men with as much tenacity as that crow had.

18

SAOIRSE

I let the door to the coffee shop close on my back, feeling the force of its pressure on me. It was like a spanking, a punishment for my lazy, irresponsible behaviour since I'd left uni. A punishment that had been meted out over the past several hours as I traipsed the streets of Dublin searching for a job. Well a job that I could manage. In the few places where I had got as far as putting in an application, I could tell by the looks on their faces when they saw that I had been let go from my previous job as a "barista" they really had no interest. I'd even tried to stretch the truth at one point, but I knew it would have been only a matter of time before they'd find out the reason I was fired. The "let go, my arse" look they gave me told me everything I needed to know about whether I'd get the job.

Now, this smack in the back was the final gesture and "will you ever cop on" warning I was going to get. It was time to give up. Wearily, I made my way to the bus stop and joined the queue of the late afternoon shoppers. My phone rang. I looked at it and saw it was Jilly. I smiled, feeling a little better.

"Hey," I said. "How's things?"

"Hey. How's the job hunt going?"

I made a mewling noise.

"That good?"

"Worse."

"You poor thing. What you need is cheering up. The session's tonight. Why don't you come? We can go back to mine after and really drown your miseries."

I'd lost track of the last week or so. I knew I'd spent a few days getting lost in the sofa, watching films on my tablet and then finally, yesterday, had decided I would try for coffee shops like I'd promised myself the first days I'd been at the house. The session had seemed too much effort then, despite the texts and phone calls from Jilly inviting me over and inviting me out and about. I finally told her that I was job searching and wanted to focus all my time on that, when in reality any searching I was doing was confined to the box set menu on Netflix.

But now, the session and some time spent at Jilly's afterwards seemed like the perfect choice to forget what had been a really shite day.

"You're right," I said. "That sounds just the thing. I'll meet you there."

"Fab! They'll be overjoyed to see you. As I keep telling you, they miss you at the sessions. And last week you'll never guess who showed up and asked after you."

For a moment a flush of pleasure rushed through me as the completely irrational thought that Smithy might have gone there looking for me. That Maura would have told him where I played.

"Luke!" she said, a moment later. "Sexy, hot Luke. Asking for you. And wasn't Eileen looking daggers when he did."

Luke. The blond surfer. Larger than life, could play the uilleann pipes so they'd make you weep with the purity of it. Could turn his hand to any instrument. Crystal blue eyes, a fringe of lashes. A body that would sing you home, no doubt.

"Did he, though?" I grinned. "Well, we'll see if he's there tonight." And if he was, there I would be, playing right along with him and I would see if he could sing me home. Smithy could go to hell, or wherever his sort went.

BY THE TIME I walked into the pub my spirits had lifted considerably, compared to earlier that day, even though it took me longer to get here and involved more public transportation than I'd liked. I'd had plenty of tunes to keep me company, ones that set me up for the evening of music and banter. Myself and my flute were ready for it all.

The music was only getting started. I could hear a few still tuning as I made my way through the pub. Finbarr looked up and saw me.

"Saoirse. We thought you'd deserted us for warmer climes."

"Ah, no. Just visiting the lower orders. Gathering tunes." I smiled at him, determined for the banter. This would be my night. A good night. I would let the music rule. Let the tunes dance outside and inside, beat a rhythm.

"Here," he said, indicating a half pulled pint of Guinness under the tap. "That's for you. On the house to welcome you back. And to make certain you stay." He leaned forward, big grin on his face. "Unless you'd rather a Murphy's, now that you strayed into Cork territory?"

I made a face in mock horror. "Now why would I be doing that? Guinness is fine. Thanks."

He nodded. "I'll bring it over to you. In the meantime your fellow musicians await you."

Happily I continued on to the back and saw Declan sorting out his concertina. Beside him was Cormac, twisting a peg on his violin. Across from him I spotted Eileen's springy curly hair.

Ah well, not every session could be perfect. Mícheal and Finbarr were there on either side of her.

I felt a tug on my sleeve.

"Hey there," said Jilly, slightly out of breath. "You just get here too?"

I nodded. "Feckin' buses. Took me ages."

"Well, you will live in the posh area. Never mind, though. You can stay at mine tonight and worry about the buses in the morning."

"I can't argue with that logic," I said. "Thanks."

She leaned in closer to me. "Well, is he here?"

"Who?" I made it innocent but, I knew, so I did. Who else could she mean? It certainly couldn't be Smithy.

I shook my head. "Probably giving it a miss tonight. But no bother. I'm happy to play with my old friends. And Eileen."

Jilly laughed and hit my arm. "You devil. But I have to agree. Sometimes I want to take those bangles and flush them down the loo."

"Ah, now Jilly. You know it's her own music she makes when the bangles get going."

"It's like being part of a Morris Dancing group. Doesn't she know that there are no bells in trad music?"

"Tsk. Are you going purist on me now?" I said.

She laughed. "There's a difference between purist and not wanting pure shite."

"And only a few wouldn't agree."

"Everyone wouldn't agree."

"What are you two discussing so intently?" said a deep voice behind me.

I turned and saw it was Luke. As usual, his long sandy hair was becomingly dishevelled and his startling blue eyes just as piercing. I smiled, thinking the promise of the evening had just increased from a mournful tempo to a reel and then some.

"Hello," I said and Jilly echoed me.

He leaned over and kissed my cheek and after a brief hesitation kissed Jilly's.

"Hey, stranger," he said, directing his gaze to me. "Good to have you back. We've missed you."

Jilly laughed. "We? You've only been the once since she the week after she left."

"That's a few more times than she has."

"Oh, but the sentiment is there, I'm sure," I said in a teasing tone.

"Of, course, what else?" He said. "Come on then, let's see what you have for us. I presume you didn't waste your time down in the remote regions of Cork and you have at least one tune to share with us. Or do they all just copy us?"

I laughed. "Ah, you are bad. I have one or two, maybe."

"Maybe?" said Jilly. "There better be no maybes about it. You owe me."

I smiled at her. "I do, of course. And I will repay the debt then with a tune, if that's what you want."

"Oh? What debt is this?" said Luke. "I hope it can be repaid tonight. I'm ready for new tunes, all right."

"She stayed with me when she came back from Cork," said Jilly. "Well, only until she could get the keys to her own house."

"Not my house yet," I said.

"Not yet your house?" asked Luke.

I shook my head. "My father's. And until the will is settled it's still technically his. I think."

"Will?"

"My father died a little while ago."

"Oh, shit, Saoirse," said Luke. "I'm so sorry for your loss. A huge loss."

And he did look sorry. His eyes were filled with compassion and the hand he put on my arm felt comforting.

I shrugged. "We weren't close," I said.

My words may have been a little sharp but I didn't want to go into it any further. He seemed to sense it because he shifted the subject slightly.

"And weren't you good to give her a place to stay," he said, looking at Jilly.

She reddened slightly and smiled. "Of course. What else would I do?"

He smiled at her. "What else." He eyed the musicians up ahead who were just beginning a tune. "We should go to the others before they think we're starting a rival session in the front here."

I laughed and followed him, of course I did, as though the flute wasn't in my case waiting to be played, but instead he was playing it and playing me at the same time. I didn't care, though. It felt good, just like the music that was starting up in my head. I would fly tonight. I was determined to.

A few hugs, "how are yous", "how's things" with a pinch of "it's good to have you backs" and I was seated, my pint in front of me, and to my surprise, a whiskey too. I raised my brow and scanned the group, skipping over Eileen and received non-committal shrugs all round except for the cheeky innocent grin on Luke's face. I opened my eyes wide and did a "you shouldn't have" shake of my head and got down to the business of unpacking my flute.

I placed the case on my lap and saw the bulge of the pocket on top and realised the low whistle was in there, where I'd placed it carefully wrapped when I'd left Smithy's house two weeks and a bit ago. It seemed like an age since then, a century, an era. In fact it seemed like it happened to a different person altogether. But there it was, the evidence that I hadn't imagined it all, as much as I might want to believe.

With a determination of the brave or foolhardy I brushed

the thoughts aside, opened the case, assembled the flute and then took a long drink of my Guinness, even contemplating the whiskey chaser. I would save that for later, when the music got going, and my body and mind were solely filled with the music.

I joined in the music mid-stride. *The Blarney Pilgrim* migrated soon enough into another set of tunes and I smiled to hear an old favourite set of *Bill Malley's Barndance, Kilnamona Barndance* and *Bill Malley's Schottische,* It was old Martin Hayes all over and I gave it welly with the sheer joy and love of the tunes and the musicians who gave voice to them.

Luke and I gave each other eyes the whole time, (sitting next to Eileen that he was, where she'd placed him), winking and laughing with it, feeling the hum run through us. Luke had picked up the bouzouki and was finding the flair and the flourish of it, the jig and reel of it, as we made our way through the set. And after a while, even the descant dissonance of Eileen's bangles faded away.

This was what I'd come for, and the set of blue eyes and cheeky smile that came with it added to the time out of time that led me away from the past and all that wasn't ever me or meant to be. I was here with the music, flirting and tapping, laughing and bouncing.

We finished with a flourish and the night went on. My Guinness never seemed to disappear nor did the whiskey that I only sipped and savoured as the night wore on. A polite request got Eileen singing and her rendition of the battered old song, *She Moved Through the Fair*, and after it, Declan declared a break.

"Not before Saoirse gives us a tune," said Luke.

I looked up in surprise. I thought it had been forgotten in the rush of the playing.

Jilly's face lit up. "Oh, yes, we need that first. Saoirse, you have at least one new tune for us, don't you?"

"I think a few tunes and an air are in order," said Luke. His eyes were full of teasing and a "go on" look.

Go on yourself, I thought. I was just about to object but Declan added his voice.

"Now, we're not having you decline, Saoirse, so just pick up your flute and work away."

I nodded and in face of their encouraging looks and interest I lifted the flute and started off with one of the tunes I'd heard at the Inchigeela session. It started out harmless enough and I ran away with it for a bit and the humming came on, the whirling inside, the jiggiddy jig and beyond. I kept on and Luke joined in with the bouzouki, Declan with his fiddle, followed closely by the others. It was a gas and I felt the smile in me and the unease seemed to disappear.

I finished the tune and went on to another, one from the other session, the one in the village, edging around the hum and the dance stirring inside. I played on, the sound growing bigger, the dance and rhythm swirling around me, filling me up inside and out, but reaching out, searching for the other dancer, the other half of the beat. A faint beat met me and the eyes I hadn't known I closed opened and found Luke's. His were wide, and filled with a glimmer of fun, a hint of puzzlement and a whole lot of wonder.

I played on, looking at Luke, making the exchange while the faint beat found mine and the jiggiddy jig continued. I finished finally, half filled with the thrill of it, but knowing there should be more. Impulsively, before the comments could even begin, I reached for the wrapped whistle in my case and drew it out.

"A new addition?" asked Declan.

I nodded. "I know my old one wasn't what it could be. So, I have this one now."

"A present to yourself?" asked Patrick, stroking his guitar, a beauty gifted to himself, much to the dismay of his girlfriend whose own left finger had needed gifting more.

"No, a friend made it for me."

"A great friend to have," said Mícheal.

I forced a nod and a smile and lifted the whistle to my lips. What tune, what tune, ran through my mind, but all I could play was one that Smithy had taught me that night. A long soft air that filled my head with everything and too much. An air that rose in my soul and stirred too much of myself. I played on and it was only after a while that I realised that Luke had started playing a low soft drone on his pipes, illuminating and illustrating the sorrowful beauty of the air. The drone played in me and wrapped me up, gave me support in the sorrow that drenched my soul and left me empty and aching. The balm was there in the low sound. Strong arms, strong sound, there to hold me up.

I finished the air before it finished me, leaving off the final refrain, a refrain I didn't want, not in a million years or a thousand fantasies. I lowered the whistle, but my head was down and I found the cloth to wrap it in. The silence was there, a hush of appreciation, but there was only "no", in my mind. The "no" of please don't mention that air, please don't acknowledge the layers I peeled back, the curtain I drew open on my thoughts, on myself.

"That's a low whistle we would all wish for," said Luke lightly. "Do you mind if I have a look?"

I took a deep breath and glanced up at him, plastering a smile on my face. His own expression was carefully neutral, taking care for me, I thought, and was grateful. I leaned over and handed it to him, glad really to hand it over to someone else, to give me time to break the connection.

He fingered the whistle and turned it around, examining closely. "A real crafted piece of work, this," he said.

I nodded, not wanting to comment further.

"Can I?" he asked, his eyes locking with mine.

I nodded reluctantly.

He lifted it to his lips and began to play an air. It was one I hadn't heard before, I thought in the one breath—and in the next, it was one I thought I knew, but couldn't find the name for it. It wasn't long, but it had a haunting beauty. When he'd done he lowered the whistle and gave me a speculative look.

"You say a friend gave it to you?"

I nodded.

"That friend wouldn't have made it, would he?"

I nodded.

"A great friend to have," said Jilly. "It has an amazing sound."

"It does," said Declan. "We'll all be lining up for one of his whistles, no matter that we don't play."

"Oh, so true," said Jilly.

I laughed uncertainly, but said nothing more. I wouldn't and couldn't add anything more, for there was no point to it. I wouldn't be seeing him again.

Declan declared the break with a voice that said "there will be no changing my mind."

I was glad for it, for all the reasons that crowded my thoughts and was glad when we all rose as one. Jilly and I threaded our way through to the toilet as a few regulars grabbed my arm and we exchanged the "glad to be backs" and "aren't you great girl, yourself with your flute." It was good, it was grand to hear those words and feel that this was home.

The warm feeling was still there with me when I'd left the toilet and a few others nodded and spoke words to me on my way back through. The seats were still empty so I veered out the side door to the alleyway. It was hot enough and the air would be welcome.

I let the cool air bathe my face when I stepped out. The light was gone now and only a dim lamp lit the area where I stood. I saw a few down at the end, near the front of the pub, smoking and chatting. In a moment I'd go for a wander up and have a chat, but for now I would just savour the feelings and music that wrapped me in their blanket.

A figure broke away from the group at the end and sauntered up towards me. I didn't need to see his face, or even his sauntering manner to know it was Luke. When he came in range of the dim light the sparkle in his eyes was evident, as was the growing smile on his face.

"Saoirse. Just the one."

"The one?"

"Oh, yes, mostly definitely the one."

I laughed and sank into the pleasure of his attention and the banter that went with it.

"Ah, no. Not the one. Without a doubt you have many more 'ones'."

He shook his head. "No 'one' who has the music in them as you do."

"Go on yourself," I said. "There are plenty of musicians who have more skill and talent then I do. You yourself have more than enough for anyone."

"Maybe, maybe not. But tonight, that was special."

"It was, wasn't it?" I said softly.

He stood in front of me, so close I could see the flecks of gold in his eyes. Had they always been there?

"That low whistle of yours is magic."

I flinched at his words, though I knew he didn't meant them literally.

"It is good, isn't it? It puts the other one in disgrace."

I said the words, but in my heart I wondered if I could ever play it again. The absolute pain and joy of the playing, the spin and whirl and utter bliss of those times with Smithy were never to be recaptured again, but still the feel of it, the sound of it, gave me a ghost of the experience that I knew I couldn't bear being repeated.

He rested his arm on the wall above my head and studied me intently. "It's more than good. You're more than good."

I stared into his eyes, felt the warmth of his breath on my face and met his lips as they descended on my mouth. It was a kiss filled with desire and promise as he first brushed my lips gently and then pressed his mouth more firmly, more sensuously on mine. It was practised and rousing and I opened up to the kiss and the possibility of him.

After a while he pulled back and said softly in my ear, "Will you come to mine after the session?"

And following that possibility I nodded my head and said, "I will."

19

SAOIRSE

His house was a two-bedroom brick townhouse that had been renovated into something approaching modern and airy. It seemed to fit Luke, and yet it didn't, but I conceded that it was hard to tell in the dim light of the arc lamp that shone on the open space of the living and dining area where we sat.

My flute case was safely tucked next to the case that held his pipes, in the corner where they also kept company with other cases of musical instruments that included unmistakably a guitar, concertina and some others that might have had a mandolin among them.

"Are you having a session here? Is that why you asked me here?" I said, nodding to the musical corner. I was sitting next to him on the sofa, holding a glass of whiskey, a "why not" move that I hoped wouldn't haunt me in the morning. It was a modest glass, I told myself, a baby's finger, well, perhaps a fat baby.

He laughed. "Ah, no, no. They're all mine." He stroked my hair, up in its usual coronet around my head. "It was an entirely different reason why I asked you here."

I smiled at him, reading the desire in his eyes. Slowly he

began to remove the pins from my hair, unwound the plait and started to loosen it. I was suddenly reminded of Smithy and I turned my face away, trying to stifle the memory.

"Is something wrong? Don't you like me doing this? It's just your hair…it's something I've wanted to do since I saw you."

He stroked it again, running his fingers through it. He loosened the hair even further, so that it fell around my shoulders and down my back. I made myself turn toward him and allowed his actions to soothe me.

"Your hair seems darker than it used to be."

I smiled at him. "It's just you and your dimly lit room changing the colour."

"Mmhm," he said. "Maybe." He leaned over and kissed me.

I opened my lips, feeling his slide against mine, first teasing and then deepening. He put his arms around me and drew me to him. I moved into his embrace, jumping, falling and full of a need to experience all of him, to lose myself in the process. I tasted whiskey and desire and let it wash over me, pull me under.

He kissed behind my ear, nibbled softly. I slipped my hand up inside his T-shirt, feeling the firm muscles along his stomach and chest. He skimmed his hand inside my peasant top. I felt the pleasure of the heat of the press of his aroused body against mine as he kissed and nibbled along my neck and down my breastbone. It was sensuous and arousing, there was no denying, and my body responded. I felt the rush of his passion, someone wanting me and that was enough. It would be enough. My body would be open to this experienced wooing and the rest of me would follow.

He pulled away, his grey eyes darkened with desire. "Will we go up to bed?"

I was careful to limit my answer to a simple nod, wanting to keep it all simple. A man craving a woman. He would get that woman.

He took my hand and pulled me up from the sofa and slowly led me up the stairs to his bedroom. He turned on a small lamp by his bed.

"I want to see all of you," he told me.

I was happy to oblige and watched his eyes as they took me in while I shed my clothes one by one. When I'd finished he pulled me towards him.

"Now you," I said.

I began to tug on his T-shirt, but he was there ahead of me and made short work of all it, until we were together on the bed, kissing and caressing. I was a woman desired and pleasured.

THE MOOD WAS on me still when I woke up the next morning. That "why not" mood that drove me to enjoy his body enjoying mine until we finally fell asleep. The "why not" mood led me to wrap my legs around him when I'd returned from the toilet, and leave a trail of kisses on his body as all of him woke up and rose to the occasion.

It became a "why not" day as we lazed in bed and then made our coffee and switched on the TV and watched a mindless show, our limbs entangled, until we retired to bed to entangle our full bodies. As the day began to fade we took ourselves out for dinner, entangling fingers so that some bit of us was always touching, woven together like the threads of one of the leather bracelets around his wrist.

No instruments or any part of music figured in the "why not" day, because the "why" would lose its "not" and lead me into thoughts and places I didn't want to go. The day belonged to those two words together, and I would keep them together as long as I could.

With a plan like that, it was impossible for the "why not" day to slide smooth as silk into another "why not" night, a night of more entangled limbs and bodies, of kisses and tongues and every part of us that would meet and unite.

The "why not" talk was filled with banter that alternated with lazy chatter about places we've been or not been, food we'd tried or not, and matters that were no matter at all. By the morning after the second "why not" night, I wandered around the kitchen waiting for the kettle and stared at the photos hung on the walls depicting the surfer side of Luke. The "catch that big wave," Luke with his sculpted body, holding an equally sculpted surfboard.

He came up behind me and slid his arms around my waist, resting his head on my shoulder. A shoulder that for most men would have been no place to pitch a chin, but to press a nose. He was tall, this surfer boy, surfer dude. As tall as Smithy, I realised, but then hid the thought behind my "why not" grin and "why not" mind.

"How long have you been surfing?" I asked.

"A long time."

"You obviously love it. How did you get started in it?"

He shrugged. "My father, well the person I looked on as my father. He and his son drew me into it."

"They both surf?"

"They do. Mon is really good?"

"Mon?"

"My foster father's son. One of them. He's like a brother to me."

I nodded, getting a better sense of Luke.

He kissed my neck. "Come surfing with me."

I turned my head in surprise. "What? Me? I've never been surfing."

He kissed my mouth. "No bother. I'll teach you."

I blinked and grabbed onto the "why not", who took the reins and said, "Good. Yeah. Okay, When?"

"This weekend."

"This weekend? That's, well..."

He grinned. "Now. Yeah. Why not? We can go by your house so you can pick up some things and we'll head out."

The "now" joined the "why not" couple and the threesome had me first showering with Luke (limbs entangled) and helping him load his board on the roof of his SUV. The threesome cheered as we headed to my house (fingers entangled) and I packed a small bag to take to the "why not" and "now" beach.

We headed west in his surfer dude SUV to the sound of "why not now" music, the threesome well and truly joined, entangled and entwined, leaving trad music and everything else that carried too much with it behind. My "whynotnow" lover sang along, raising his hand from our periodically entwined, entangled fingers to shift gear or stroke my hair, which now fell everywhere and nowhere, entangled in itself. I'd come undone in Cork, and now I was wrapped up, entwined and entangled with my fingers, limbs and hair with this "whynotnow" man.

Smithy brought his motorbike to a stop, resting his feet on the ground. He stared across to the house. "The Rookery". She was known as "Maura the Rookery" for a reason, and that reason was circling overhead, cawing. A murder of crows. Isn't that what they called the collective, thought Smithy. Appropriate, he thought. Though at the moment it was more likely he would murder her and her crows. Well, he would if he could. And therein lay the crux of it all. The reason that "rookery" and Maura, who she was, were synonymous. Why she thought her name was a great joke. And so it was. And the joke was on them, on him and anyone else who didn't like war, didn't like armed confrontation, or was so sick of it and its consequences. For people who would rather try other things before war. Because war was Maura's food, it was her life's blood, it was who she was. She was Morrigan.

And because Smithy knew who she was, he also knew that her love of conflict had drawn her into this little scheme of Anu's. This ridiculous crazy notion that she could bring the real Bríd back to life and lure him from his stance. Had Anu known he'd lost the magic? He'd kept it as hidden as he possibly could.

Maybe she'd sensed it, or Morrigan had. But regardless of what had driven Anu, Smithy knew what drove Morrigan. She must have enjoyed every moment of his encounters with Saoirse. And he knew without a doubt she'd contrived to bring Saoirse into contact with him at every possible situation. She probably had a hand in sending Saoirse down to him the first time they met. The thought of it drove him through the gate and along the foot-path to the door. He banged on it loudly. He knew she was in. Her main henchman was up in the tree overhead, cawing down at him loudly. He looked up and glared at him, lifted his arms as if he had a bow in them and was releasing the arrow. The crow cawed louder then flew up to a higher branch.

Behind him, the door opened.

"Goibhniu."

No, "hello, how are yous"—they were beyond that and more. It was an exchange of looks, of eyes that spoke amusement and fury, dancing around each other like too ill-timed partners. Smithy crossed his arms over his chest to stop reaching for his sword that wasn't there. That's what she wanted, and regardless of the fact it wasn't there, he cursed that it was his first instinct and told him everything he wanted to deny.

"Smithy," he said, voice tight.

She laughed, her eyes alight and full of spirit. This was her territory, a battle of wits almost, almost, but not quite, as good as any battle of swords, spears and fists. It was the "not quite" that had her placing a hand on Smithy's shoulder. He flinched and shrugged it off. More laughter came, though the eyes danced an angry rhythm and he thought, good.

But still she touched him again, this time gripping his upper arm. "Did you come to see me or fight with me? Because you know which one I would prefer."

"I would never fight you physically," said Smithy.

She laughed again. "Why would you? You know the outcome."

His anger flared again and he grasped it, grateful that it reined him back onto the path he meant to go.

"You had no reason to meddle with me. No reason at all. This will not get you a battle, a war or any other conflict you might be yearning for."

He'd tried to keep his voice even, hard, the way it had all sounded in his head on his ride over. A ride that been like those Furies from Greece, the hum and roar of his motorbike acting like a voice for his rage. It was a rage that told him he could still come alive with it, his body become a fire, a furnace that would forge once again the fighting man, the warrior he'd left behind. It flared in him now and gave fire to the words and phrases that spilled out of his mouth, bitter and awful.

"I am not one of your battle toys to be tossed about and thrown into the fray to see what would happen. I am not someone to provide amusement for you. I've done nothing to you to deserve that, but I can assure you that I won't take your meddling lightly."

Her eyes sparkled and he bit his lip and reminded himself that he'd just given her something to savour and delight in, ah the pure feck of it. The pure, shittin' hell of it. He couldn't win.

"Just stop it. There's no point," he said finally. "I told Anu I won't have any part of it. Even with her attempts to recreate Bríd."

She made a tsking sound. "Oh, Goibhniu, Goibhniu. Don't lie to yourself, or me. You know that's not true."

"It is true. There's no point in any of this."

"Ah, no, you're wrong. And you know it. There's a large point. A huge point. He's come back. It's time to stir ourselves, wake up to the facts and see what he's doing to us. To all of us. Everything could die. It's happening now, faster than we'd like and we must do something."

Smithy gave her a sceptical look. "You don't care. You only want the means that gets that end. The end has nothing interesting to offer you."

She snorted, frustrated. "You fool. You think I'll be able to exist if there's nothing here? I can die just as easily."

Smithy contemplated that, and not for the first time wondered what could kill her. Did she mean that the lack of conflict, of war, would render her null and void? Kill her, in essence?

"So you want to help," he said, his tone still doubtful.

"Yes, of course I do."

"And not just because your assistance would contribute to bringing about a monumental battle with leftover Fomorians and whoever else has joined Balor since then. A battle more terrible than anything seen before it. More terrible than the first and second battles of Magh Tuireadh."

She grinned. "I can't deny that holds certain appeal, but I do realise what's at stake and that compels me, too."

Smithy shook his head. It was still difficult to believe, but for now he would take her at her word, because he knew she would admit nothing else.

"Well, how nice it is you've developed such a helpful spirit this late in your career, Morrigan," he said, enunciating her name slowly. "But you can leave me out of your helpful efforts."

"But my efforts have aided you, Goibhniu. That's my point. My other point. She's drawn your magic up. Admit it. She's entwined with you, become your other half again. It was obvious to me even at the Inchigeela session what was happening. I can only imagine now...after you slept with her. Well, you didn't sleep at all, did you, really?"

He stiffened. "You're wrong. She's a girl. Just a girl, nothing more."

"Oh, Goibhniu, it would be amusing if it weren't so tragic."

He turned and started to walk away. He'd had enough of her taunting and besides, he'd said what he'd come to say. There'd been no victory, but then he hadn't expected one. It was Morrigan after all.

"She's gone, you know."

He halted and turned, even though his mind said to keep on walking. To get on that motorbike, feel the thrum and roar of it, the rage and power of it and ride back to his forge. His own source of being just Smithy and put that "justagirl" out of his mind. But his body betrayed him and he turned to look at her. At Morrigan with her glittering eyes, knowing that she was enjoying this just as much as she'd enjoyed every event that had involved himself and Saoirse.

"Gone?" a voice said. It was a voice his mind knew was his, but at this moment he was disowning it, emphasis on the "dis" because his mind wanted nothing to do with it.

"She left a few days ago. Right after she spoke to Anu. Right after you dropped her off, or so I've heard." She glanced up at her henchman and smiled softly. "A little birdie told me."

I glanced up at her henchman, Rook. "Don't pretend you had Rook keep an eye out and not you. You wouldn't have been able to resist watching the moment I took Saoirse back to her *grandmother* and discovered just who she was."

She shrugged. "I can't pretend it wasn't deliciously fun. And later, when she walked down the road like the Hounds of Hell were after her."

"Hounds of Hell? Really."

"Great expression, isn't it. And so apt in this case. I did manage to speak with her. So dotey, she is in her glamour. Though I have to say Anu needs to do something about that. It's fading." She gave Smithy a speculative glance. "Perhaps too much *not sleeping* with you?"

Smithy reddened. "What do you mean, her glamour is fading? She doesn't look like Bríd at all. Not really."

"Come, come, Goibhniu. Even Anu couldn't create a glamour that would fully disguise the height of her, the colour of her hair, the eyes. All of it still has a vague suggestion of who she was. Or, I mean, is. And now she's even more so. Her hair, even when I saw her walking down the road was a darker red. No longer the Titian colour she likes to describe it. I didn't get a close look at her eyes, but her body, well," she made a gesture towards her chest. "Fuller. More mature. Like the woman Bríd was."

Smithy stared at her, tried to make sense of it, to see the way through what Morrigan had just said. His mind still at odds with his body, reprimanded and yelled, but the body still wouldn't answer. Finally, when any terms of unification seemed impossible, his body agreed, turned and strode to the motorcycle.

No FIRE LIT THE FORGE, but the heat was unmistakable. It wasn't the kind of heat that, spinning whirling dancing, created a keen edge, a flawless shape that wove two metals and magic, the tra la la and fiddle dee dee that set a blade to light. There was no light about it. It was a dark and heavy heat. A heat that emanated from him and filled the place with bile, bitter and strong. It was the heat that looked at all the blades, half made swords and other articles of war and said "beware."

But his mind reared again and fought for its place at the helm with reason and caution. It issued orders in a firm and calm tone. Smithy unclenched his fists. Put on his safety glasses. Lit the forge and slipped on his gloves. He was a smith. He would practise his craft. It was a slip, what had happened. But that slip jumped around, jiggled and poked with a snicker. "Practise." He muttered a mental "feck off" and set to work.

He took a bar of metal and turned and ran it through his gloved hands to get a feel of its weight. To understand its shape and the shape it was to be. This was him, this was how he fashioned and created the objects of beauty and purpose. He made a careful choice with each one of those words and ran them through his mind, thought them to himself, the himself that was paying attention, or so he hoped. He grabbed his tongs and gripped the metal bar, placing it in the forge. He watched it heat, himself and his running, humming mantra. The words "creation and beauty" stood out and he liked their boldness, thought it showed who was boss and what would come of things.

The metal bar heated. He took up his hammer and began to pound the metal against the anvil. The sound of the pounding rang out with a ding and ding. But the ding and ding didn't become the ding, ding, ding of the dance, of the weaving, of the whirling. There was no spin, no hum or anything near it as the metal became flatter and flatter and flatter. It wasn't like before. The before of Saoirse, his arms wrapped around her, feeling her back against his chest, his mind filled with the stars and all the lightness they brought. The hum that whirled so hard it lifted him up, fused him to her and created such energy, an energy that he knew could be only one thing and one thing alone.

He threw down his tongs and hammer on the counter in disgust. Where was the magic he'd had before he'd been with her, made love to her, entered her body physically just as she entered his metaphysically? It had been faint. But it had been there. It had come on its own, without her. No, it was nothing to do with her. It was his and he would coax it back. He started to pick up the tongs and the hammer and stopped, the realisation that was rising slowly like a balloon on a breath of wind, gradually emerging. The magic that had come the first time had been after he'd met her. After he'd talked with her, shared a cup of tea, brought her into his house. Touched her.

He looked at the blade they'd fashioned together. The beauty of it, in its design, its creation and the way he knew it would function. They made that. Together. If he worked with her, would she be able to bring his magic back in full? To enable him to craft any weapon, any tool the way he wanted, with or without magic? He allowed the possibility to enter his mind which now had softened its hard line of before, but only some. The Saoirse he'd met, the Saoirse he'd talked with seemed hardly possible. The Saoirse he'd played music with, the Saoirse he'd touched, kissed and made love to, seemed all too possible.

His body responded to the memory, recalling it all again, another magic spell of a different kind, but one he couldn't resist.

"Bríd," he whispered, as if saying it would conjure her up right at that moment, as if all the other times he'd done that, whispered her name and nothing had happened. But this time there was a kernel of belief. A little seed that was sprouting, and with just a little bit of tending, nurturing, would blossom forth into the full bloom of notion that Saoirse might actually be Bríd.

What had that crow of a woman said? That her glamour was slipping? Fading away so that she resembled Bríd more? He shook off that knowledge. Such knowledge would lead to other thoughts and maybe other dreams. Dreams he couldn't afford.

21

SAOIRSE

W e've pulled up to a tiny old stone house on a hill
with the long beach stretching out below us. The
salt air breeze blew cool against my cheek and I
inhaled deeply. It was hours since we'd left Dublin and we were
in Connemara, on the tip of the land. At the edge. There was
nothing but sea in front of me and little behind, and that was
perfect in every way. Especially in my "whynotnow" life with my
"whynotnow" man.

This "whynotnow" man drew up beside me and draped an
arm around my shoulders.

"Feels good, doesn't it," he said.

I nodded. "It's lovely."

He kissed the top of my head and then took my hand.

"Come on. We'll get the jeep unloaded first and then we can
relax and have a swim. We need it after the long drive."

I gazed a little longer at the sea, then pulled myself away
from it and helped him unload.

It was a quick enough task, light hearted and full of promise
in the backpacks, bags and other bits we brought inside. I
laughed and made much of it, this impulsive act, this glorious

day in the hope for many glorious other days. The glorious days stretched longer and wider in the lightness and brightness of the open plan stone house with its stripped light wood floors, the light-filled Velux windows along the roof that met the sun beaming in from the large patio doors facing the sea.

I gasped and smiled widely, dropping my bags and lifting my arms out in celebration of the space and the moment just behind me and just going forward.

"Oh, Luke, this is grand," I said. "Did you do this?"

Luke shrugged. "It was a project I enjoyed."

"My god, aren't you the talented one," I said, my eyes still taking in all the details of sofa, chairs, tables and the spiral staircase that led to a mezzanine bedroom.

"Oh, you like my many talents?" he said.

I looked at him, at the gleam, the light that was in this "whynotnow" man who was mine in these glorious days of light. I tilted my head, all coquette and "go on with you", and raised my brows.

"I love them all so far, but will you be showing me more?"

With a laugh and an arm-around-me squeeze he had me spinning again. I looked up at him and he kissed me, fully, on the lips. The light filled me, shining right through and I knew then that I wanted this "whynotnow" to last longer, to detach the "now" send it off away home and just keep it the two, the "whynot" because they paired so well.

THERE WAS HARDLY anyone on the beach when we arrived. The tide was on its way out and the day was starting to fade, but the light that shone from Luke let him take me by the hand and run towards the water, hand in hand, with just the swimsuits between us and the water.

"The sea," he'd told me. "You have to feel it on your skin, all of it. And then you get the connection, the why of it, the spirit of it. To become part of it. At least the first time you get in."

"But what about our swimsuits? There's no direct contact there."

He grinned at me. "Once we get in the water, I'll make adjustments. You'll see."

"Adjustments?" I stared at him a moment, a little uncertain in the whole tidal strength of his light, his pull. And then I realised. "Ah, no." The words came out of my mouth, but his fingers caressed the back of my hand as he held it.

"Trust me," he said, softly. He leaned over and kissed me again.

And so I did. Trust him, as he led me running towards the water, into the water up to our necks, so cold, so cold. And I trusted him as he folded his arms around me, gently, and removed my bikini. First the top, and then the bottoms. And then his own swim trunks, balling it all up in his hand. He wrapped my legs around his waist and gently pulled me under the water. The moment was brief, it was electric while the cold, the fear just washed away and we rose again still entangled.

"See?" he said. "The sea has enveloped you. Made you part of it."

He lowered his lips on mine, teasing, brushing and then kissing deeply. I was drawn into the kiss, another tidal pull, and he pressed me tighter against him, so we would be fused to each other as we fused with the sea.

It was an experience like no other and one that came less as a "whynot" moment and more of being caught in the strongest, deepest undertow of yearning and wanting. A moment made larger and larger by many moments strung together, but no time was passing, yet all of it was.

And when we emerged out of that time as we emerged out of

the sea, our swimsuits intact, the light of the glorious day was nearly gone and we became nearly shadows as we walked back to the stone house in a silence that had no need to be filled.

I STARED at the painting above the small fireplace. It was large in every way. Stunning. Full of impact in its drama as it mirrored the scene through the patio doors. But this seemed more real. Perhaps because there was nothing but beach and sea. The sea in all its colours, textures and movement. The large rolling waves swept in to the edges of the foreground, the world, the power nearly forcing its way off the canvas into the room. And at the edge of the water, with the sea breaking all around him, stood a naked man, strong and muscular, a silver band around his arm and a torc around his neck. His hair blew wild and loose around his head and shoulders. He was startling and striking. Compelling.

I kept studying the painting, wine glass in one hand, the cheese and bread of our simple fare in the other, poised, waiting and waiting. The eyes of the man held mine, assessing me just as I was assessing him. There was something about him I thought I should know, felt I should recognise. I sighed.

"The painting," I said. "It's very...striking. Powerful. Where did you get it?"

Luke looked up from the cheese he was cutting to place on the small plate he had balanced on his lap and regarded the painting.

"I didn't. It's mine."

"Yours? You mean you painted it?"

"Yes. A while ago now, though."

I stared at him. The talents of the man. It was too much, nearly. Too much to comprehend, to see how this surfer, this "whynot" dude with his "whynot" surfboard could have made the glorious house, mastered the number of instruments as well as created an incredible painting. Because the credible of "incredible" was severely tested when looking at such a wonder, a painting like no other. "Whynot" and "wonder" seemed so at odds. Could you blend them into to the "whynotwonder"? I didn't know and didn't know how to know.

"You leave me speechless and senseless," I said finally.

He laughed, leaned over and picked up a strand of my hair that had fallen from the loose plait I'd fashioned after we'd swum.

"I could say the same," he said.

His eyes darkened, but the light was still there, pulling me in. In the now watchful eyes of the man by the sea, I felt a stirring. A tidal pull of a different sort.

"Who's the man in the painting?" I said, looking back up again at the canvas.

He paused a moment, glanced at me and then towards the painting. "Manannan."

"The sea god?"

He shrugged and nodded. There was a strange intonation when he'd pronounced it, one hard to describe, but nearly foreign.

I studied the man in the painting carefully and I could see of course that it could be no one else but the sea god. Manannan Mac Lir.

"I like your depiction of him. He seems so powerful, so real. As if all the myth has been stripped away and you just have him, Manannan."

He smiled and the light shone in his eyes. "That's exactly what I was trying to achieve."

"Well you achieved it."

"I know," he said.

I laughed and nudged him, all thoughts of the man forgotten. I picked up my wine and drank deeply and set the glass down. "If you're done, will we go explore some of your other talents?"

"Yes, we will," he said.

He took my hand and pulled me up the spiral staircase, away from the painting and to the bed.

A GLORIOUS MORNING joined the glorious day before it. We woke up early, well Luke awoke and roused me with an urgent kiss and a "let's be off" to catch the surf, or the wave, or whatever that was out there in the sea, the wide ocean waiting for us. My limbs moved sluggishly while I tried to arrange them in my swimsuit and later, on the beach, into the spare wetsuit he managed to find for me. Lots of "what was I thinking" streamed through my mind but his encouraging voice, magnetic smile and coaxing hands saw me through a perfunctory surfing lesson.

Giggles took hold of me, though, halfway through. Giggles saw me collapse in a heap as I tried to slip my legs through quickly to the squatting pose that was the beginning of "rising to your feet while catching that wave". I was on land.

"Oh, Luke, the only thing I'll catch is a mouthful of water," I said, still giggling.

"Ah, no. You're doing grand, you'll be grand, so."

"You're such a liar." I giggled again but rose amiably to try once more.

"You just need to focus. Feel your body move. You'll get it."

"In my eye, I will," I said and giggled again.

He gave me a pleading look and I knew then it was important to him. I'd seen the way he looked out to sea, watching the other surfers, paddling, gliding, surfing. And he was patiently trying to give me a chance to enjoy something of what he experienced.

Sobering a moment later, I straightened and tried to concentrate. To make this more than a "whynot" moment, live this glorious day for all that it was meant to be. After a quick peck on his lips, I lay on top of the spare surfboard, feeling the flat hard surface beneath me. I gave myself a mental check along my body to the outermost part of my limbs and imagined the sea beneath me. I imagined the rocking, the gradual swell and rise of the sea as the wave was about to come under me and I rose to a squat in one smooth motion and then stood, arms stretched out.

"Yes!" said Luke. "That's it."

I looked at him and beamed. It had been enjoyable to imagine and feel that idea of the surf, the whole build-up to when the moment arrived and I would be on top of the sea, riding it hard, the surfer girl sea goddess.

This surfer girl sea goddess, after several more practices and encouraging praise, followed the surfer dude god out to the sea to try and put those moves and feelings in the sea and on the sea. There were an ocean of waves given to me and I paddled my board towards them, following Luke until he pointed and we both turned to begin our ride.

My ride was short, but filled with promise and joy. My mouthful of sea became plural but I tried again and again until I found one that I rode through the distance. It was tiring, it was joyful, but my limbs and lungs were not yet up to the goddess standard and I eventually pulled up the board and headed up the beach towards our things. There, I sat, my wetsuit peeled away and my clothes restored and watched, my "whynot" sea god out on the waves.

And he was as glorious to watch as the day that was in it. So graceful, so powerful, the mage of all surfers, except for perhaps one. This other mage joined Luke in the riding, in the conquering of the waves that roiled and rolled in, crashing and thundering, growing larger as the time wore on. They were like two riders of the Apocalypse minus two, their synchronous actions like some water ballet that had me mesmerised and everyone else who was on the shore. I sat there, enchanted, wanting it to never end.

But they came in, and there was some applause and a few cheers, a gesture that I could appreciate and did join. Why wouldn't you for such a performance? It made me smile and laugh to see that beautiful man who shone so brightly create such a display. The other surfer, his mate, his companion in riding, was nearly as large and broad as Luke, his long blond hair nearly snow white. He looked familiar as he stood there in his wetsuit at the edge of the sea, talking at the edge with Luke. The foam lapped at their feet and he put his hand on Luke's shoulder, the serious nature of his words evident even from this distance.

I was startled when he nodded towards me and Luke turned, stared at me. I raised my hand and waved, but he didn't wave back. He just looked. Even from here I could see the "whynot" leaving his body, the gloriousness of the day retreating out to the wide ocean. The few clouds that had rolled in seemed to grow larger and darker.

Luke turned back to his friend, placed his hand on his neck and leaned his head against him. A moment later he pulled away, nodded and then with a "bro" clasp of the hands they parted and Luke started to head towards me.

Unease seeped in, then poured in, fast and furious like a flood tide. It spilled into every part of my body and by the time Luke arrived at my side and the steely expression in his face became evident, the unease filled me completely.

"What is it?" I asked. "What's wrong?"

"We're leaving," he said, his voice hard.

"But why? I thought we were enjoying it. I was. I loved surfing."

"We're leaving. Get up, let's go."

I rose and followed him silently up the beach and then to the house. Once inside, the silence continued. Luke went upstairs and I could hear him packing his things, and when I joined him he took my backpack from the floor and tossed it to me.

"Pack up. We're going back."

"I don't understand, Luke. Why?"

"No questions. Just pack."

I began to utter a fresh plea but closed my mouth. His expression was shut down, as was the rest of him. Time to go. The door was shut, my "whynot" man and everything else that went with him had left. I sighed and started gathering my things, stuffing them into my backpack with force as anger began to build.

It didn't take us long to reverse the course of yesterday's unpacking and resume our seats in the SUV, surfboard strapped to the top and on our way eastwards. No music, no loose and lovely feeling. Just silence. The "whynot" time now replaced with the "whatthefeck" and "pissoff".

22

SMITHY

Smithy stared out through the shed door. Behind him the forge lay untouched, as it had for the past week. It was a bleak day, the sun never quite cutting through the mist that had gathered that morning. It reflected his mood perfectly.

He'd managed to get himself to the forge, a feat after days of either sitting inside at the kitchen table scrolling aimlessly through his phone, only to pause and snort at YouTube videos of various smiths posting their demonstrations on sword making, or riding around on his motorbike along back roads. His behaviour frustrated him, disgusted him and his mind tossed constant mental reprimands his way. That he'd made it as far as the forge today made him quite proud, until he ended up standing in the doorway, staring across at the hills.

Was it fear, or pure procrastination against the inevitable? The knowledge that he was going to eventually have to either make the feckin' sword and fashion a handle for that dagger blade and just hand over whatever resulted, or come out and tell Anu that the magic was gone and what little chance it had of returning had disappeared back to Dublin, or who knew where.

Who was he fooling? It was neither, said his mind, which

tossed that fact his way just as it had the reprimands. It was pride and hurt and hurt and pride. And hurt pride. Untangle that, said his mind. Untangle that and get hold of yourself. Cop on.

"Goibhniu."

Smithy blinked and looked across at the gate. Anu. The sight of her was startling on so many counts. She had never sought him out here at the forge. Never. His forge was his demesne, his place that was him and she'd let him be there. Always met him or contacted him through others and out and about. So the sight of her there, standing at his threshold, gave him pause.

"What is it?" he asked. He studied her carefully. There was nothing in her expression or her manner that suggested anything but one neighbour calling to another.

"Am I welcome in?" she asked, her voice pleasant.

"Of course," he said. "Come away inside."

He led her into the kitchen and offered her a chair at the table. Hastily, he cleared away the clutter and piled it on the counter and in the sink.

"Cup of tea?" he asked. What else would he do? What other hospitality could he possibly offer in this strange world of inbetween and not? There was no protocol for this, no rules of welcome cups and platters of food. Servants waiting, a harper at the ready. Nothing royal or high table about this tidy little house with its tidy little kitchen.

She laughed, sensing his thoughts, he had no doubt. He shrugged the shrug of helplessness, frustration and bewilderment that this scene had created and waited for her cue.

"Tea, of course,"

He made the tea, not in the cup as he would usually do, but in a teapot he dug out from the back of the press. He didn't realise he was doing it and still wondered that he'd done it until he poured the hot water in there and waited for it to steep. Did that mean the milk went in the jug? He sighed, retrieved the small jug and put it on the counter, then poured the milk into it. All the time he was conscious of Anu, sitting, watching, assessing.

Eventually, the teapot, jug, mugs (not cups!) were on the table along with a plate of biscuits. It was the best he could offer. He never had fresh cake or anything else that might usually be on offer. As it was, he'd had to endure her smile and eyes as each item was placed on the table. Was the smile because she recognised his indecision about the kind of hospitality he should offer? A "what was right" series of moments that left him feeling foolish? Or the even deeper reason in that it put off the moment when they would have to talk. When he would have to listen and then reply. To make the refusal, to make the explanation.

It was probably and undoubtedly both. Anu knew. Knew him, knew the parts that made him up.

She lifted the teapot and poured the tea first into his mug and then hers. Delicately, but not. It was a manner that was wholly hers. She pushed the mug towards Smithy and he grasped it like a lifeline. Like something to hold on to that was more than a mere mug of tea.

"This is important, Goibhniu," she said, her voice calm and even.

"I know," he said hoarsely. He cleared his throat and indicated to the table. To the fact that she was here, enjoying his meagre hospitality and only something vital would draw her here.

"It's Balor."

"What about him?"

"He's here."

"In Ireland? On this land?"

She nodded. "He's getting bolder, more aggressive in his reach and his exploits."

Smithy shook his head in disbelief. "The bastard. He knows he's not to set foot in this world on Eire. He knows it."

"We've allowed him to establish himself across the ocean, in America. I hoped he would be content with that and it would give us time."

Smithy frowned. He knew about time and how it tricked you, made you feel you had it and then you didn't. He'd learned that bitter lesson to long ago. The long ago that no longer figured in numbers.

"He outwits us again, it seems," said Smithy. "He has darkness and vitriol as his power."

"All the more reason that we must defeat him. Soon. Now."

"So the time is now?" Smithy said sceptically. "And does time agree with that statement?"

She frowned at him. "Goibhniu, I know you suffered terribly. First from losing Bríd, your heart's mate, to Bres, and then losing her again in death."

"You don't know."

"You don't think I suffered with her loss? With all the losses? With the pain and misery that I feel every day as this land is assaulted and tortured in so many ways?"

Smithy stared at her and tapped into something deep. It was there waiting to come up, spill forth. "You have experienced loss. Of course. It's who you are, it's what you are." He took a deep breath. "What I am experiencing.... What I am living is loss, but not loss. It's living and not living, it's guilt and not guilt. It's an emotion for things I did and things I didn't do and things that were not of my making. Events that weren't of my making. The force of magic and power that run through my body are destroyed, poisoned, shrivelled and dried up. I am a husk of nothing."

Anu leaned forward and placed a hand on Smithy's. "I say

again. It wasn't your fault. You did all you could and more. The only poison is within you."

Smithy snatched his hand away. "You. Know. Nothing."

Anu sighed. "But still, you can help. Balor is here, now. In this land where he should never step foot."

"What can I do? Did you not hear? I have nothing. No magic."

"He's in Cork," she said, ignoring his words. "Visiting one of his subsidiaries. Apparently he wants to form a company and join one of the other petrochemical companies and begin fracking."

"Fracking?" Smithy said, sidetracked. "That's a new area for him, isn't it?"

"He's started doing it in America. He has a company set up for it there under his energy company."

Smithy shook his head. "That's crazy. He wouldn't get approval, surely?"

"Oh, Goibhniu, you know better than that. The way business and government work, it will only be a matter of time."

Oh, that tricky bastard "time" again. He sighed. He did know better. But it still made him angry. Furious, in fact. That bastard and his poison was still trying to create chaos and ruin. His vengeance for long-ago ills and grievances over events that happened and were from his own making, truth be told. Balor's daughter was long dead and any shame attached to an unwanted birth lived on in her glorious son, Lugh.

The irony of the situation suddenly struck him and he snorted. Bríd's story was not dissimilar.

"What is it?" said Anu.

He shook his head. He wouldn't say it. Until his thoughts drifted sideways. "Saoirse. You're certain she's in Dublin?"

Anu looked at him curiously. "Yes. Well, she was last week. Why?"

He shook his head again. "No reason in particular, except that if Balor's wandering around it's best if she's far away from him."

Anu cocked her head, a small smile on her face. "And why is that, Goibhniu?" she said softly.

"The glamour. Morrigan said the glamour is slipping. And if she's looking more like Bríd now..." he stopped and frowned. "Well, if it's true and she is Bríd, then she's in danger."

"It is true."

It was true. The words echoed in his mind. That same mind that had tossed reprimands and all sorts at him now agreed with Anu. She was Bríd. And his heart, the one that had been through quite a bit in the last while, ached.

Anu leaned forward again and this time took up his hand. "Goibhniu. We need to make sure she's safe."

Smithy raised his eyes to hers. "Yes. We do."

They both knew that Balor, once he'd seen Bríd, would stop at nothing to kill her and ensure that there was no bringing her back this time. Bríd was key. Bríd was his key. His life's blood. His magic's life. And together their magic was so very powerful in what they could create together. One magic, whole.

"I'll send Morrigan this time. We'll check that she's still in Dublin and keep track of her."

Smithy nodded. "I should go to her, though. Try to make it right. Try...."

Anu squeezed his hand. "Yes, Goibhniu. But first, we'll send Morrigan."

Smithy nodded again. His mind said "practical" but his heart screamed "no, go now." It was a war he didn't know who would win.

ANU WON. At least that's what it felt to Smithy as he rode his motorbike east towards Cork. She talked him in circles and sideways and every way that led to the bike heading east. Morrigan had headed towards Dublin on Anu's instructions, her wings taking her there in no time, but still, that feckin' beggar time hadn't provided enough for him to wait to hear what Morrigan had to say. It was "now" that took over and here he was, the mobile phone in his T-shirt pocket, pressed against his chest so that he would know if Morrigan had news. As the crow flies, even in its literal sense, hadn't been quick enough.

The road was busy going through Macroom. He snorted impatiently, crawling up the hill and then through the bottleneck narrowed street curves to the other side. Once free of the bottleneck, it seemed to slow down again, only to eventually free up. He longed for the open stretches and then to the bypass where he could really make good time. But this was a day for stop-go systems, happy shoppers and "must make the appointment" people all heading to the city, and any progress was thwarted among the myriad cars that lined the roads.

The slow progress only contrasted to the busy thoughts that warred in his mind. No reprimands issued this time, only contradictory thoughts and feelings who tried to box clever with each other. The feelings didn't explain or rationalise, they declaimed, they emoted and displayed all their intuition to show him that he could never doubt who Saoirse was. The thoughts were cool and calm with just a hint of disdain that arguments would ever be proven on such flimsy platforms as feelings. It was all about what was possible, what could happen. But Smithy knew. Smithy knew that the platform was built on something stronger. It was magic and it was Bríd.

SMITHY PULLED his bike up and slipped into a parking space just along the quay. It was just about big enough for his bike. He removed his helmet and stared out across the river to the high rise building. If he'd been in any doubt about the location of Balor's offices, the placard-holding protesters outside confirmed it. He could hear their shouts and chants from here. It wasn't quite a mob, but they certainly weren't the happiest bunch. He didn't know if that was a good sign or bad. He certainly wouldn't be upset if one of them chose to maim Balor.

He swung his leg over the bike and locked his helmet to the frame. His curiosity grew and he began to walk along the quay to the bridge and then across it. As he drew closer to the protesters he could see that it was more than just your usual enthusiastic environmentalists, but a mixture of ages, genders and types. Their signs decried not just the fracking but the destructive evil of Balor Energy Group. Smithy allowed himself a satisfied grunt of appreciation that finally people saw through this charlatan who spouted jobs and prosperity. Who boasted of the number of school computers he'd purchased, of the schools he supported in so many ways they were beholden and, in his mind, enslaved to his view of the world.

He approached the crowd and tried to peer over their heads to the door of the building. There was no sign of Balor as far as he could tell, or anyone else that might be representing him and his company. But the protesters were obviously here for a reason.

He moved towards a woman who seemed fierce enough and old enough to have some idea of things.

"Anything happening?" he said. "Is there going to be an announcement?"

She turned to look at him and nodded. "That bastard should be out any minute. To address our concerns." She said sarcastically. She snorted. "It's all talk. Talk, talk, talk. Serious about concerns, in his hole."

Smithy fought back the urge to laugh and managed a nod. "He's a bastard all right. There's nothing to argue there."

She looked at him and grinned. "You sound as if you know that personally."

He shrugged. "No need to know him personally to realise that."

"Did you want a placard?" she asked.

"I'm just here to shout. I think that's enough for me," said Smithy.

She laughed. "I've come down from Dublin, so I feel the need to carry a placard and shout."

"Dublin, eh? Your commitment is admirable."

"Ah, no. They are protesting up there, but they sent most of us down here because he's here. He's due to fly out tomorrow. That's if the deal goes through." She emphasised "deal" with a sneer.

"Ah. Of course. I'd heard something like that. Well, I'm all for lending my voice," he said.

He scanned the crowd and saw that it had grown even in the time he'd had the conversation with the woman. He even saw a few cameras and members of the media. It stirred something inside him. Was that hope? He tamped it down, because, unlike anyone else here in this crowd, or among all the activists in this country, the government and the businesspeople who made deals with Balor, Smithy knew how completely evil Balor was. And even worse, how powerful he was. And no one else, except for the Tuatha De Danann that were left in this world, could come even close to hope to defeat him.

A roar went up in the crowd. Smithy looked over their heads to the door of the building. A group of people emerged, among them a powerfully built man with dark, greying hair, a beard and an eye patch. Smithy stared, paralysed by the intensity of seeing this man after such a long time. The time that stretched and bent and kept you waiting so it seemed like forever. But it wasn't forever, and Smithy now knew it hadn't been long enough. The hatred, the vitriol and the utter rage rose up inside him and it was all he could do not to rush forward and take the man down with whatever he could bring to hand.

23

SAOIRSE

We neared Galway and the silence still reigned. No word, not a sound came from Luke's tightly pursed mouth, so it was left to me to imagine and create the narrative in my head. The "why" taken from the "whynot" to do a solo flight and zoom around in my head to parse out actions and words.

It had all gone wrong when we surfed. That much was clear. Up until then, there had been nothing but joy and more joy in our actions and interactions. The lesson, though awkward at first, was nothing but fun and eventually successful. I'd ridden the waves, then watched him glide and ride like a conqueror. The joy was evident in every lean and sway of his body. When he'd emerged from the shore, sleek as any seal, his friend had reinforced and celebrated his success and prowess. But then the friend had pointed, gestured and talked. It was at that point it had all collapsed.

I didn't know this friend, not from Adam or any other man that had crossed my path. He couldn't know me, could he? I allowed it was possible here in Ireland, where the degrees of separation were no degrees at all. But what person could he know who would paint me in such a light that Luke would react, no recoil, to such a degree? There was no one I could recall.

The "why" hung out and crossed lazily back and forth, wearing a path but going nowhere. I sighed and tried to toss it aside, look at the view out my window and plan what I was going to do.

"I'll let you off at the railway station at Galway," Luke said, breaking the silence. "I-I'm not going back to Dublin. I have to head away north."

I stared at him, too astonished for any response.

"I'll pay for your fare, not to worry about that," he said. He didn't look at me. He kept his eyes on the road, gripped the steering wheel for dear life and fell silent again.

I turned to my window again and nodded my head. The "why" grew bigger and was almost mocking me as it danced about and swung back and forth against the lie he just uttered. "Head away north" in my eye, I thought. The silence continued its barrier and the wall of it turned from brick to granite as I spied the railway station building up ahead. A few minutes later he pulled up outside, drew out some twenties from his pocket and tossed them towards me.

"Oh, feck off with yourself," I said.

I got out of the jeep, retrieved my backpack from the seat behind and slammed the door, leaving the twenties on the floor of the SUV. It was a gesture I could ill afford at the moment, with a dubious credit card and a debit card on hazard red, but I wasn't going to do anything to ease his conscience.

Inside the station, my prayers I learned at boarding school all lined up and ready to go in my head, I waited in the queue at the ticket counter and hoped those prayers would join those wings and make me a woman with a ticket. It wasn't until I got to the counter and the man asked me the "where" that realised I had assembled the wings and prayers for the payment but the not the destination. Would I go to Dublin? Or would I go elsewhere? And suddenly I knew. Or maybe the wings and prayers told me.

"Cork," I said.

The name came as if it had been pulled from the bottle that had contained my anger and frustration, not only from Luke and his outrageous behaviour, but everything else. The Lukes be damned, along with the Smithys and grandmothers who weren't grandmothers. To fathers who behaved like business supervisors, and the years of boarding school holidays, and a useless degree that saw no blossoming talent but a barista as its crowning achievement.

And there I was—suffused, infused and exploding with anger, seated on the next train to Cork.

I EMERGED from the station in Cork, backpack on, flute case in hand, and was caught up in a stream of people. I was surprised at their number. It was a Saturday, but still, it seemed more than would be expected and so many more than the number of people who'd been here the two other times I'd been in the station.

The tide of people carried me along from the entrance and eventually up the road. They couldn't all be headed towards the bus station, surely? It was then I noticed that some of them held placards emblazoned with words in vibrant colours. I tried to make out some of the words, and with a bit of craning and head tilting, saw words like "fracking" and "poison".

I went up alongside one of the people, a woman who was not much older than me, holding a short wooden post with her placard affixed to it.

"Protesting?"

She looked at me and smiled. "Yeah. You should come. It's important that this man hears all our voices."

"Fracking, right?" I asked.

She nodded. "This time. But that man and his company are poison. Literally."

I suppressed the English degree person's urge to explain that she was mistakenly using the term "literally" in this case, as so many people were wont to do.

She frowned and eyed me warily. "You're not in favour of fracking are you?"

"Oh, god, no," I said. In truth it wasn't ever something I'd considered, but this didn't seem to be the time to mention it.

Her smile returned. "Good. Because it's a terrible thing for this country and this planet."

"It is, of course."

"And this man, with his billions, is trying to rake in more billions for him and his cronies by exploiting the earth and its treasures. But we won't let him, will we?"

I shook my head, though I felt such assurance was dubious given the record of this country and the other governments of the planet. The "we" had proved always too weak against "them". At least it had seemed so to me.

She linked her arm through mine. "You've nowhere more important to go, have you? Because this is the most important thing you have to do, today. Any day."

We were heading down across the river, this stream of people of which I was now part, and I looked at this woman and nodded, trapped by her arm and words And sure, what was the harm? I could go for a short while and then catch the bus west. It was Saturday, it wasn't raining and wasn't this the most important thing I had to do today and any day?

"I'm Saoirse," I said.

"Ciara."

She introduced me to a few of the others around her as we moved in our herd towards the building Cíara told me belonged to the literally poison man.

"What's the company?" I asked after a while that had been taken up with fragments of crimes and misdemeanours.

"Balor Energies Group," said Cíara.

I murmured the name. "Seems appropriate. Though maybe Baleful Energies Group might have a better ring to it."

Cíara laughed. "I like it. Pádraic Balor of the baleful eye patch."

"Pádraic Baleful eye," I said. "Why eye patch?"

"You'll see. Can't miss the bastard because of it."

"Oh, he sounds a proper villain, so," I said.

Cíara nodded. "Oh, proper villain."

We traded a few more remarks as we moved along, a comfortable rapport settling between us. It was a nice feeling and one that had gone some way to defuse the anger and settle the cork in Cork back on top of the bottle. Not all the way in, but just a bit. Enough that I could enjoy this exchange and perhaps direct any seepage out of the corked bottle towards this baleful eyed man of literal poison.

We drew up by the building, the crowd large and thick around us. There was a definite energy here from the mixture of angry mutterings, strident comments, gesturing and gesticulations, all directed at the building entrance. An occasional shout or demand was issued for baleful-eyed man of poison to show himself, to give an account of himself. To face his accusers who charged him with crimes against Mother Earth.

The term "Mother Earth" (capitalised of course) echoed through me and I flinched. It was close to home, and the home that it was close to was one I wasn't prepared to entertain in or around. I wanted far away from that home. Suddenly, it all seemed to close in on me. This crowd with their indignation, their outrage and call to battle on behalf of the planet that they'd name as their mother. I had no mother, not one in any sense but literal/biological and so it held no meaning for me. Gone. I was gone. I worked my way through the crowd who seemed to surge forward at that moment, pushing me with it. A roar went up and I turned, just as I was shoved and pushed and in that forward momentum I spilled out onto one side of the crowd.

I turned and saw the man himself. Mr Baleful-eyed man of poison, standing there in his Armani suit, grey haired slicked back, beard perfectly groomed and a large black eye patch covering his left eye. I gaped, drawn by the sight of him, the presence of him larger than life. Broad of chest. Broad of everything. And filled with power. He smiled. A smile of genuine disdain, dislike, and all the other "disses" that could knock a person back.

"Bríd!"

I turned at the shout, for no reason other than it was what my body did. A body that had no cause to betray me like that, would hear nothing of the silent scream inside my head as I saw Smithy approach me, his face filled with all kinds of worry, fear, joy and something else that couldn't be, but my body knew and made its response.

He grabbed me and wrapped me in his arms and kissed my head. "Oh, feck it, Bríd. What the hell are you doing here? It's not safe."

I tried to pull from his arms, because I had to, the cork was rattling. His arms felt good, though and I tried to deny how good they felt. How warm and right and true. "Let me go. I'm fine."

He held me tighter. "No, you're not."

I struggled against him. "Leave me be."

"Hey," said a man near us. "She said to let her go."

Smithy gave me a frustrated look, releasing me except for one hand that clutched my arm.

"Please," he said his voice softer.

He said a few more words, but I couldn't hear him for the crowd who were pushing closer, moving us forward towards the entrance. I tried to keep my balance and looked around me, Smithy's hand still clutching one of my arms.

"Oh, feck it all," said Smithy. "Quick, we need to leave. He's seen us."

"What?"

"Balor. He's seen us."

I looked over to Mr Baleful-eye of the Poison, Baleful Poison-Eye. The name was getting better and more improved as it repeated itself in my head. Until I looked at him and the humour and wit left me, but the name remained as it swelled and congealed into the poison that it was and could even almost literally be. For that face, with its patched baleful poison eye was directed at me. The good eye, or the eye that had no patch, because good seemed to have no part of his eye or any other part of his face, was looking at me. It wasn't a benign look, but a look filled with rage and hatred so incomprehensible except when it was coupled with the word "poisonous", being active that it was. Active in a way that I didn't resist Smithy when he grabbed my hand and took off running. We ran fast and hard and I knew nothing about our direction, only that I wished that I could run faster and that my backpack wasn't bouncing so hard against me. I threw it off and tossed it aside, kept my precious flute case, my breath coming hard and fast, my legs striving for bigger and faster lengths.

Smithy suddenly pulled me inside a building and to a short, dark hallway where he hugged me tight to his chest, my head buried in his shoulder while we panted, trying to catch our breath.

"Did we lose him?" I whispered.

Smithy put a finger over my lips and shrugged. He motioned for me to wait where I was and quietly made his way to the end of the hallway. I could see now that it was some kind of office building, all but one office locked and dark for Saturday. I waited and listened hard when he disappeared around the corner, my breath held, chest tight.

When he returned I could just about see in the dim light that his expression had eased somewhat. I released my breath.

"Is he gone?"

He shrugged and took my hand again. "For now, maybe, but we can't take any chances. We'll go out the back and circle around the building."

"Where will we go? Did you bring your bike?"

"Shhh. No time for questions, just do as I say."

We made our way out of the back entrance, past the one lit office, a solicitor's, whose blinds were thankfully drawn. Once outside again, Smithy walked rapidly along the road, heading towards the river. We crossed over, finding a stream of people heading towards the shopping district. Once there he cut through one of the buildings, and then out through the back, until we were once more out on the road.

He made a winding progress through various buildings and out again, and eventually came along the river once more. It was a slow and laborious progress, but I made no complaints, my sense of urgency picked up from him.

Eventually, he stopped by the river. There was a small patch of ground that was more dirt than grass, and further along the river I could see longer and greener stretches of ground. He gave a low whistle and then a short one, murmured a few words and somehow a boat came from somewhere.

In view of what I'd experienced in the past few months it seemed ludicrous that I should question the somehow and the somewhere, but my mind kept trying to make sense of it. I opened my mouth to voice the somehow and somewhere questions but Smithy put a finger to my lips and shook his head.

"No questions, remember? Just do what I say."

I shut my mouth, the somehow and somewhere questions lost in my throat because of Smithy's look, the desperate, fearful look that had lurked there, and the voice that matched it.

He got into the boat, helped me into it and pushed off with one of the oars. We drifted a moment and then the current caught us, strong enough to take hold, but not fierce enough to give me pause. There were no seats, just the empty boat, a few cushions and the oars. Without a word, Smithy laid down in the boat and pulled me into his arms, laying my flute case beside us.

24

SMITHY

"Close your eyes," Smithy said.

He watched as she slowly did as he asked. He nearly grinned. He could see that she was at war with herself about whether to challenge him at every point, to ask all the questions that were so obviously racing around her head. That was his Bríd, he knew that without any doubt now.

He pulled her under him, protecting her from the sight of anyone who happened to see them at this fragile juncture in their journey. His hair and the back of his jacket were nondescript enough. Her eyes flickered open at the movement.

"Not to worry," he said softly. "It's just anyone looking can only see my back." He smiled. "A very unimportant looking back."

She frowned, not entirely convinced. "But if he's looking for us, he would think it odd."

"It's all right," Smithy said. "It's only for a few moments. After that we'll be safe."

She opened her mouth to say something more but he shook his head. "Wait. For now, just close your eyes."

With doubt still present in her eyes she closed them and once again Smithy could view her face without the querying and piercing looks she gave him through eyes that he saw in the light of day were indeed now Bríd's. Even the feel of her against him now, the softer limbs, bigger hips and breasts were hers. But the face was even more so, now. The fuller lips, the precious nose was all and more of what he remembered, what he knew to be Bríd.

He ached with the knowledge, with the pain of her, here, under him. His beloved. He could feel his body respond to her, to the physicality of her, but also the spirituality of her. It rose up and seeped right through his skin to the depths of his soul. It joined his and spun and wove again, the joy of it, the purity of it just wrapping around him inside and out.

With great effort he tried to disentangle it. Not yet. He knew that. He uttered the words instead that would begin the journey, the path that he knew must be and it must not involve her.

As if sensing his shift and the next, Bríd's eyes flew open and met his. Above them, the sky yawned, bright and filled with a light that was more. A light that was pure and shone around them and in them. There was light all around, nothing but light. They floated, the current beneath them soft and almost unde-tectable.

"Where are we?" she asked.

"The Time Between Time."

She blinked. "The Time Between Time. What do you mean? What's that?"

He kissed her forehead lightly. "It's the place where no time is present. The place between worlds. We're safe here."

"You mean Balor can't follow us here?"

Smithy shook his head. "No. Only one of the Tuatha De Danann can access it."

She blinked at him, bit her lip and nodded.

"And he's after me."

"Us. But especially you. He knows without you I am nothing. I can do nothing. My weapons are useless."

She opened her mouth to speak, but he put his finger on it. "I know it. I've known it for a long time. Without you I'm not whole, the magic is gone. Surely you know that now?"

"But the whistle," she said softly.

He smiled sadly. "The whistle was made with your music still singing in me, the touch of you, however briefly, still spinning and vibrating in me."

She stared at Smithy, filled with confusion mixed with disbelief, but at the corners, at the back of it all, there was a growing knowing.

"Oh, Smithy," she said.

"Goibhniu."

She pursed her lips. "Goibhniu" she said softly. "I know nothing of this. I promise you. There is no memory of any of who you claim I am."

He sighed. "There's no 'claim' about it, Bríd. It just is. You just are. And Balor wants to destroy you. Destroy us."

"But why me in particular? Why not you? I have no memory of any of it, so why would he go after me?"

He turned away from her. "Not only are you key to my magic and I the key to yours, you were there with the Fomorians. You know all their secrets, their weaknesses."

She inhaled sharply. "Did I betray the Tuatha de Danann? Is that why I was with the Fomorians?"

He shook his head and started to speak.

"No, wait, it's coming back to me."

He looked at her hopefully. "You remember?"

"No, no. Not in the way you mean. I remember what my grandmother said. I mean what Anu said," she corrected herself. "Or whatever the hell, she's called," Saoirse muttered.

He grinned, charmed for just a moment by the small petulant outburst.

"So Anu explained it to you all, then. Good."

She sighed. "I suppose. Though there's so much that I don't know. I feel as though I'm coming in at the end of the show. Or the drama play."

He snorted lightly and stroked her hair. Oh the feel of it, silken, just as he remembered. "I can imagine. And I'm sorry. But hopefully this will end soon and you'll be safe."

"Are we to remain here, so?"

"In Time Between Time?"

"Yes. You said yourself it's a place only the Tuatha De Danann can go to."

"There are many of the Tuatha de Danann who would seek us out and bring us to either world."

"Either world?"

He gave her a sorrowful look. It was all that she'd lost the understanding, the depth of knowledge and the rhythms and joys blended with sorrows that made all its parts.

"The Otherworld *mo croí*."

She stilled and he didn't know if it was the endearment or the mention of "Otherworld."

"Otherworld?" she said softly.

"We are in the place and time between the world we just left and the Otherworld. The world the Tuatha de Danann inhabit. Or the *sídhe*, as some call us."

"*Sí Beag, Sí Mhor*, little fairy mound, big fairy mound," she said, musing. "Like the music air. Those *sídhe*."

He gave a light laugh. "I suppose. It's been trivialised."

"And paddy whackeried, to be sure, to be sure," she said with the most exaggerated vaudeville Irish accent he'd heard.

"Hmm," he said. "I didn't know you were a leprechaun."

"No," she said eyes wide. "But sure, wasn't that you in the film, *Finian's Rainbow*?"

"You mean the one holding the pot of gold? Ah, no, that was Fred Astaire. A different kind of little people, but so very big with his dancing."

It was good, this feeling right now, this bantery, jokery light exchange that just made him joyful and happy and so filled with her in his arms, able to love her in a light but wonderful way that wove them into each other but left the weft and warp of the pain strands out on the edges.

"Is that where we're going?" she said. "To the Otherworld? To Sí Beag, Sí Mhor?"

"Well, it's more a medium sized fairy mound, rather than a small or big one."

She laughed again, nestling down into his neck. "Will it take long to get there?"

Not long enough, he thought. He forced a smile that would push away those weft and warp strands of pain that had suddenly crept into the weave. "Are you asking are we there yet?"

"No, not at all. In fact, I would like to stay here for hours. For days. For weeks. Can we do that?"

He kissed her lightly on the lips, stealing it quickly in case the theft of such a kiss would produce a rejection and retribution he wouldn't be able to afford.

"No, *mo grá*. We can't stay here that long, because in the two worlds time moves on and in measurements that are far outside of what you may think. As it is, we are stealing time from our lives. In both worlds. It may only be a few days in the Otherworld, but in the world we just left it could be weeks. Or months."

She stared at him, eyes wide, filled with confusion, disbelief and finally acceptance. "Ah, not so bad, then. In some fairy stories, it's centuries."

He smiled at her. "Yes," he said, softly. "Not so bad."

The boat jolted slightly and he looked up to check, though he knew what had happened, he was still just hoping it wasn't time. But it was. Time was taking them now. They'd hit shore.

Slowly, he rose up in the boat and steadied it against the bank. Bríd sat up, and he thought of her now as Bríd. If only it gave him the courage and will that he needed. He stepped up on the bank. This "if only" joined the other "if onlys" he'd accumulated.

Bríd started to rise up and reach for his shoulder, but he stopped her.

"No," he said. "Stay in the boat."

She gave him a puzzled look. "What do you mean? Are you returning to the boat?"

He shook his head. "No. I'm staying here, but you have to go back to the other bank. To the world we just came from."

"No," she said, her brows lowering. "No. I'm going with you." She started to get out of the boat but he pressed firmly on her shoulder.

"Bríd, you can't come with me. It's too dangerous. Balor will look for us both here first. He'll know that's where we'll go."

"He can come here?"

"Yes. With help from those who have Tuatha de Danann blood, yes." He kept his voice neutral, even. He wouldn't tell her any details. "But he can't access Time Between Time. Only those of Tuatha de Danann blood can."

"Then return with me to the other side. Time will have moved on enough that he will think we're gone. We can go north, away from Cork. We could travel to another country."

He shook his head. "No. This is the safest way. For me to lead him away from you. He would know that I would never willingly leave you once I found you."

"Then why are you leaving me now?"

The pain and fear in her voice almost broke him. Especially the pain. Was it for him, did she have enough of him woven in her soul still that it could make her feel pain at the thought of losing him?

"Because it's best," he said. "Because I have to."

"No, you don't have to."

"Yes, I do. I didn't save you last time, but I can do it now."

"I don't care about then. I don't even remember it, so it doesn't matter," she said, her voice rising, urgent.

"It does matter, Bríd. I let you go, and I never went to you even when I knew I should. And then when they told me you were dead it broke me, hollowed me out, so that I was nothing. I've been nothing for too long. Until now." He looked at her, pleading in his eyes. "I have to do this, Bríd. Not just for you, but for me, too. For us."

Tears welled in her eyes and she finally nodded. Slowly, she sat down in the boat. Smithy leaned over her and kissed her on the lips, sliding his hand around the back of her head. It was a bittersweet moment for him, her lips so soft and willing, so tender and full. Eventually, he pulled away and stroked her hair. After one final kiss to her head, he pushed the boat off with all his love for her tucked inside it, and he prayed to all the gods and Anu that it would be enough.

25

SAOIRSE

O nce I hit the bank I crawled out of the boat, a *Lady of Shalott* returned, bedraggled and heartbroken, the mirror assuredly cracked, a curse definitely come upon me. I felt a wail rise up inside me. A *caoine* pure and perfect that would put any keening banshee to shame.

I could see some walkers in the distance, heading towards me on a winding path and I hastily moved away from the bank and made for the trees that were scattered over to the side of the path. Once there, I leaned against a tree to catch my breath and orient myself. Another wail rose silently up inside me. A wail born of confusion, despair, fear and grief.

I was caught up in something that wove a web so tight around me I could hardly breathe. The fantastical fantasy of events I'd experienced since my father's death were just too overwhelming for me. Had he even been my father? Had he even died? Was he ever real? All those questions so unthinkable a few months before were so very plausible now. But worse than contemplating all that, was the very real ache inside my heart when I thought of Smithy. Goibhniu. Even as the name Goibhniu echoed in my mind, I knew it was true. He was true.

I stood back from the tree, only now noticing it was an oak, a young one, but still an oak. Fitting enough I thought. Strength, wasn't it? Or perhaps more fitting as the tree everyone leaned back on in every folk song that had heartbreak in it. Well, not every song, came the retort in my head. That voice would have to get me to Anu. That voice would help me find my way to the bus so that I could take it to her village and eventually to her. Bus was all the few notes stuffed in my jeans would get me. For a brief moment I wished a different action when Luke had thrown the money in my direction in his SUV, but it was only fleeting and I didn't really mean it. Luke seemed long ago now and almost, the "feckin' shit head" feeling, a distant memory.

I dragged myself to the path, flute case in hand, the voice of reason filled with oaken strength pulling me forward. One foot placed in front of the other, a two-four rhythm with whole notes wanting to be quarter/quavers, take your pick, hoping and wishing for a reel, but getting a march. A tune came, placed by something other than the oaken voice. The phone, lost long ago in the mad dash was not its source. The source was outside, yet inside. Around me, yet in me. It wove around me and wrapped me up, set my pace. The pace was a happier, faster one and I found a road. The road led me to another, turned me right and then left, went uphill then down, and eventually, I recognised the buildings. The church spire. Capitalise all the letters of the church that made Cork its own. Bells and all. I hadn't heard them, those Shandon bells, but I knew I wasn't far from a place I could find my way. At least to the bus. The rest would have to wait.

ONCE SAFELY BOARDED on the bus heading west, I sat back and leaned my head against the window and cradled my flute case.

My head was crowded with the thoughts that had overtaken me once I'd reached the bus station and seen the date. Two weeks. A fortnight. Fourteen days. All of them had lapsed since I'd stood outside Balor's office building. Goibhniu had been right. It didn't seem possible. I laughed at the thought of those words. None of it seemed possible, but yet it was. And nothing could change the fact of the date. And even though a fortnight had passed, my heart was still aching. Another fact that hadn't changed.

I glanced out of the window, even now looking for signs of Balor, or someone who might be connected with him. It was stupid, I knew that, because how would I know? All I could really check was that it wasn't Balor. No one could miss that man in a crowd, especially with the eye patch. Eye patch. Ah, the sin of it. Jaysus. How had I been so dim? Dim of course, because who would think that someone with an eye patch would be an actual mythic enemy from a past lost in the mists of time? And the fecker had been so confident he hadn't even thought to change his name, for feck's sake. Balor of the Evil Eye. Sure, it was one of the myths Anu had mentioned. Or had I read it in a book? The poisoned eye that was so powerful it would strike dead anyone within its sight. And me, the numpty, had even joked about "poison eye", or something along those lines.

The train of recrimination and "should haves" which was long and contained many cars of baggage, kept winding through my mind as the houses passed and became open space and bypass. It continued on through the open rural spaces and little villages along the main route. It was a distraction, all of those "I should haves" cars especially slow, with its passengers even waving as they lumbered through my mind.

It was a thought train that kept on going, even as I stepped down from the bus and began the trudge to Anu's house, with no possession but my flute case and no phone to keep me company. Just that endless train. And the main passenger now on that train was the thought that I had to go back. Go to the Otherworld. Find Goibhniu, because something inside me, something deep and woven so inextricably into all of me was saying, screaming that it wouldn't be all right. That Goibhniu wouldn't be all right.

I CLIMBED the road that led up to the house. I passed Maura's house with its crow filled trees and was thankful that there was no sign of her lurking about. I walked at a fierce clip to minimise the chance she might pop out suddenly and waylay me. There wasn't much she wouldn't see on my face, and at this moment, I didn't want her advice, her comments or her questions.

Once safely past her house, I hurried onward towards Anu, so anxious now to arrive I could hardly fight the urge to run. It was the feeling inside of me, grown so large now it nearly jumped ahead of me, leaping in great bounds.

When I arrived at Anu's I could see some of the cows in the nearest field milling around, but there was no sign of her. A quick nip past the house to see if she was in the milking shed. It seemed about the right time, but again, no sign. I backtracked and made for the door to the house and nearly fell through it when she opened it just as I was about to.

"Bríd," she said.

Her voice held no surprise and her intonation left no doubt that she was done with any pretence about my name. Pity I hadn't her certainty. Pity many things. Pity the state of circumstances that brought me to her door, asking for help. It wasn't pity that had me thinking of Goibhniu, the reason why I was here. That reason had me squaring my shoulders.

"You know why I've come? You know what happened to Goibhniu?"

"Come in, child. Don't stand there on the threshold."

Her words held meaning, they always held meaning, I realised. I just never knew that meaning and felt equally helpless now. But I did feel "threshold" hang heavy and thick in the air as I stepped across or through the doorway to Anu's home. At that moment it was more "across," but in time, it would become more "through" as I slid into the life that was and would be.

THE MUG of tea was a formality, a thought gatherer, a calming pause. Whatever it was, it didn't suit me in the slightest, but Anu made us go through it. Wait for the kettle to boil, wait for the tea to steep. Wait for it to be poured and then handed out and then to sit at the table. A ritual I wasn't in the mood to appreciate, especially in the silence in which it was conducted.

"Oh, Bríd," she said with a gentle smile. "A few moments in this world mean very little when laid aside the momentousness of the subject matter. A subject that must be given all the care and understanding that can be brought to it."

I frowned and gave her a frustrated look. "Sorry, now. But cryptic talk isn't what I'm after. Do you know what happened with Goibhniu?"

Anu sighed. "I know that he went over to the Otherworld."

I leaned closer. "Do you know the circumstances that took him there?"

She cocked them slightly. "No, not directly."

"Well, let me tell you...directly." I took a deep breath, wondering where to start.

"Start at the beginning," Anu said, as if hearing my thoughts.

I narrowed my eyes. "Yes, well. The beginning. Funny that,

isn't it? There are so many beginnings. But this is the one I'll choose. I was in Galway, on the coast. I was with someone, but we had a falling out. He left me at the railway station in Galway and I decided to come here because I somehow wanted to lay some of my issues with you and all that's happened to rest. I was angry at him, but really, I think it had much more to do with you and all that had happened recently. When I arrived at Cork I was caught up in some group protest outside of an office building. Balor's office building."

She raised her brows, a mixture of horror and sorrow on her face. "Balor's? Oh in the name of all that's sacred."

I looked at her after her remark and cleared my throat. "As you say. Balor. That Balor. And he was there, emerging from his building. And just when he did, Goibhniu saw me. I have no idea how he knew I'd be there, but he did. He grabbed me, but I was so startled…" I trailed off, another train of recriminations bundled with "what ifs" trundled through my head. "Balor saw us. We ran. Goibhniu took me through a maze of shops, paths and eventually we came to the riverbank."

"And he summoned the boat," Anu said.

I nodded. "We drifted for a bit. And then he told me." I stopped, suddenly unable to complete the sentence.

"He left you at the bank of the Otherworld and told you to return here."

I nodded again, words still impossible. She leaned across and took my hand away from the mug of undrunk tea and held it. She murmured softly, words of endearments I thought, though they were uttered in a language I didn't recognise, let alone understand.

I breathed deeply. "Why?"

"Why?"

"Why did he have to go on his own? I mean he gave reasons. Balor would expect us to go there and it was safer for him to go and me to come here. But I don't see how I am any safer." I gestured to myself. "I'm not even the me I know anymore. Not really."

Anu stood up, came over to me and pulled me in her arms. "He was right. There is much we can do to protect you here and there is much to do here. We have to prepare, Bríd."

I allowed her embrace for a moment only. A moment to derive comfort and strength. A moment to reach down for the anger I knew was there. The anger would see me through, would draw me across and through that threshold to where I needed to begin.

I pulled away. "Prepare what? Prepare to let Goibhniu get killed? Prepare to let Goibhniu sacrifice himself for me? We have to bring him back. That's what we need to do."

She shook her head. "No. Goibhniu is better where he is."

"You must be joking. He could be at the mercy of Balor or one of his henchmen at any moment. He could be under threat from who knows what over there." I had no idea of the perils of the fairy mounds, the Otherworld, but if the tales held any particle of truth, danger in the most unexpected forms existed there.

"You underestimate Goibhniu. And you forget that he's inhabited that world on and off for centuries. Since the banishment. He has friends and allies there. He'll enlist their help. We need their help, now the time is upon us. We need every advantage here and in the Otherworld."

She was so calm, her voice and words so reasonable, but my instinct shouted against it all.

I shook my head. "I'm sorry, but this time it isn't enough. I know it." I knew it so deeply, so truly and I couldn't find the words, because the words weren't enough to describe the depth of the knowing that I felt.

Her eyes filled with compassion and she tried to embrace me again, but I resisted.

"Bríd, there is so much import in the tasks ahead of us. Tasks that must be completed soon. Now. You are key in these tasks in ways you can't imagine. And you must trust me to know that this is right. This choice for you to come here."

I shook my head, still resistant. "I can't believe that. I won't believe that."

"Oh, Bríd, you have no choice." She kissed my head. "Now, why don't you go have a rest? You must be exhausted."

I looked at her. "I have no things with me. No phone. My backpack and everything else are gone. All I have is what I'm wearing."

"Don't worry about that. I'll find you something until we can get all of that sorted out."

I let her lead me to the stairs and take me up to the bedroom I'd used before. I sat on the bed and waited as she made her way back downstairs. I went to the window and stared out to the yard with its milking shed, the piggery, and the field to the side of it, but my eyes didn't see anything but the images in my head of Goibhniu. Smithy. Anu could try all she wanted to convince me that he would be fine. I had noticed, though, she'd said nothing about Goibhniu returning at any point. But I would make it happen. Because the knowing had become stronger than ever and it reached across the worlds, grabbed me hard and wouldn't let me go. Goibhniu needed me. He was in danger and I was the only one who could help him.

26

SAOIRSE

The morning was filled with well-meaning words and comforting pats from Anu. I just went along, my shoulders sagged and my smile resigned, though I wanted to scream my fury, my desire for action. How could I manage this journey? The knowing was there, but the abilities, the craft, the steps that would get me to his side were so very elusive and complicated.

I was dressed in a pair of dark jeans and top that belonged to Anu's wardrobe, though I could never imagine her wearing them, so different was it from her size and her usual clothes. My Doc Martens suited the look and the mood, dark, dark, dark and I'd felt a grim satisfaction when I pulled them on earlier.

"I'm going for a walk," I said, pulling on my dark jacket. The weather was fine, but I knew there would be a breeze this early in the morning. "Unless you need my help."

"Ah, no you're grand. Go get some fresh air. You'll feel better for it."

I nodded, found a wan smile and put it on. "I don't know how long I'll be."

She nodded. "I'll see if I can get another phone for you, in the meantime."

"That would be good," I said, though I had no interest in a phone. And for now, I didn't care. I had no one I wanted to contact and no interest in social media or any Internet exploration. Unless it told me how to get to the Otherworld. And if it did, that advice would lead nowhere.

I COULD SEE the house from the distance as I walked down the winding road. I walked faster, my destination in sight, until the road dipped below and it was no longer visible, and then I broke into a trot. There was an urgency on me now. I couldn't explain it, I could only feel it. It was as if the house drew me to it like a magnet, even though I knew he wouldn't be there and the tiny kernel of hope that he would be was foolish.

My steps slowed as I neared the house. It looked quiet, silent. No smoke emitting from the chimney, no hammer ringing its beats against the anvil. I opened the gate to the yard and walked across it, noting the closed door to the forge and the other sheds. Once I reached the back door, I tried it, but it was locked. I looked around for a place to hide a spare key, hoping against hope he was of that ilk. I lifted a few rocks nearby, a spare bucket and found nothing. I spied a pair of wellies tucked under a little stone outcrop protected from the elements, held my breath as I reached in and felt around the inside of the right and then the left. It was in the left that I found it. I broke into a grin.

The key turned in the lock with ease and I pushed the door open. The kitchen was cold and I shivered a little when I entered. There were some unwashed ware in the sink, which for some reason brought tears to my eyes. He'd not long been gone, it said to me. An "I'll be back" promise of washing up. I moved through the kitchen to the sitting room beyond and looked around me. The stove was cold, the fire there long burned out beyond embers. I picked up the book that had been placed face down on the table with its pages open. It was a fantasy. I nearly laughed with the absurdity of it.

I moved over to the fiddle, shut up in its case and lying in the corner of the room. Carefully, I opened the case and withdrew the fiddle. I put it up to my chin and moved the bow across its strings. I played a little tune, badly, because I only had only the rudiments of a notion how to play, but it somehow made me feel closer to Smithy. I couldn't help but think of him as Smithy when I tried to conjure him with the fiddle. That was who he was to me when we'd played.

The notes resonated mournfully inside me. It was a keening of sorts, the sort of sound that shows all the aches that are too awful to say. It reached out and connected with me, communed and commiserated. It understood and allowed me space to feel the loss and the pain of what we had been and what I had rejected.

After a little while I put away the fiddle and went into the bedroom. The bed was unmade and full of promises of later, too. There were clothes draped across a chair and at the end of the bed, as if he had changed hurriedly.

I hadn't been here since those few nights we'd shared together. Those special, wonderful nights when I'd become one with him in a way I'd never done with anyone else. I knew that it was special and there was something between us that was strong, a bond that no man or anything else could put asunder, not even death. I just didn't recognise it for what it was because it didn't seem possible. But it had nothing to do with possibility, it just was.

One of pieces of clothing draped on the chair was a black hooded sweatshirt. I picked it up and held it to my nose. I inhaled deeply. I could smell him in the fabric, his scent embedded deeply and difficult to describe. Not a man given to aftershave or cologne, but a scent that was just him. On impulse I removed my jacket and pulled the sweatshirt over my head. It settled down around my body, big and bulky, but it felt good. I placed my hands in the pockets and snuggled into it, trying to draw his scent around me. It gave me comfort, made me feel as though he was here with me. I closed my eyes, drew in my breath and let it fill me up, give me strength.

I grabbed my jacket and made my way to the sitting room and then to the kitchen. Once there, I had a quick glance around to see if I needed anything and decided I didn't. I locked the door and made my way to the forge, used the other key to open it. Once inside I flicked on the light. It came on with a hum and I stood there, blinking in its brightness and surveyed the space.

It was so neat and tidy. So much more so than the house. A place of a man who loved what he did. Despite the number of blades scattered across one of the worktops, it was a place of work, a place of creation and craftsmanship.

I moved over to the worktop holding the blades. I picked up one of them and realised it was the blade we'd created together, polished and finished, all except for a hilt, in the time when we spun, twirled and wove ourselves together. I felt something stir in me as I held the blade in my hand, felt its weight. It was beautiful, almost mesmerising, and so balanced. I don't know how I knew that but I did. The only thing lacking to make it perfect was a hilt. I looked around for something that would suffice, knowing all the while I was so very ignorant of all of this.

In the end I spied a ball of string and began to wind the string around the hilt end of the blade so that each line of string lay next to the other. I kept winding, building up the layers until I ran out of the string and tucked the end inside the layers. It wasn't perfect, but it would do. I slipped the blade with its string hilt into the pocket of the sweatshirt and looked at the other blades on the counter. There were no others that approached a finished state.

I turned my eyes to the various items hung on the wall. I spied a small shield, nearly as small as the targes I'd seen in films of Scots fighting on the battlefield. Next to it was a sheathed dagger, the hilt displaying stylish embellishment, as if it were a prop for a film. I took the two items down from the wall and examined them.

The shield was on the heavy side for me and it seemed bulky when I slipped my arm through the leather straps. I clasped it firmly, spread my feet apart and bent my knees slightly in a defensive stance. I took up the dagger, removed the sheath and pretended to lunge and stab. A moment later I dropped the stance and rolled my eyes, thinking how ridiculous I looked. Was it all just a farcical idea?

I looked at the dagger, still held in my hand and realised there was something different about this one. It didn't feel like the other, the one for which I'd fashioned the string hilt. The one we'd made together. That one felt almost alive, part of me. Ready to do what I bid. It had talked to me, told me things without anything other than a knowing. It gave me a knowing. A knowing of its wants, a knowing of "should dos" and "will dos". This dagger, well it was just dead. It lay heavy in my hand, telling me nothing, imparting nothing.

It was a weapon, though. I couldn't dispute that. I needed it. I replaced the dagger in its sheath and tucked it inside the pocket of my sweatshirt with the other blade. Maybe it would learn a thing or two from the other, I thought with a little laugh.

I picked up the shield and headed for the door. I'd got what I'd come for. Once the forge was locked I headed back to the house. I unlocked the kitchen door once again and headed directly through the kitchen to the sitting room and then on to the bedroom. I could only hope what I needed was there. It took a little searching among the clothes in the wardrobe, but I finally found two belts. One of them I buckled around my hips, using the last hole and placed the two daggers, side by side through the loop of the belt end that I'd tucked up. I pulled the sweatshirt over it, satisfied that the weapons were more or less concealed. I slid the other belt across one shoulder, under the sweatshirt and slung the shield along my back under the sweatshirt. It was awkward and bulky but I had little choice about it.

I caught myself in the mirror, the long plait of hair I'd woven that morning bright in the strong light of afternoon. Impatiently, I stuffed my plait down the back of the sweatshirt and decided I looked like a maimed hunchback with all the bulk back there. It had to be done, though. It kept my hair out of the way and made me less conspicuous. Or perhaps not conspicuous because I really did look like a deformed hunchback, but at least I was less recognisable. I left the bedroom and made my way to the outside door, giving everything only a brief glance as I passed. I inhaled one last time, imprinting his scent in my mind and in my body. I hoped that soon I would replace the memory with the real thing.

27

SAOIRSE

I stood in the yard, glancing around one last time. I was suddenly startled by a large crow that landed almost in front of me. I gaped as I watched it transform into a woman.

"Maura!" I said, her name escaping from me. If I'd had time to collect myself I would have given her true name. Morrigan. I was under no illusions now, and if I had been they would have vanished the moment she shapeshifted in front of me. No more pretence. She wanted me to know. Maura the Rookery, indeed. No wonder Smithy had said her name with such irony. Goibhniu, I corrected myself.

"What brings you here?" I asked.

She studied me carefully, her eyes taking in my clothes and my stance, which had assumed a slightly defensive posture.

"Going somewhere?" she said. She smiled slyly, leaned forward and touched my waist where the daggers were hidden. She arched a brow.

I hardened my gaze. "Perhaps."

"Oh, Bríd, don't be coy with me. I'm here to help you."

I remained silent, my expression settled into distrust. "That's very kind of you, but I don't need your help," I said eventually.

I was fairly certain that any help from Morrigan, the Goddess of War, would lead to nothing good. I was also fairly certain that she'd had a good hand in all things concerning Goibhniu and me coming together. That should have made me glad, for I was happy that the two of us had come together, I had no doubts about that, but anything with Morrigan involved was bound to have unforeseen dubious complications.

She tsked. "Bríd you're armed with weapons I doubt you know how to use, most likely to go to a place you've never been before. You need my help. It's what I do."

"Warfare? I've no intention of going to war. And as I understand it, you enjoy fomenting conflict. That's not what I want."

"Fomenting?" She laughed. "You sound like you're narrating one of those hero cycles of the mythic tales. Morrigan foments conflict among the Fíanna." The last phrase she intoned with a deep voice of an onstage narrator.

I frowned. "I mean the words, whatever you may think of my choice."

Morrigan sighed. "I have no intention of creating any new conflict. We have enough brewing for me to handle."

I remained silent, waiting for her to leave. I could wait, I had no problem with that. I knew, with that knowing, I needed to do this by myself.

Perhaps she sensed my intransigence because she softened her stance and her face took on a pleading expression.

"I want to help," she said quietly. "Because it's important that you stay safe, that Goibhniu returns quickly. The two of you are important to our chances of succeeding against Balor."

"So, you've chosen to support the Tuatha de Danann again?"

I had tried to assemble all the pertinent facts about Morrigan as soon as I'd seen her. Facts? Really? I nearly laughed.

I supposed they were facts, to the extent that it was the only information available about Morrigan. Daghda had persuaded her to choose to side with the Tuatha de Danann in the second Battle of Maigh Tuireadh. Had Daghda persuaded her again this time, or had she never shifted her loyalties since the battle? These were all things I didn't know. I had yet to encounter Daghda and knew nothing really about his current status. Was he back in the Otherworld? My ignorance overpowered me for a moment.

"I am with you. All of you. So, yes, I want to defeat Balor as much as you do. He has no liking for me after the last battle. You must realise that, at least."

I nodded, not so much that I believed her, but because it made sense.

"So, let me help you. At the very least I can show you how to wield the dagger."

"Wield?" I said mockingly. "Are you out of a novel set in medieval times, my lady?"

She widened her eyes in annoyance and gave a momentary flash of anger. "I have lived centuries. You have not. Well, at least in your present form and with the memories you have currently. My speech is my own."

I nodded an apology. That was as far as I was able to go. "Right, fine. You can show me how to use the dagger."

Before I could utter any more words she had whipped the hilted dagger from my waist, the blade drawn from its sheath, and was holding it up against me.

"See how vulnerable you are?" she said. "Anyone could disarm you in a few seconds."

"You've made your point," I said, flatly. "Just get on with it."

She smirked at me. "Just showing you what can happen. It's part of the lesson."

"Okay. Got that point."

She raised the dagger and took my hand. Carefully she showed me how to hold it, how to draw it quickly, how to safely store it. Once I had those actions proficient enough to satisfy her she showed me how to use it, the best manner for defensive use, and then as an aggressor. She moved with lithe grace, her body easily finding the rhythms, her strength more than I expected, even for knowing who she was. I couldn't match her strength or her quick movements, but after at least an hour spent practising, she finally gave me a satisfied nod.

"That will do for now. It might serve to get you to Goibhniu. Then he can keep you safe."

I hoped her words were true. "So you know where I'm going and what I intend to do?"

"Of course. Didn't I say as much?"

I shrugged.

"Do you even know how to get there?"

"I watched Goibhniu. I was there in the boat and then went with him to the banks of the Otherworld."

"But you don't know how to summon the boat."

I shook my head.

She nodded and bit her lip. "Okay. I hope your memory is good. If so, I'd say you'll be able to manage it."

"Thank you," I said sarcastically.

Sarcasm was all I had at this point. My "whys" and "hows" and "what ifs" and all those clauses that crowded my head were nearly making me sick with anxiety and I knew that I must put all that aside. I had to push into the "will do" territory and leave all those others in the dust of doubt and impossibility. I couldn't afford any of that.

She gave me a doting smile that nearly patted me on the head by itself. I flinched a little at the condescension so evident there in her.

"What do I have to do?"

"Okay. Listen carefully."

She began to repeat a string of words. I had no idea to their meaning, their language, or even if they made any sense at all. I listened with all the attention I could muster, using my experience picking up tunes to imprint the sounds, the rhythms and every other clue that would help me to remember the words.

"Is it an incantation?" I asked when she was done.

She laughed lightly. "I suppose. Just think of it as a summoning and direction."

I nodded and left it at that. I didn't want any distractions from my efforts to memorise the summoning. Slowly I started to repeat the phrases she'd intoned, doing my best to replicate her. Finally, when she was satisfied I had it down sufficiently, she nodded.

"Good," she said. "You're as ready as I can manage at the moment." She eyed me up and down. "Take off the hoodie," she said.

"What? No."

"Take it off." Her voice was sharp, permitting no refusal.

"Why? I put it on because it disguises the fact I'm carrying daggers. And a shield."

She laughed. "All it does is make you look ridiculous. And suspicious." She removed her black leather jacket. "Here, wear this, if you must."

"But it doesn't have a hood," I protested. "My hair. I can use the hood on the sweatshirt to cover my hair."

"Do you think you're the only one with that hair colour in the Otherworld?" she laughed again. "Just tuck your plait inside the jacket. That's good enough."

"But the shield. I can't travel to Cork with a shield on my back. Did you think I would put it in a shopping bag?" My anxiety gave an edge to my voice. This direction I was taking was suddenly becoming so real and dangerous, I wanted to remain as inconspicuous as possible.

"Of course not. Why do you need to travel to Cork? It's risky. Too close to Balor. What's so important that you have to go there?"

"To summon the boat from the River Lee in the spot Goibhniu used," I said impatiently. "Why else?"

"There's no need," said Morrigan. "I'll show you a place near here, where it's more secluded."

I frowned at her. "Really? There's more than one place to summon the boat?"

She nodded. "There are several scattered all over the country."

"There's one near here?" I asked. But of course there was. Why else would they cluster here? Goibhniu, Morrigan, Anu. And for all I knew, others. "Where?" I asked.

"Just over the hill. Just outside of the village. We'll go the back way. Through the woods."

"Fine," I said.

I removed the hoodie silently and handed it to her while I took off the shield slung across my back. The daggers hung at an awkward angle in the belt, but at least they were secure. Morrigan eyed the hiltless dagger curiously, then looked up at me. I shrugged. Her eyes widened a moment, but she made no further comment. The shield removed, I put on her jacket and for a moment I was surprised at how well it fitted, but then my body had changed from the slender figure of months ago. The jacket felt safe, thick and quilted, almost like padded leather armour from medieval times. It was long enough, ending at my hips and just covering the points of the daggers.

Morrigan came over to me, made a few adjustments to the belt so that the daggers hung low to my left side, below the jacket.

"There," she said. "You can reach them with more ease."

I nodded, uncomfortable with her meaning, but acknowledged the wisdom of it. I took up the shield and belted it across my shoulders again. I was ready.

We set off, Morrigan tying the hoodie around her waist and leading the way, up along the small track and then heading into the woods. They were mostly silent, the only noise a few birds twittering and singing, and the sound of our feet treading along the ground. I fell into a kind of reverie, reviewing the words she'd had me repeat, and eventually they led my steps, created a rhythm that I fell into as if it was drawing me to where I was meant to be.

And when we emerged from the woods, crossed a field, and then another we came to the river bank. The Sullane. The only male river in the whole of Ireland, or so I'd been told. Would he take me to where I needed to go? To the right time? I could only trust that he would.

"I leave you here," said Morrigan.

"You're not going to wait until I summon the boat?"

She shook her head. "It's best if you do it alone. It will be sure to come, then. Sure to take you to the right place."

I gave her a puzzled look, but who was I to doubt her? She turned and retraced her steps and I watched her retreat. She didn't look back, she'd made no parting comment. No words of encouragement. I wasn't certain if that was a good or bad thing. I suppressed my momentary feeling of abandonment and turned back to the river. I had been prepared to do this without any help, so I shouldn't mind her need to leave.

I looked at the river, flowing calmly and slowly at this point of the summer. So innocent and sweet. I took a deep breath and spoke the words in an even voice, hoping that would be sufficient. I'd barely heard Goibhniu when he'd spoken back at the Lee, I rationalised. I waited, not sure what to expect or when. Or from which direction. Would it suddenly appear, or come drifting down from upriver? I closed my eyes and then opened them. Nothing. A moment later though, the boat was there. The same one. I blinked, surprised, though I'd been expecting it. I got in, lay down and stared up at the sky, hoping it would take me to the right place. Not the little fairy mound, or the big fairy mound, but the medium sized one.

PART III

SÍ BHEAG SÍ MHOR

28

SMITHY

He could feel them. They weren't far behind, he guessed. Even if he kept up his gruelling pace he knew they'd catch up to him within the next quarter of an hour. They were on horseback. Fomorians. He knew it was them. He could hear it in the hoofbeats. The anger, the determination. The need to kill him. There were a few Tuatha de Danann with them as well. Of that much he was sure, if only by way of managing to get the Fomorians here now. He wasn't certain who and how many, but certainly more than one. But he wouldn't know, because he didn't plan on being captured. He needed to leave this track, though.

He would have to take to the forest, something he'd been reluctant to do, because he knew of the hidden dangers there. He weighed those dangers against his imminent capture and headed towards the trees. If he kept to the edge, just far enough in that the riders wouldn't see him, he would probably escape them.

The dark canopy of trees closed in on him sooner than he expected. He felt the small pocket knife in his pocket, his only defence against whatever might decide to throw themselves against him. Laughable, really, since it had no ounce of magic to it. He would have to rely on his wits for the most part.

He slowed to a jog and allowed his breathing to calm. Despite the danger, he felt alive, filled with purpose. His body hummed and he knew the tune. It was their tune. His and Bríd's and all the love they'd felt oh so long ago. It was awake, alive and coursing through him now, wrapping him in its own kind of protection and love. He would do this for her, no matter the outcome, but the power of their tune would help him to keep her safe.

A slow smile spread over him, his mouth just a hint of what was going on inside his whole body. His breath was even and steady. Through the forest, and back onto the track. In a little while that would wind him slowly to Daghda's place. A day or so and he should be there. Daghda would need to know where things stood.

He kept on, the slow jog becoming a regular rhythm, his body remembering how to be fighting fit. He'd kept up his sword practice but not as often as a warrior would, and his regular jogs around the back roads weren't quite the same as the training he'd undergone in times past, but he wasn't bad, he conceded. A light rustling made him tune into the forest more intensely. Whispering began and grew louder. He glanced over his shoulder, but could see nothing.

He turned around and a small man stepped in front of him, dark eyes filled with menace, a long spear held in his hand. A moment later five other men of the same size, same black hair and eyes joined him, all armed with the same type of sharp spear. Smith stopped, nearly tripping over his feet to avoid running into them. The Hunters. They were offshoots from the Fir Bolg, gone to ground in the forest during the wars after the majority of them had fled to the islands. They avoided the Tuatha de Danann as a matter of course but they took offence at anyone who invaded their territory. They'd taken on a legendary quality under the guise of The Wild Hunt, but he'd only known them as The Hunters. Whatever name they had, they were dangerous and they rarely discriminated in who or what they hunted in their forest, taking great pleasure in the kill at the hunt's end. An end that was never doubted or contradicted.

He bowed low, hoping a measure of respect might give him some leeway with them.

"My lords of the hunt," he said. "I beg your leave."

They narrowed their eyes, almost in unison. "Who are you and why do you beg our leave?" said the first man who'd appeared.

"I must ask your pardon for that," he said. "Goibhniu is my name, and I meant no offence. I intend to leave the forest in a short time. As soon as my pursuers have passed."

"Goibhniu?" said the first man. "The smith."

"Yes, my lord," said Smithy.

"Who are your pursuers?"

Smithy thought quickly and made a decision. "The Fomorians and some traitorous Tuatha de Danann."

"It doesn't surprise us that some of your people are traitorous," said the first man, as Smithy now thought of him.

Smithy shrugged. "It's the way of things."

"And why are the Fomorians pursuing you?"

Smithy took a deep breath, weighing up how much to reveal. He sighed. "Balor. He wants me dead, because another war is brewing and he knows I have great power in swordcraft.

"Yes, we've heard that. And with other weapons as well." The last statement was made in a thoughtful tone.

Smithy nodded. "I forge many things in metal."

"And they have power, these things you forge?"

"At times. In certain circumstances."

Smith felt a growing unease, knowing where this was heading, but it might be his only choice to avoid death or something darker. The history between the Fir Bolg and the Tuatha de Danann was not amicable. Though distantly related by merit of their shared descendancy from Nemed, the Fir Bolg had arrived in this land now called Ireland before the Tuatha De Danann, and had only been forced to leave after they were defeated in battle and their king dead. The Fir Bolg had little reason to like his people, and by extension, him. His only hope lay in the fact that that his people had not pursued the Fir Bolg, but had let them leave and remain in peace on the islands and in the forest. The Fomorians, on the other hand, hadn't been so kind in their years of rule, oppressing both his people and the Fir Bolg.

"And you ask our leave to travel in our forest so that you may avoid capture?"

"If you please, my lord." He knew he'd lathered on the courtesies heavier than lard, but it was all he had in his arsenal.

The first man turned to the others and they exchanged words in low tones. Smithy studied their expressions, hoping to discover their plans and feelings about his intrusion. The first man pursed his mouth and nodded and faced Smithy once again. He crossed his arms against his chest. Smithy's heart sank. Whatever the verdict, he was certain not to like it.

"We have decided we will grant you leave to travel in our forest for a short time. On one condition."

"What is the condition?" He steeled himself for the answer. Waiting for the axe to fall in a more metaphorical sense than what he'd expected when he first entered the forest.

"That you make us a magic spear," said the first man. There was whispering behind him. He frowned and sighed, nodding. "Six magic spears."

The groan was in him and it wound around inside him, squirming to get out. Jaysus feck. He'd expected maybe a knife, but spears? Six of them, even. He had barely managed a blade back with Bríd. It had felt good, though, and only the beginning of what they could do. That thought rose up, but he still couldn't be certain it was true, nor could he be certain of the future. Still, he must strike a bargain. And a hard one at that.

"One spear. And a guarantee that you will join us against the Fomorians."

The first man's face darkened. Behind him, the whispering started up again. He turned to them and the whispers became heated. Finally the first man turned back and stared at him, clearly unhappy.

"We will join your people against the Fomorians, but only if you give us four spears."

Smithy crossed his arms, forcing a neutral expression on his face in order to hide his dismay. He grabbed on to that tune, their tune. Tried to anchor himself to it, look for that pledge, that hope he knew it could promise.

"Three spears," he said, and hoped that he'd heard the tune right.

The first man thought a moment and then nodded. "Done."

"Done." The bargain was struck. No person would dare break a bargain made in this manner. And he knew he was bound to it. But facing its implications would have to wait until later.

DESPITE HAVING SECURED permission to travel the forest, Smithy still felt unease. He knew they still watched him, in ways that only they could do, with the trees communicating his presence through root and branch. At least that's what he'd been told, and now he had little reason to doubt it. They weren't termed "The Wild Hunt" for a mere whim. Though a bargain had been struck, they were a canny bunch and just as the so-called "little people" were renowned for finding ways around any bargain that kept to the letter of it, it was The Hunters who were the real cunning ones.

He knew he would find his side of the bargain uncomfortable at best, but more than likely dangerous. He also knew that if anyone, such as Anu or Daghda, found out, their anger would be uncontainable. He didn't need to be told that if he made those spears, he could very well find them used against him and his people—and who knows where else or on what else they would find to put them to use. Spears, *his spears,* in their hands was unthinkable. He knew all that. And he knew that he must find a way to employ their own methods to approaching a bargain and work around it.

He found himself emerging from the forest. The track he'd been following which he thought paralleled the road at a safe distance seemed to curve outward now. Gradual enough that he hadn't realised it. He looked around, puzzled why it had. There seemed no reason for it. He stood there a moment, on the forest's edge and tried to read his unease. He looked at the trees, soughing lightly, but there was no breeze. He looked down at the track which had ended so suddenly. The trees rustled and shifted. Conversing. He had no doubt about it. They were conversing. And he also had no doubt that he was the main topic of that conversation.

He turned to plunge back into the forest, but the track that had led him to this point held roots that tripped him up and he found himself sprawling on the ground, hitting it hard. He remained still, the wind knocked out of him, and tried to think.

Hooves thundered in the distance. Smithy tried to scramble to his feet, but the roots just tangled him more. Half on his knees, he twisted to look to the road, though he really didn't need to do that to know exactly who was thundering towards him.

The horses drew to a halt. A few men dismounted and headed towards him, grabbed his arms and hauled him up. The roots released him, suddenly retreating back to their origins. Smithy cursed The Hunters and their love of tricks and twists. Didn't they realise that their actions harmed their chances of securing their spears?

He shook his head against their behaviour, against the traps and trouble that ensnared anyone who came to the Otherworld unprepared, lacking knowledge and vigilance, canniness and all the other qualities necessary to survive here. And he was the biggest fool, because he'd known all that was required and had still made basic mistakes.

All these thoughts flagellated him as the men dragged him back to the mounted men. He looked up and scanned their faces. Balor hadn't deigned to come across, but then again, he hadn't expected him to. Smithy only hoped that he was so taken up in his concerns back in Cork and elsewhere that he wouldn't think to search the city and the county. That there would be enough time for Bríd to go to Anu and her protection before these men informed Balor that Bríd wasn't with him.

One of the men bound his hands and ankles before dumping him unceremoniously across a horse. The move nearly knocked the breath out of him once again and he coughed. Someone swatted his head hard with the hilt of a sword. The blow rang in his ears and he cursed.

"Just be glad it wasn't one of your magic swords," said one of the men. "Keep your mouth shut and do as you're told."

A few moments later the horse moved forward, slowly gathering into a canter. It was all Smithy could do to remain on the horse and keep himself from hurling the contents of his stomach. They continued on and Smithy increasingly felt like he was being beaten from the inside out. He considered his options and on impulse, he followed one that at the time seemed attractive.

With the last of his strength he reared up and threw himself off the horse and onto the track.

He hit the ground with a brutal thud. The horses ground to a halt, but not before one of them managed to stomp on his left arm. Pain roared up and blinded him, so that any thought of quickly untying his ankles became impossible.

Someone kicked him, hard in his side. He groaned. Another kick, a little further down. Pain filled his thoughts, roared its sound and was all he saw.

29

SAOIRSE

I climbed out of the boat and scrambled up the bank. No grace involved, only anxiety laced with a hefty dose of fear. I tried to hum one of my tunes, a jaunty one called *Lucy Farr* and laughed. "Saoirse Far", more like. Saoirse very, very far. I looked down at myself, at the almost unfamiliar shape that I seemed to have. Tall, yes. But definitely different. Less clumsy. Even as I'd scrambled up the banks and now, as I stood here wondering where to go next, my gait, my carriage felt different. It wasn't just the leather jacket that stretched across my shoulders and chest in a manner that was bracing and yet showed curves I never knew I had, it was the different sense of being that I felt.

"Bríd Far" echoed in my head. I sighed. "Saoirse/Bríd Far". I was still Saoirse in my thoughts, my music, my memories, no matter what my body said.

With that settled, I looked around again, searching for some indication of the best direction. Behind me, I heard a whisper. I turned and saw that the boat was gone. Had the whisper been a warning, or a goodbye? Whatever it was, there was no turning back. No return to the other bank and a different world. Not just yet, anyway.

I headed inland, skirting the forest that loomed thick and heavy to my right and the path that led into it. I had no inclination to enter. Besides the fact that it was dark and I wouldn't have a very good sense of where I was heading, it made me uneasy. Nothing good came from a forest in any fairy tales I knew.

There was no real path or track along the grass, though it had been well trodden, and that gave me some hope. Up ahead, I saw a gradual rise in the land which was comprised mainly of open grassland with some shrubs. In the distance were some sheep as well, and I took comfort from that normal, familiar sight. The sun shone warm in an azure sky above me, something that seemed so displaced from Ireland. Another world, there was no doubt, I thought wryly.

I broke into a trot, feeling the urgency of the open land and no sign of any human. Were they humans, I mused. Was I human? That thought made me uncomfortable. Best not to question these things. Not at present. I felt less than magical and more than a little vulnerable, even with two daggers in my belt and a shield strapped to my back. I had no plan, just an urgency and deep-seated feeling that I had to find Smithy...Goibhniu... soon. That I still didn't know what to call him seemed part of my lack of plan. But I knew how I felt.

I kept trotting along, trying to steady my breath and keep my pace even. I was amazed at my fitness, my ability to keep up the pace I'd set. I was no marathon runner, no fitness fanatic who spent hours in the gym. Walking was my gym, I'd been too awkward for anything else. But now, it was as though I'd spent years training.

The trot followed a rhythm that reminded me of tunes I didn't know I had. Not a jig, slip jig, reel, or polka. Especially not a waltz. Not even a slide, but maybe something in between them all. The in between step kept going, in this in between moment, interlude, and I could only hope for a destination that was more than in between.

I reached a small rise and began the descent when I noticed a small farm tucked away at the side. I brightened at the thought of a farm, which seemed a safer, less threatening prospect than, say, an encampment of soldiers. Or a castle filled with them. Still, it would pay to be cautious.

I slowed my trot and headed toward the farm. I could see some cows in the yard and what might be pigs as well. The whole farm looked to be in good repair and that reassured me too. I drew up in front of it, allowing a hopefulness to rise inside me. A man was in the yard standing by one of the cows. I put my hand up in what I hoped was a friendly manner and waved.

"Hello," I said in my best "just paying a call" manner. "How are you?"

The man looked up, his face puzzled and wary. He was tall and wiry and wore a knit cap, a stained brown leather jacket, dark wool trousers and leather boots. His hair was fair and hung scraggly from his cap and his eyes, lined from hours of squinting, were light in colour.

There was no wave returned. He spoke, but the words were in a different language. The language I'd memorised for the boat summons, but still had no meaning attached. Feckingfeckingfeckit. It never occurred to me that I wouldn't be able to communicate with anyone over here.

I gave a weak smile and assumed the friendliest body language I could manage. Arms akimbo, loose limbed, loopy smile, seemed to be the one that found me.

"You wouldn't speak English, by any chance, would you?"

The man shook his head. A shake that meant he had no idea what I'd said. "Gaeilge?" he said.

Feckingfeckingfeckit. It was my own fault for not really applying herself to my Irish. If I had, now it would have been useful. But who'd have thought? Would you even feckin' believe it? The best I could manage would be to sing him a song. Somehow, I didn't think the words of *An Binsin Luachra* could accurately convey my questions and needs. A maid out looking for rushes meeting a young lad hardly contained anything useful.

I shook my head sadly. "*Níl.*"

He nodded and his expression eased somewhat, which seemed a positive. He looked behind him, towards the house and called out a name. It sounded a bit like Finn, but I couldn't be sure. A moment later a young lad burst out of the house and approached the man. They exchanged a few words and then the young lad went haring off up the road. The man turned to me and gestured towards the house, then beckoned me towards him. He went to the door, turned around and beckoned me again.

I made the decision before I even thought about it. What choice had I? Stumble around for a while longer, looking for someone else who didn't speak English? Maybe some clever gestures and drawing would get me somewhere, and it seemed a possibility that I might be able to do that in the house, with this man.

Inside, the house opened up into a large kitchen with a sizeable working hearth, deal table and benches. Shelves against one wall were lined with sacks, earthen pots and dishware. Bright light filtered in from the window at the back. A woman sat at the table, a white kerchief covering her head, dressed in a wool gown of dark green underneath a wrapped sleeveless apron of white cloth. She gave the man, presumably her husband, a quizzical look and then turned her gaze to me. Her expression was cool, considered. She spoke to the man, her words sharp. He answered her and shrugged. She sighed and rose, gesturing me to take a seat on the bench.

I moved, still in my loopy goofy version of friendly, and sat on the bench. I began to nod, why, I didn't know, I seemed not to be in control. This was no "in between" rhythm and anything approaching my "whynot" or "whynotnow" mode that was so easy and part of me. This feeling, this rhythm in my body was the experimental mode that only some godawful modernist would understand or appreciate and I certainly wasn't one of them.

So I sat, my face arranged in a most ridiculous expression, a shield strapped to my back for all the world to see, including this farmer and presumed wife, and two concealed daggers at my waist. My hair was still tucked in my jacket, though my chest I hoped indicated I was definitely not a man. Such a threat as I might pose was surely defused by my womanly curves and absurd demeanour.

It seemed that it had, because she eventually placed a cup of something warm in front of me, along with a plate filled with what appeared to be slices of meat and some bread on it. I nodded my thanks and placed my hands together in Namaste pose, knowing as I did so how I was adding another silly to the already bursting tally of silliness I'd offered these people.

The food looked really appealing and I heard my stomach grumble in agreement. I hesitated, wondering if I should eat it, as all the tales of visits to fairyland shouted warnings. They all seemed to agree on the perils of eating in the Otherworld. Bound there forever, or was it return a thousand years later? I didn't know. But did I really count as human travelling to Fairyland with a large capital? This was the Otherworld, the Sí medium-sized rather than little or big. This wasn't *Tam Lin* or even the Tir na N'Og story.

My stomach made the decision for me and I picked up a fork, noticing for the first time that it was a proper fork, made with some kind of metal. And the plate was earthenware, the type found in any kind of rural idyll dabbler's kitchen. I don't know what I'd been expecting, but apparently not this. It somehow gave me an encouragingly more positive outlook and I began to eat.

The food was plain, but no less tasty for it. I reached for my cup and was pleasantly surprised to find a kind of warm mead. It was lovely and it was all I could do not to make a pig of myself, downing the cup in a matter of moments. I left it half full and returned to my food. The mead made me pleasantly relaxed very quickly and I looked up at my hosts and smiled.

"Very good," I said, pointing to the food. "It's grand. Thank you very much. *Go raibh mile maith agat,* I added in Irish. I could at least manage "thanks a million". "*Tá se an-mhaith,*" I said feeling braver and pleased that "very good" in Irish had suddenly come to mind. I wasn't so pathetic that those phrases from school hadn't stuck in my mind.

The couple beamed at my words and I beamed under their pleasure, feeling I'd made some progress in allaying their unease and caution.

The door opened and the lad came tearing in, words tumbling out of his mouth. The farmer nodded and frowned. He glanced at me, said a few words to his wife and left, closing the door firmly behind him. She gave me a nervous glance before busying herself around the kitchen, taking down plates and cups and putting together another plate of food. Her son looked at me and then his mother quizzically, before finding a place at the table facing the door and watching it expectantly.

I wasn't allowed much time to speculate on his expectant look, the wife's actions, or the farmer's exit. A few moments later the door opened and a man came bursting through. He was tall and broad, with a dark hair and beard and appeared to be in his mid-thirties. A scar ran across his brow which was pulled down into a frown. He came to stand in front of me by the table in an imposing manner.

All of this would have sent me from unease to alarm on its own, but when coupled with the padded and studded leather jacket and heavy boots that seemed straight out of some medieval battle re-enactment, as well as the dagger at one side and the sword at the other, it was all too much. I sat there, eyes wide, stunned. Any soft and fluffy connotations about fairyland were off the cards. They had definitely marched out of the room and left me there, stupidly ignorant and clueless.

"*Dhia's Mhuire dhuit*?" I said the common greeting impulsively and then cursed inwardly at saying something so stupid as "God and Mary be with you." What was wrong with me, for feck's sake? It appeared all my sense had deserted me.

"Ah...." I searched the Irish for excuse me, but came up blank. "*Conas a tá tú*?" It was all I could manage, all my memory could dredge up, asking how he was. Feeble, feeble, feeble.

He narrowed his eyes and then fired off some rapid Irish at me. I shrugged my shoulders and shook my head. His face darkened again. He jerked on the shield strung across my back. Spoke again, this time both in Irish and the other language. I shook my head and tried to look apologetic. He dragged me to my feet, pulled me away from the table, knocking over the bench I'd been sitting on. He stared down in my face, anger clear in his eyes. He spoke, slowly, loudly, still gripping my arm vice-like.

"I don't know, I don't know," I said, knowing my fear was evident.

He gripped my other arm, shook me hard and spoke again. I looked at him, willing myself to understand, an exercise that only caused more deficits in my mind. My gaze drifted down from his face and a little kernel of my self-defence class came back to me. Do I aim for the groin, bring my knee up to him with a hard thud? I gauged the distance and the possibility of its success. But he must have read my intentions on my face because suddenly he had me turned around, my arms gripped behind me and my legs spread apart. In the quickness of his movement he caught the edge of one of my daggers and it went flying to the floor.

He shouted at me, the pitch of his voice making my head ring. He uttered a few words to the farmer, who moved to the dagger and picked it up. He placed it on the table and began to pat down my legs and then unzipped my jacket. The other dagger, the hiltless one, rested in my belt clearly for all to see. Behind me, the man snarled, snatched it out of my belt and threw it on the table.

He barked some words to the farmer and after a moment's hesitation left the room and came back with some rope that he handed to the man, who used it to tie my hands behind my back, after which he dragged me out of the house and over to a stone shed. He opened the door and tossed me inside, shutting it securely behind him. I heard a latch slide into place. I couldn't see a latch on this side, or any other way to open the door, but then again, I couldn't see much, because there were no windows and it was pitch black. I could, however, smell quite a lot and most especially the heavy, heavy stench of pig shit. And I could hear rustling, soft at first, and then a bit more insistent. I tried to assure myself that rustling sounds were better than snorting, better than snuffling. Rustling could mean mice. Mice I could handle. Rats, not so much. But they seemed more mouse-like, surely. Just a few mice to wait out until someone saw sense and released me.

30

SMITHY

S mithy groaned when he tried to sit up. His side was bruised and he wouldn't be surprised if there wasn't some internal damage. Broken ribs at the very least. His arm throbbed, too, no doubt broken where the horse had stomped on it. The pain came in waves, though they had eased somewhat now, compared to when he'd first been thrown in this cell.

He opened his eyes again and looked around in the dim light to apprise himself of the cell from his vantage point. Though he was on his back for the most part, he could still feel the straw underneath him, scratching the bare skin of his palm. Above him was a wooden ceiling and around him stone walls. There was a small window high up on the wall opposite the door. Too small to warrant bars. At a guess, he'd say he was in a tower keep. One of those built to defend all comers, back in the time when the Tuatha de Danann were uncertain about their safety in their new lands, where any minute a Gael, Fir Bolg or Fomorian would see fit to attack. Things were more peaceful now, but these towers were still inhabited, though usually made much more comfortable in the living quarters. Except apparently, in this tower.

Smithy blinked, trying to gauge the time of day through the window. It seemed to be sometime in the afternoon, judging by the light pouring in and if he'd correctly guessed the window's direction. But he could be wrong about that and he had no idea what afternoon it was. The afternoon of his capture or later? Judging by the state of his stomach and his throat, it might be the next day or the day after that.

He tried once again to ease himself upright to a sitting position. The pain seared through him, but this time he managed it, supporting his injured side with his right hand. He paused and tried to catch his breath. He gathered his energy again and this time aimed to stand. He staggered with the effort, nearly falling to the stone floor, but finally found his balance and stayed unmoving while the pain in his side and the sudden roaring agony in his arm eased.

Once he'd recovered, he slowly moved to the door, feet dragging along the straw. When he reached the door he raised his right hand into a fist and pounded on it.

"Guard!" he shouted.

He pounded again, the effort sending more waves of pain through his side. He could feel the sweat gathering at his brow. His breath came in pants. He leaned against the door, waiting for the pain to subside, waiting for a guard. He closed his eyes.

He didn't know how long it was, but eventually he heard the sound of someone outside the door and a lock turning. He backed away from the door, catching his breath at the sudden jab of pain at his side from the movement.

The door opened and a large beefy man with a grizzled beard and braided hair frowned at him. Another, slighter man with fair hair and a ruined face stood behind him.

"What's all the shouting about?" said the large man.

A Fomorian. Smithy just knew. It was evident by the flattened nose, but also the biker jacket with the big fat F stitched on the left side. One of Balor's tough lads. Probably from America, where he posed it up in some sort of biker gang. Smithy refrained from rolling his eyes. Anu had said Balor travelled with a coterie of security men of every ilk, ready for every kind of situation. So that was who he'd sent here to get him. But why were they holding him? Why not kill him outright? Smithy's unease grew. Did Balor think he could convince him to work for him? To create magic swords, or whatever he had in mind? Smithy frowned.

"Don't you frown at me, boy," said the Fomorian.

Oh for feck's sake, thought Smithy. Did he think he was in some backwoods town in the American south? Or some TV show?

The Fomorian shoved him and Smithy groaned with pain. "I said, what's all the shouting about?"

"Water," Smithy said with a gasp. "Could I have some water? And a bit of food." He tried to keep his voice pleasant.

The Fomorian grunted and swung the door shut. Smithy stared at the closed door and listened as the steps retreated. He sagged against the door and sighed. He glanced around the cell and noticed there was a pot in the corner, presumably to relieve himself. In another darker corner was a small cot. That surprised him. But then again, the possibility of Balor wanting him for something rose up once more.

He hobbled over to the cot and eased himself down on it, wincing. He needed to find a way to bind his chest and to create a sling. There were no sheets on the cot, but he wouldn't have expected that. And he knew he would never be able to create anything out of his T-shirt. Not for a while anyway. He reached inside his jacket with his right hand and felt his left arm, carefully. No bone protruding, which was good. There was definite swelling, though, and he could only imagine what it looked like. Hopefully a clean break. He prodded lightly and gasped. Closer investigation would have to wait.

Footsteps sounded outside the cell and the lock turned once again. The door swung open and the man with the ruined face stepped in. He wore the cloth tunic, leather trews and boots of the Otherworld and his greasy fair hair was tied back. A Tuatha de Danann traitor? Smithy wasn't certain, but he bore all the marks and guilt of it. He approached Smithy, his head down, a scowl on his face, bearing a tray with a platter, jug and cup on it.

The Fomorian appeared at the door, his arms crossed along his chest, a menacing look on his face. Smithy turned his attention back to the man with the ruined face and nodded to him.

"Thanks," said Smithy.

The man scowled harder and put the tray on the floor. He reached inside his tunic and pulled out a lump of cloth and tossed it on the cot. "Bandages. For your arm. And your side."

Smithy nodded and gave him a quizzical look. "A bit of mercy from a traitor?" he said softly.

The man's face darkened. "Watch it, or I'll stick Dog on you."

Smithy's glance flicked to the Fomorian. "Dog?"

The man scowled again and shrugged.

Smithy shook his head and looked once again at the Fomorian named "Dog", and barked. He couldn't help it. Sure, it was too much for anyone, and he was probably punchy from lack of food and the shock of recent events.

Dog strode forward and hit him across the cheek. Smithy shook his head with the force of the blow and tasted blood.

"Any more of that and I'll take that food and you won't get no more," said Dog.

He looked at Dog, his expression now neutral. Dog grunted and, with a last dark look, went to the door, the man with the ruined face close behind. A moment later the door clanged shut and the lock was turned.

Smithy sighed, rubbing his jaw. He knew he'd been stupid to bark even before the sound had left his mouth, but somehow it had just tumbled out. But in the end, it had been worth it, if only for the pure craic of it all and the day that was in it.

SMITHY OPENED HIS EYES. The light from the window told him it was early morning and the day was fine. At least for now. He could hear birdsong in the distance and the sound of cows. Milking time?

He'd noted these various details in the past few days since Dog and his minion had come to his cell. Now the minion brought him food at regular intervals, with Dog standing guard at the door. No words were exchanged beyond a grunt or two, but Smithy could sense the waiting and watching from Dog. A sense of expectation.

But today was different. He didn't need to have the presence of the two henchmen to know that the expectation had heightened and there was something imminent about it. Today, he thought. Balor would arrive today. He wasn't certain how he knew this, but there was no doubt.

Smithy rose from the cot, his arm still feeling the effort and his ribs aching too. He put his hand to his arm. It felt hot to the touch. He frowned and, with effort, slid the makeshift sling from around his neck and attempted to remove his jacket. He panted with the exertion and beads of sweat formed at his brow. He tried to keep his concern at bay and steeled himself to make the effort once again. This time he succeeded, but it left him nearly exhausted. He paused a moment to catch his breath, then lifted his T-shirt to reveal his abdomen and chest, a substantial bandage wrapped around it.

He tugged at the bandage's end where he'd securely tucked it. It came away and he began to unwind it with awkward motions, using his good hand. When it was finally removed he examined it carefully. Livid bruises of violent blue, red and a hint of green were stamped on his left side, where they'd kicked him. The bruises looked worse than before, but that was to be expected. He pressed at them tenderly with the fingers of his right hand and hissed at the pain. A bit improved, though, on the searing sharp pain that had assailed him when he'd first sustained the injury.

He reapplied the binding, an even more awkward under-taking that took him several tries before it remained in place, all the while conscious of the throbbing in his arm. When he finished, he closed his eyes to gather strength and prepare himself for the next examination. A few moments later he lifted the sleeve of his left arm and looked. It was as he'd feared. The arm was still red and swollen and it had taken on a very angry look. He walked over to the window and peered at it closer. A small, faint red streak traced its way from the swelling. Shit. He knew it was serious. In fact he'd suspected that it was developing into a very bad infection and now it was spreading. He shoved away the further implications of blood poisoning and the dire results of that if it was left untreated. Smithy took a deep breath. He couldn't put it off any longer. He had to do something. The state of his arm and Balor's imminent arrival were red flag warnings that couldn't be ignored.

He went back to the cot and sat down, trying to think, to assemble some kind of plan. He was weak, injured and unarmed. He'd allowed himself as long as he could to regain some of his strength, but the tipping balance had been reached, and it would be downhill from here. He wondered how long before he became feverish. Not long, he thought.

Footsteps and shuffling sounded outside the door. Then the tell-tale turn of the lock. It was later than he'd thought. Time for his meal. His stomach grumbled in response. Bread and cheese and a cup of ale once a day was hardly going to keep hunger at bay, but it was better than nothing, he knew.

The traitor minion entered as usual, bearing the tray with its predictable fare. He made his way over to the cot, his eyes cast down, avoiding Smithy's gaze. Smithy had decided not to bait the man but still, it rankled that one of his own people was working for Balor. The minion put the tray at the end of the cot, keeping his distance.

"My arm," Smithy said. "It's bad."

The minion looked up at his words, glanced over at him and away.

"My arm needs attention. There's infection in it now, I'm sure of it."

The minion stood there looking down at the tray, his body language screaming uncertainty.

"Look," said Smithy, his gaze directed toward Dog, "I need a healer. Now. It's very bad. If you don't get me a healer I could very well lose the arm or even die."

Dog frowned at him sceptically. Smithy sighed. Big, but not much wit. What was it that Cornish man said to him one time, "In with the bread and out with the cake?" That was Dog. Half baked.

He tried again. "If your master wants my services, which I presume is the reason I'm being held here, then I'll need the full use of both my arms." He'd said the words carefully, slowly.

Dog grunted, his eyes narrowing.

"Sure, if you don't believe me, come have a look for yourself, over by the light."

Smithy got up and went back to the window and waited. Dog hovered uncertainly by the door until he frowned again and stomped towards Smithy. When he reached Smithy's side, Smithy turned his shoulder towards Dog, and under the guise of showing his bad shoulder, he used the motion to bring his right arm back and swing at Dog. He hit him square in the jaw and Dog moved backwards with a grunt. Smithy shoved him hard, towards the cot where the minion was cowering in a huddled position. Dog tumbled against the minion and they both fell on the cot. Smithy ran for the door, still left open by half-baked Dog and hared it over the threshold and towards the stairs. Behind him he could hear a roar of anger.

The stone steps were slippery and he fought to keep his balance. His side was screaming now with a pain that matched the one that took hold in his arm. He clambered down, trying to take the steps two at a time, where possible. He turned at the switchback and saw the light of an opening up ahead. He shoved on, conscious of the footsteps closing in. When he reached the entrance, he paused a moment to get his bearings, searching for the door that would lead him outside. The room was empty, save for a table, chairs and two cots placed against a far wall. A few sacks slumped along the floor in another corner. He saw that he was too high up and realised there must be another set of steps to take him down to the ground level. He spied the steps and headed towards them. They were steeper than the other set. He started down, the film of slime that covered them slowing his progress. He reached the end and saw the outside door and halted.

A large length of wood was along its middle to bar anyone entering. He made his way to it and using the last of his strength, tried to slide it back with one great shove, but it only moved a fraction. He tried again and it was nearly free of the brace on the door frame. He gathered his breath for one more shove and a large hand pulled him away. He turned to see Dog, his face contorted with anger and his fist drawn back. Smithy roared in his face. It was instinctive and it stunned Dog for a few seconds, just long enough for Smithy to reach for the dagger at Dog's side. He withdrew it, brandishing it in front of Dog, who roared back, rushed Smithy, grabbing the wrist that held the knife. They wrestled for control for only a short while before Smithy's hold gave way and Dog had the knife. Dog shoved Smithy and he lost his balance, falling to the floor, and as he fell, his feet caught Dog's and Dog tumbled on top of him. Smithy felt a sharp severe pain to his bad side. He opened his mouth to scream his pain as the force of Dog's body falling on him drove the dagger deeper into Smithy's side.

31

SAOIRSE

I began to slow my pacing. It had seemed the best strategy since being shut up in this dark shed. I'd sung songs, hummed tunes, danced a few steps of long forgotten set dancing, all in a bid to keep whatever scuttling present in this shed at bay. Now, I was tiring a bit. I'd no idea how long it had been, but judging by the number of songs, tunes and dance steps it had been at least a few hours.

I dragged myself around the room a few more times, before sinking dispiritedly to the shed floor. Outside, I could hear the lowing of some cows and perhaps the bleat of a sheep. I ran through the few ideas budding in my head on how to get out of the shed. The brief moments of hard hammering had gone nowhere. Perhaps when, and I was very hopeful about this "when", they came to feed me, I might be able to make them see reason. The laughter that came with this plan now could hardly control itself. Pointed fingers and clutched bellies full kind of laughter. Hardly a plan. No plan at all.

I sighed, drew myself up once again and headed to the door. Once there, I felt around the edge, trying to slide my fingers between the door and the frame. If I could find a way to lift the latch on the outside I could get myself free. I had tried the metal end of my belt before, after the hammering, but that had been too thick to manage it.

Now my eyes were fully adjusted to the dim lighting of the shed. Too much so, I thought wryly as I spied shifting and moving little hillocks of straw in the nearest corner. My boots are thick, I told myself. In that corner, leaning against the wall was a long piece of thin metal rod, presumably used to prod the pigs.

I went over and picked it up, tested its weight, and brought it back over to the door. I poked the edge of the door to see if I could find a place to fit it in and use the rod as a lever. I tried first in the middle, but I had no luck. I moved it further down and tried again. I kept trying, moving the rod just a little on the edge of the door and finally, about two thirds down, I managed to squeeze the rod between the frame and the door. I took a breath and swung back on the rod with all the strength I could manage. There was a real resistance. I pushed harder against it and suddenly it gave way. I flew back onto the shed floor with the force that had been released. Breathless, I sat there for a moment, staring at the open door and the awaiting freedom outside. I grinned.

Rising slowly, I dusted myself off and headed into the light. The sudden burst of brightness caused me to hold my hand up against it all while my eyes adjusted. I blinked a few times and then looked around. I could see the farmhouse not far away and the track that had led me here. I moved from the shed, through the small muck filled yard, hoping to skirt the farmhouse and get back on the track. I knew I'd be forfeiting my daggers and shield, but there was no help for it, as the chance of retrieving them safely was nil.

I moved stealthily, hoping my movements wouldn't attract any attention. I heard voices. Shouting. The door of the farmhouse burst open and a man came striding in my direction, the farmer, running close behind. I froze.

The man stopped, looked at me. "Br— Saoirse!"

I peered at the man. Wiry ginger hair, high cheekbones. A memory stirred. Inchigeela, the guitar player. "Finn?"

A wide smile broke out on his face. He closed the distance between us and wrapped me up in a hug. I stood there, too stunned to react. He pulled away.

"Thank God you're safe," he said.

"God?" I said. "Really?" It just spilled out, the irony with all the attending confused emotions and disbelief.

He shrugged. "Figure of speech."

I lifted my chin and gave him an ironic look. "What brings you here, Finn? Or whoever you are." I squinted at him. "Don't tell me. Fionn Mac Cumhail."

He laughed and shook his head. "Not likely."

"Why not likely?" I said and then held up my hand immediately after. "Never mind. I don't want to know."

"Ogma," he said. "But we'll leave it at Finn. That's for the best. For here and especially across the water."

I sifted Ogma through my mind, but came up with nothing. No half learned lesson of Celtic tales or anything else that might clue me in to why he preferred Finn. But this wasn't the time or the place and there were more important matters at hand.

"Goibhniu," I said. "We have to get him. Balor chased him here and he's in danger, I'm sure of it."

He glanced across at the farmer. "Smithy?" he said, his eyes telling me more. "We'll have to see if we can find him."

He turned to the farmer and spoke. The farmer listened carefully, nodded and headed towards the farmhouse.

"What language was that?" I asked.

He turned his gaze to me. "The language of the Tuatha de Danann. The True Tongue."

I nodded. "I couldn't make them understand that I meant no harm. They don't speak English."

"No, not many of us do. That's one reason few cross over. The other is, well, it's forbidden for the most part. Though no Gael would probably know that anymore."

I smiled. "And I bet they wouldn't care. Not really."

He gave me a serious look. "Maybe not now. But over the centuries it has been dangerous. Religious people often saw us as a threat. That's why many more have the language of the Gaels, but so few have English. Many more slipped through and travelled there before Christianity became dominant and even more when English was the primary language. It's been left to us who have been charged as sentinels across the water to learn and maintain our English and know the customs there."

"Sentinels?" I asked. "Is Smithy one?"

He nodded. "A reluctant one, but nevertheless he was charged with it a long time ago, well, a long time in your world." He pulled himself up. "Well, not exactly your world, though, really."

I gave him a speculative look. "So you know?"

He looked me up and down. "It's difficult not to know. There's no mistaking who you are, now."

I looked at the farmhouse with puzzlement. "But they didn't know me. Not even that soldier."

He followed my gaze. "No, well. They weren't at Tara. At the court. I was."

"Ah, right." It all made sense and yet all of it didn't make any sense. Not one bit of sense in all that I'd understood all the years of my life in Dublin.

"How do you know Smithy is here? And that Balor has him?" asked Finn

I took a deep breath and focused once more on the important issue. "He is. I saw him get out of the boat and enter this world." And I told him all that had transpired in Cork and since I'd returned to Anu's. As I relayed the tale, his face grew more and more troubled.

"We have to let Daghda know," he said finally.

I gave him a puzzled frown. "How will that help?"

"He can help. And it's important he knows how serious things have become across the water."

"How will he be able to help, though?"

"He'll be able to find out where Smithy's being held and verify who's holding him. And he'll send men. Warriors."

"But that could take a while, surely. Unless you can transform into something?" The last question I'd asked in a hopeful tone. Because that was the best answer. I knew in my bones we needed to go now. That Smithy needed help, now.

Finn laughed. "No, I have no ability to do that. My strengths are elsewhere. But I can get a message to him quickly."

"Quickly, as in as quick as a text? You have mobiles over here?" The look on his face gave me the answer. "No, well, I didn't really think so."

"It will be quick, I promise. We should find out where Smithy's being held by this evening. Tomorrow at the latest."

I nodded. I had no choice but to hope that it would be the case.

THE MORNING DAWNED grey and overcast. I'd hardly slept. The feather tick, though not the worst on offer, hadn't helped as it was laid on a plank bed that left me in no doubt of the increased size of my hips and other parts of my body. My mind was equally unable to rest and I spent most of the night staring at the wooden ceiling and listening to the snores of the others in their small rooms above the kitchen.

It had been a curious reunion in the kitchen when I'd entered with Finn. The farmer and his wife both gave me their apologies, speaking through Finn. To Finn, their deference bordered on obsequiousness, and it wasn't long before I realised they regarded him as their chief, overlord or something along those lines. I vaguely knew the structure of ancient Irish society, but what would be ancient to me was probably not even conceptualised in their structure. He was wearing the clothes I'd seen him in when we were in the pub, but with a sword hung awkwardly at his side, and his movements told me that it wasn't something he felt accustomed to.

There was no sign of the soldier. Warrior. He was gone and when I asked Finn about him, he only said that he'd told him to go, that he wasn't needed. It was only after a bit of prodding that he told me the man was a steward of sorts. His steward. There was more to the story, but I failed to muster the energy to ask for it.

After the apologies were made, the farmer brought some paper, ink and pen to the table at Finn's request. Finn took a seat and composed a message. The script was a series of characters and slashes that seemed indecipherable. When he'd finished, he went outside. From the window I could see a small bird (wren?) flying down towards him to land on his arm. He placed the rolled-up paper in its beak, though it seemed overlarge and too heavy, and the bird took off. No shapeshifting, but quick enough, I thought.

There was no reply by the time we'd gone to bed that night and now, in the light of the next day, I found myself praying that there would be one soon. I had no clue who I was praying to. All my ideas, what I'd rejected, what I'd accepted, had been turned upside down and I knew only the shape and form of the religion I'd been raised in and that prayer was part of it. I rose from my bed and tiptoed quietly down the stairs and outside. The door creaked when I opened it, I paused, listened for stirring above, but there was nothing.

The light was breaking over the horizon and the grey day grew a little brighter. I was surprised when I saw the farmer, whose name I now knew was Diarmuid, emerging from the shed. I shouldn't have found it unexpected, because it was evident he'd just done the milking. But then Finn trailed out after him and my astonishment became even greater. I just couldn't make Finn out. I couldn't reconcile the stellar musician I'd seen in Inchigeela with the overlord/chieftain persona he assumed here. The clothes, now a mishmash of trendy jeans and practical boots no doubt from the hands of an Otherworld craftsman and the sword that had been at his side yesterday, only served to confuse me.

Spotting me, he raised his hand in greeting and began to head towards me. He was nearly by my side when a bird flew towards him, something in its beak. He looked up and held out his arm. This bird, which I could see now was a large rook, landed gracefully. Finn removed the scrolled paper from its beak and released the bird back into the sky. The rook took flight with a loud caw and then vanished from sight a moment later.

I watched as Finn unfurled the scrolled paper and read it. It was all I could do to contain my impatience. Finally he looked up and frowned.

"What is it?" I said drawing up to his side. "Is there news about Smithy?"

"Yes. Daghda has found out where he's being held." He felt silent a moment, deep in thought.

"Where? When can we go there?"

He turned, looked at me. "A place just north of here."

"Not far then?"

He shook his head. "A half day's ride, if that."

"Then let's leave now. We can be there before noon."

"No, Saoirse. We wait for Daghda."

"But surely we can meet him there. He'll be coming from Tara, right? Wouldn't Tara be north of that place, if you say it's not far? Are the distances different? The place names?" I floundered a bit. The geography was potentially another handicap I hadn't contemplated.

"Yes, Tara is the Tara you know in terms of direction and distance."

"So, we can do that. It would be what, meeting them about halfway? Where is he—somewhere in Tip? Or its equivalent here?"

He gave a small laugh. "Close enough, but never mind. Yes, I suppose we could meet them there. It would save time."

I smiled, relieved I'd been able to convince him. "Good. Then let's get ourselves ready and underway."

He looked down at me and sighed. "We'll have a bite to eat and then go. I'll let Daghda know of our plans."

32

SAOIRSE

We ate quickly. The farmer's wife had already risen and was in the kitchen by the time we'd returned after reading the message, the farmer ensconced at the table, his son beside him, so that it took her no time to serve us a quick meal too. Once fed, I looked to gather my things, realising that I still hadn't recovered my daggers and shield. I asked Finn about it and he spoke with the farmer, who looked abashed, rose and went upstairs. A few moments later he returned, the daggers and shield in his hands. He handed them over to Finn. They exchanged a few words before Finn examined them carefully and then looked over at me.

"He said that he took them upstairs after Riangabur took them from you. They looked to be valuable since Riangabur seemed to eye them with longing."

"Isn't your man trustworthy?" I asked.

"To the extent that he covets his position."

"But didn't he send for you?"

Finn shook his head. "It was Díarmuid. He sent the lad after he roused Riangabur. He knew where you'd come from and thought it best that I be informed."

I nodded and then held out my hands for the daggers and shield.

He hesitated. "I can understand why Riangabur wanted them." He held up the one without the proper hilt. "Especially this one."

I eyed him curiously. "Why?"

"They are all Smithy's work. Without a doubt. But that one in particular," he indicated the hiltless one, "that's different. He made it, well, he was involved in making it, because I can sense him there, but there's more to it. It's contains the most power I've ever felt in any weapon. Including any of Smithy's old work, from before."

I looked at him completely puzzled. "We made it together. Well, he helped me create it. Across the water. I didn't really know what I was doing, but it was..." My words dropped off. I didn't know how to describe how it had been between us and all that I'd felt during the dagger's making.

Finn looked at me in wonder. "It's as they always said. The two of you. The power. The magic."

I looked at the dagger. "Magic?"

He held up the other dagger. "This dagger and the shield. They're made recently. It's craftmanship of the highest order. A blade honed perfectly. The best weapon possible, across the water. The weapons Smithy made here, before. For battles. They had a power. Magic. Anyone who wielded that weapon would not suffer death." He held up the hiltless dagger. "This dagger, or rather blade with its improvised hilt, is even more powerful. I can sense it. And if it's as you say, that the two of you made it together, then..." he looked down at the dagger, "it's probable its user won't even suffer any injuries, and anyone stabbed by this blade will die instantly."

We stood there in silence while I digested his words. I reached for the dagger and held it, trying to feel all that he'd said it contained. I did like the weight of it in my hands. It seemed to feel more at home there than the other one. I had been able to wield it easier during Maura's lessons. I inhaled and clasped it tighter. A small hum vibrated up my arm. It startled me so much I nearly dropped it. The humming spread through me. It felt good. Right. I looked up at Finn, my eyes wide.

"You feel it?" he asked.

I nodded. Carefully I placed in the belt where it had been before. I could still feel the humming, though it was muted now.

"Look after it," he said. "That's powerful and unique. Others will want to have it, if they find out."

"We'll have to make sure they won't," I said. "Do you think Riangabur knew about it?"

Finn shrugged. "Possibly. It's hard to tell."

"All the more reason to get to Smithy as quickly as possible."

"Agreed," said Finn.

I took the other dagger and the shield and slipped them into their respective places.

THE STONE WALLS loomed above me as I crouched in the nearby shrubs. "Loomed" was the only word for the dark and forbidding edifice standing Bronte-like with glowering clouds surrounding it. No tune could compensate for its presence. No tune at all. And the songs had long since fled my head, taken flight with the jigs and reels and the jaunty dancing. It was the time for battle cries to stir the blood, but my blood remained unstirred and only anxious, worrying and filled with dread.

"He's in there," I said. "I can feel it."

Finn nodded. "It shouldn't be long before Daghda and his men are here."

I pursed my lips, biting back the words that came to me. La

di da, la di da, I said in my mind. But it was no real tune and any "la" and "di" and "da" that tried to masquerade as a tune were stiff and unconvincing, and would be thrown out with disgust any moment. But they persisted, obeying the commands I'd forced out there.

I shuffled, switched positions and squinted at the tower. I hadn't noticed any movement since our arrival an hour or so ago. I presumed it was an hour. The only clock I had was the sun overhead. Any internal one I might have possessed had been wound backwards, sideways and smashed. And a "La di da" to that. Finn had patiently explained the general layout of the towers scattered across the land, certain that this one conformed to the old original patterns established, since he could see no evidence of modification. I'd argued for immediate confrontation, but he vetoed that idea. "Foolhardy," he'd said. "A watchful eye is what's needed." At this point I was all for "foolhardy" and wanted to give "watchful eye" the back end of a shovel.

The door to the tower opened at that moment and my body went on high alert. Finn put a hand on my arm, a calming measure that did little to help my tension. A man stepped out, holding two buckets. He was thin with scraggly hair. He trudged wearily away from the door towards us, liquid sloshing from the buckets. The pungent smell of urine wafted in our direction.

Finn pulled me down further behind the shrubs. I could hear the man shuffling closer. He stopped not far from us, set one of the buckets down and threw the contents of the one remaining in his hand at our shrubs. He set it down and picked up the other bucket, emptying its contents in the same direction.

I wrinkled my nose. Fortunately the shrub was thick and little of the urine had penetrated the area where we were positioned. Still, I rose to a squat, reluctant to test the shrub's filtering. The man, his task complete, turned around and headed back to the tower. I looked at Finn, fire and meaning in my eyes.

He shook his head and mouthed "wait" to me. The fire was in my belly now, angry and stirred that he would miss such an opportunity. I rose quickly and raced after the scraggly-haired man, shoved my body into his limbs and brought him down with a thud. The buckets fell with a clatter on either side of him. I took one up and caught him on the side of the head with it, hard. He went still.

I scrambled up off him and headed towards the open door. I could hear Finn at my heels and increased my speed, unwilling to have him interfere. A "why didn't I use my dagger" mantra cycled through my head as I rushed through the tower door, my eyes blinking at the dim light and encountered a small flagged area and a set of stone steps. I climbed them carefully, trying not to make a sound. The steps were slippery and I nearly fell a few times, but eventually I reached the top. The door leading to a room stood ajar.

The fire was still there, inside me, but stilled at the sight of the large man sitting at the table, his back to me. He was studying the cards in front of him which were spread out in a game of Solitaire. A large collection of jittery nerves joined that fiery belly of mine. I withdrew my dagger, took a deep breath and ran towards the man, who could have easily found a place among any biker gang. I stabbed him in his side, all Maura's training forgotten in the panic of the moment.

The biker roared and rose up, turning towards me. I backed away and he came after me as if he'd had nothing more than a pinch to his side. I held up the dagger and reached for the other one at my belt and began waving the both of them in his direction. He approached me warily, circling, roaring his anger. I felt one of the daggers begin to hum and the hum vibrated through my body, spinning, swirling, linking with the fire, unravelling the nerves. I circled with the biker, my eyes suddenly focused, my body filled with its own movement, a pattern ancient and unforgotten.

A flicker of fear appeared in the biker's eyes, but then it was gone and the rage was back. He moved forward, shouting his war cry and I feinted and went for his left side, directing the blade with accuracy. The biker roared again, held his hand towards his side and fell. I looked at the dagger, still embedded in his side, its hilt already showing blood. The other dagger remained in my hand, its temporary hilt now stained with my sweat.

Behind me, the door clattered open and Finn came rushing in.

"Saoirse!" He stopped, spotted the biker lying on the floor and made his way quickly to my side. "Are you hurt?" he said, looking me over.

I shook my head. "I'm fine."

He frowned at me. "You were lucky. You could have easily been killed."

"Maybe, but it was an opportunity." I shrugged off his look and glanced around the room eager to get on with the search. "Smithy must be upstairs somewhere."

I nodded over to the only other door in the room and headed towards it. It opened easily and revealed another set of stone steps leading upwards. I started up them quickly, my sense of urgency increasing, the other dagger still in my hand. All the worry and anxiety that I'd tried to keep at bay for days began to overtake me. When I reached the landing and saw the door with its lock, I knew he must be on the other side.

"Smithy!" I called through the wood. There was no answer. "Goibhniu!" I shouted louder. Tears began to form in my eyes, created and fuelled by the worry and anxiety.

I turned to Finn who was coming up behind me. "The key. We need the key to unlock the door."

Finn nodded, turned around and went back down the steps. I waited impatiently, pounding on the door and calling Smithy's name. The tears were coursing down my face now, certain that I wasn't going to like what I found on the other side of the door. Finn returned a short while later, key in hand. He moved me aside and put the key into the lock. It turned easily and I released a breath I didn't know I'd been holding.

We entered the room, Finn leading. I quickly moved in front, scanned the room and saw a figure lying on the cot. I rushed to it and knelt beside it. In the dim light I could make out Smithy's face, pale and sweating. I put my hand to his face. It was burning up.

"Smithy," I wailed.

His eyelids fluttered for a moment and then went still. I glanced down his body, taking in the bloodstained T-shirt and the swollen arm. Carefully, I lifted the T-shirt and sucked in my breath. A series of mottled bruises surrounded a deep gash at his side weeping blood. I looked up at Finn, now standing behind me and he shook his head, a grim expression on his face.

I lifted the sleeve of his T-shirt where his arm was swollen. Violent red streaks ran the length of his upper arm. I knew only that the streaks were a very bad sign.

"Broken arm," said Finn in a low voice. "Gone septic, I think. We need to get him out of here and to a healer as quickly as possible."

I nodded, too choked to speak. Together, we managed to lift Smithy off the cot, supporting him on either side, and make our way to the door. The fact that such movement didn't rouse Smithy at all had me even more worried, but I could do nothing about it except try to get him to a doctor before it was too late.

Slowly and awkwardly, we dragged Smithy down the steps, pausing occasionally during our slow progress. Finally, we reached the bottom and went through the door into the open room where the large man lay bound on the floor. He hadn't yet stirred. A small pool of blood was beside him, but his chest was rising and falling, so I knew he wasn't dead. At least not yet.

We headed across the room to the next set of steps. The door was still ajar as we left it, but I could hear noises below. Daghda and his men? I hoped so.

A moment later a figure appeared, large and bearded. For a brief second I thought it was Daghda, until I saw the eye patch. I halted in my tracks. Beside me Finn tensed. He looked at me, his eyes conveying a message as he slipped the key into my hand.

"Go," he mouthed.

I shook my head slightly. I wasn't going to leave Smithy. Not again. Finn glared at me, his meaning clear. I shook my head slowly. I would face whatever there was to come at Smithy's side. Finn made a noise of frustration and dropped his hold on Smithy, who fell against me and I staggered under his weight, until he slipped to the floor.

Balor gave a shout and began to stride across the room towards us, but Finn grabbed my hand and made for the steps going back up the room above, dragging me behind him. I tried to resist, but his hold was firm and I stumbled after him. At the top he handed me the key, shoved me in the room.

"Lock yourself in," he hissed. "I'll try and fend them off until Daghda and his men arrive. Balor mustn't get hold of you as well as Smithy. It's too dangerous."

He turned and left, pulling the door behind him. I stood there, stunned for a moment, until his words provoked action and I locked the door.

33

SAOIRSE

The sounds of clashing below became louder. I paced the room once again, unable to stop. The need to act, the need to help the fight below was so urgent I could hardly contain myself. There was no music in me now, only desperation, despair for Smithy and frustration that all fed an anger, a rage whose only music was battle.

That the clashing continued gave me some hope. If Finn was down, they would be mounting the steps, trying to break down the door, but that hadn't happened yet. I went to the window again, even though I knew I wouldn't see anything of use. I could hear some faint shouts, but that was all.

I paced again and began to pray to that unknown. I added a request to Anu to look over Smithy, to make this come right. I had no idea if she would hear, if she could or would act, it was just what came to my mind.

A loud thud sounded at the door. I turned and stared at it, wide eyed. The thud came again and then a muffled voice. I made my way closer.

"Finn?" I said tentatively.

"Open up," shouted an unfamiliar accented voice.

I backed away. "Who are you?" I shouted back.

"Daghda."

I breathed a sigh of relief, then hesitated. "How do I know?"

A noise of exasperation came from the other side of the door. I heard a shout. A moment later, another voice shouted my name through the door. Finn. I raced to turn the key in the lock and threw open the door. Finn stood there, a broad chested fair haired older man behind him. He had piercing blue eyes and a strong nose. They both held a sword loosely in their hands. I hugged Finn briefly and he gave me an awkward smile in return.

Daghda stepped in front of Finn and grabbed me in a fierce embrace, murmuring words I didn't understand. I pulled back awkwardly and looked at Finn.

"How's Smithy? Has Balor been taken? Is everything okay, then?"

The questions flew from me, my eyes going back and forth between the two men.

"Smithy is still alive," said Finn. "We need to get him to a healer quickly, though."

"And Balor? Is he alive?" I hoped that he was dead, killed in as painful manner as possible.

Daghda shook his head. "No, he escaped with a few of his men."

I frowned, disappointment filling me. "Bastard," I said.

"We'll get him, don't worry," said Finn. "It's only a matter of time."

"Yes, but it would have been so much better if we could have done it now," I said.

"Well, that's for later," said Daghda. "We must get Smithy to a healer. Now."

He looked at Finn. "Airmid?"

"Diancecht is back at Tara still, then?"

Daghda nodded. "He is being punished for his actions against his son."

Finn narrowed his eyes and glanced at me. "I see."

I watched the two of them, puzzled. "Will this Airmid be able to help Smithy? Won't he be better with a proper doctor? Back in the real world?"

Daghda gave me a flat look. "What is real? You think this world isn't real?" He shook his head. "Come, we've no time to lose arguing."

Finn whispered in my ear. "Listen to him. Show respect. He knows better than you think."

I said nothing and followed them down the steps. At the bottom, I saw men sprawled across the floor. Some bleeding, others unmoving. To the side, against a wall, I finally spotted Smithy. I ran to him and knelt by his side. He looked paler than before. His breathing was barely discernible. I looked up at Finn and bit my lip.

He shrugged. "We'll do the best we can for him."

"But will we even make it in time to this Airmid?"

Finn looked over at Daghda.

"We'll have her come here. Let her know, Finn" said Daghda. "I'll send the boat."

Finn nodded and left.

I knelt beside Smithy, raised my hand and brushed the damp hair from his face. The skin there was clammy. Should I hold a wet cloth there? It didn't seem the best idea but I wanted to do something. Anything that might help to prolong his life until help arrived.

I HELD the cloth against Smithy's wound, willing the bleeding to stop completely. It had eased to a slow trickle and I took heart from that and used it against the growing greyness in his face, the ragged breathing and the blue tinge to his lips.

I leaned down and whispered in his ear, hoping that would rouse him, give him the will to fight, to stay alive. "Goibhniu. It's me, Bríd. I've come to take you home."

There was no response, no stirring, not even a flicker of an eyelid. I stroked his forehead. It felt even clammier than before. I leaned down and kissed it and then pressed my lips against his, willing my energy into him. A small puff of air escaped his mouth and I lifted my head, searching his face for confirmation that he'd heard me and that breath of air was his response, but there was nothing. And as I stared I saw that nothing was bigger than any nothing I could imagine. There was no rise of his chest. Nothing. No trace of a pulse. Nothing. Not a breath from his mouth, his nose. Nothing. Nothing. Not a thing.

A small wail rose. It was another 'not a thing', it was a power. A power filled grief, stifled for a moment when Airmid came in. She entered like the breeze that I supposed carried her on the river to this place, graceful but determined. She was only a little older than I was, with grey eyes and dark hair. I could see she was taller than me as she strode towards us, her bag held in one long, slender hand, her other hand raised in greeting.

She shifted her gaze to me. It faltered a moment and then it brightened. "Bríd," she said softly. "So good to see you. I understood you walked among us again."

I had no patience for pleasantries. "Do something," I wailed. "You have to help him."

Airmid glanced past me at the figure that lay beside me and I saw the disappointment and sorrow on her face a moment later. She looked at me, eyes filled with compassion. "There's nothing that can be done now. Nothing I can do."

"No," I said, shaking my head. "No. It can't be true. There must be something."

Finn came to my side and tried to pull me up. "I know it's difficult, Saoirse. We all loved Smithy. It seems impossible to let him go."

I resisted his efforts. "No. We can't let him go. I won't let him go. There has to be something we can do. Anu didn't bring me back for nothing. For this."

"She didn't plan for this," said Finn. "It was something that happened."

I sniffed and wiped the back of my hand across my nose. I rose and took a deep breath, glaring at Daghda. "If it's as Anu says, then she brought me back. With your help. With the help of many of you." I glanced at Finn and Airmid. "So if I could be brought back, after years of being dead and buried," I said, my voice hard. "Then you can bring Smithy back. Goibhniu. You need him." I held up the hiltless dagger, now safely replaced in my belt. "Don't you agree, Finn? You've held this dagger. You know what we can do, the both of us. Smithy and me. Together. If you've any chance against Balor you know you need us. Both of us."

Daghda looked at Finn. He gave a nod.

"Let me see the dagger," said Daghda.

I strode across the room and placed the dagger in his hand. He clasped it, felt its weight, waved it in a circle and then looked at me, his eyes gleaming.

"I can't deny its power," he said.

"No," I said. "It's the only weapon we have so far. But there could be more."

Daghda frowned.

I looked at Airmid. "Who was responsible for bringing me back? Was it you?"

"No," said Airmid, softly. "Diancecht."

"Then take me to him." I cast my mind back, trying to remember the details of Anu's explanation of what had happened with me. "Slane," I said. "The Well of Slane. They bathed me in its waters." I looked at Daghda. "Where's the well?"

"It's blocked," said Daghda. "We blocked it up again after Diancecht dipped you in the well."

"We'll have to unblock it, then," I said. I looked at them all, their expressions filled with scepticism and something else. Fear. I looked at each one. "What is it?"

Finn looked at Daghda and then spoke. "It's an uncertain, the well. It may not succeed. And the outcome, well, it might not be all that you hoped."

"What do you mean?" I demanded tersely. "Surely it's better than being dead."

Finn sighed. "He may not be all that he was. Half alive. His memory, his strength, his power could be gone."

I took a deep breath. "Well, I'll take that chance. I can't accept the other alternative."

Daghda heaved a weary sigh. "Very well. We'll leave in the morning."

"No," I said. "We'll leave now."

"Shall I let Diancecht know to meet us there?" asked Finn, looking at Daghda.

"No," he said. He glanced at Airmid. "Fetch him yourself. I would rather not allow him the freedom to move around unaccompanied. And he'll understand better that just because we're asking his help, his punishment still stands."

Finn turned and gave some orders to the other warriors in the room. They left, I presumed to prepare for our journey. Airmid came over to me and we knelt beside Smithy.

"Here," she said. "I'll help you get him ready for the journey.

"Thank you," I said.

We worked in silence for a little while, binding the wound at

Smithy's side and crossing his arms over his chest out of the way of the men who lifted him onto a makeshift litter.

"Why is Diancecht being punished? What did he do to his son?"

"He killed him," said Airmid flatly.

I recoiled slightly in horror. "Killed him, but why?"

Airmid frowned. "Jealousy."

"Jealousy? What was he jealous of?"

"His power. My brother was the most powerful man of medicine. He knew every herb and every treatment. Diancecht couldn't live with that."

I stared at her, digesting her words. "He was your brother? Diancecht is your father?"

"Yes," she said, her eyes awash with tears and a mixture of emotion. "Much to my shame, Diancecht is my father."

I exhaled slowly, the connections nearly too much for me. This man, this healer, Diancecht, wasn't all powerful as I'd thought. He was a man full of pettiness who could murder his own son. Was he the right person to give Smithy over to? I wasn't certain at this point I could have faith in him to ensure Smithy came out of this whole and alive. I placed my face in my hands and sighed. What choice did I have?

34

SAOIRSE

Daghda sat silently up front, his eyes on the horizon. Directly behind him lay Smithy, grey and still, a blanket wrapped tightly around him. A sharp breeze created by the speed at which we travelled caught a lock of Smithy's hair. It was enough to fool anyone who might glance at him for the first time to think he might be only be very ill, rather than beyond help.

But he wasn't beyond help, I assured myself. It was an assurance I'd repeated the whole of the journey to the well. I pulled my jacket tighter and buttoned it up further. I was more than grateful for Maura's jacket and that she had the foresight to give it to me. I was grateful to her for more than that and I could only hope that I would be able to return the jacket and favours with it.

"Is it much longer now?" I asked.

I'd refrained from asking this question for a good while, conscious that it sounded like the whiny cliché it was. But at this point I was beyond caring. My care of how it sounded had vanished several kilometres back. Now my patience had jumped ship as well.

Daghda looked back at me. "Not long. We should see the fort at Slane shortly."

The fort. It was a landmark at least. I looked anxiously ahead. We'd travelled by boat for the most part, I'd realised, because the waterways would allow the speed the horses couldn't. But even when we were mounted, with Smithy's body slung across Daghda's saddle, the horses suddenly appearing out of nowhere, the horses seemed to possess a speed and stamina I didn't think was normal. I was no horsewoman. But somehow I was able to ride with grace and agility, as if the skill had been stored in my body, somehow.

But the boat had appeared when we reached the next river that would take us closer to our destination. The current seemed to favour us, even when it shouldn't. I had stopped trying to question all of it, to forget any application of the rules and probabilities of the world I was used to and just accept it. But it wasn't always easy. And that difficulty fed my own doubts about any success with Smithy. And the doubts about the truth of my own existence. I would have to just hope, trust and believe, like any good Wendy clapping for Tinkerbell.

"There it is," said Daghda. "Slane Fort."

I followed his gaze and could see a curved stone wall up ahead. Slane Fort, I presumed.

"Slane Fort," I murmured. "Slane. As in Slane Castle?" I don't know why I hadn't linked it before, but since I hadn't ever been to one of the famous concerts or even visited the area around Slane Castle, I hadn't put it together before now.

"Yes. That's what's there, in the time across the water."

"But here, in this world, Slane Fort is on that rise. And the well is there, too?"

Daghda nodded. "It's in both worlds. And blocked in both worlds."

"So, we're in County Meath? Doesn't that mean Tara isn't far away?"

Daghda turned and levelled a glance at me. "Yes, why?"

I smiled. "That means Diancecht wouldn't have that far to travel."

Daghda nodded. "He should be there when we arrive."

I sat back, pleased, even though I knew that Daghda still had grave reservations about this whole undertaking.

We approached the bank near the fort and I could see figures standing there, waiting for us. Finn and a thin, bony man with a craggy face and long, white hair. His dark, piercing eyes glittered at Daghda. Diancecht, I presumed.

Finn pulled the boat in with the rope that Daghda tossed him, and secured it to a ring embedded in the bank. I stepped out of the boat with Finn's help and watched as, between them, Daghda and Finn lifted Smithy to the riverbank.

Diancecht knelt down beside Smithy and began to examine him, lifting the bandage on his arm and the one at his side to see the extent of the wounds. All the while Smithy lay there, pale and grey. The skin had begun to sink into the body and the limbs were stiffer than they had been when Smithy was placed in the boat.

I looked at Diancecht and his face held nothing but annoyance.

"How long dead?" he said in English, looking at Daghda.

Daghda shrugged. "A few hours, maybe a little more."

Diancecht nodded and pursed his lips. He spoke to Daghda in their own language and I watched, frustrated. Daghda's tone was matter of fact. Diancecht raised his brows and then looked at me. I gave him as firm and stubborn a look as I could muster. He gazed down at Smithy, seeming to weigh the possible options.

Finally, he stood. "There's a large risk with what you

propose, given that it's been such a long time. And the state of him. Some of those wounds had been festering for days."

Daghda looked over at me, his expression telling me that he had concluded the same thing before we even started this journey.

"I want to try," I said in a loud voice. But I wanted to make it a statement, not a debate. "We'll do this." I looked up at the fort. "Where's the well? By the fort?"

Diancecht frowned and then looked at Daghda, who shrugged again and nodded. Diancecht sighed.

"If you're set on this course, we should go quickly. It's nearly dusk and we want to have the task complete by dusk. It's the best time to recover his soul, to sing it back to his body."

I paused a moment, his words startling me. Singing? There was music involved with bringing someone back to life? To call his soul back? It was a concept that was surprising and at the same time it seemed right. Especially to someone like Smithy. The Smithy part of Goibhniu who was filled with music that could enchant the soul.

"Come, child," said Diancecht, sharply. "There's little time to lose."

I moved towards Smithy and helped them carry him towards the stone, using the blankets as a makeshift litter once again. We trudged to the fort and around it, towards the back, to a sheltered place. We headed for a clump of trees and the small clearing within it. Diancecht signalled for us to put Smithy on the ground. It was then that I could hear the faint sound of water and I spotted a small pool, half-filled with rocks. Across from the pool a pile of rocks was stacked in a haphazard manner. The pool itself was more of a spring, though it looked to be the height of my waist and not very wide.

"I started clearing the well before you arrived," said Finn. "I think there's enough in order to submerge Smithy."

"Perhaps a few more," said Daghda. "What do you think, Diancecht?"

Diancecht nodded. He looked across at me and frowned. "This is your last opportunity to change your mind. The man you know might not be the man that returns. You must be prepared for that."

I straightened. I'd made up my mind. There was no turning back. There was no other choice. "I understand. We still go ahead."

I watched as Finn and Daghda cleared more rocks from the pool, Finn submerged to his hips thrusting the rocks towards Daghda, who took them and placed them on the grass. After a little while Daghda called a halt. Already the light by the pool was growing dim and I could see to my left that the sun's rays had just disappeared from the fort.

Diancecht issued his orders quickly, in their language and Finn, now out of the pool, helped Daghda lift Smithy into the water. Diancecht slid into the pool, robe hitched up around his waist to expose his bony legs, and aided Smithy's body into the water. Finn came back down beside him to hold Smithy and on impulse, I decided to join him there, splashing them all in my haste.

Diancecht gave me a dark look but I faced him down, my own glare matching his. "I am going to be here whether you like it or not." Somehow, I knew I needed to be part of this process to help Smithy's soul return. That with my presence, my touch, he would find the true path back. That I would get the true Smithy back.

"I'm his *anam cara*," I said.

The words didn't feel trite or "New Age" on my lips. It was truth. I was his soul friend and he mine. I would help his soul come back, rather than ensure its journey from his body to its home at death.

Diancecht gave me a resigned look and then turned once again to Smithy. He raised his hands palms outward and began to chant. The chanting echoed around us and continued for a while. My body began to hum in response. I could feel the whirl and twirl of a tune. A rolling, lilting sound of a flute and fiddle. I began to sing it. Sing it as notes that were stretched and full like waves on a long and a calming shore. A lullaby of notes, a waltz of notes that echoed again and again. I'd closed my eyes without realising it, the whole experience was just unfolding and unfolding without an effort.

I had no thought to time or place, it just happened and continued and filled me until it stopped. It was then I opened my eyes. I looked over at Diancecht, whose arms were still raised upwards. He was silent. He lowered his arms and placed his hands on Smithy's head and then pressed it down, so that his whole body was submerged. It lasted for what seemed an eternity as I watched anxiously, until suddenly, Smithy's head burst through the water's surface with his eyes open, his mouth spouting water. He was alive.

I threw my arms around him, uncaring for the others. "Smithy," I cried. "Thank god."

Smithy looked at me. "Thank God? Really?"

I laughed a laugh that was more hysteria than humour. "Thank Diancecht. Thank the Well of Slane."

I kissed his mouth. It was cold and his lips were blue. "Let's get you out of there, before you catch cold. I don't want to go through this again."

"There will be no 'again'," muttered Diancecht, stepping out of the pool with Daghda's help.

I looked at him. "What do you mean?" I said tersely.

"This time and no more," he said.

I looked at Smithy. "This time, then. I only need this time."

Finn led Smithy to the edge of the pool and Daghda helped

him out, followed by me and then Finn. Smithy stood there, shivering and I placed the blanket around his shoulders.

"How do you feel?" I asked.

"Fine," he said.

"Your arm? Your side? Are they paining you?"

He shook his head. "I'm fine. Really. There's no pain."

Diancecht moved the blanket aside and began to examine Smithy. He grunted a few times and then looked up at Smithy.

"You were lucky," he said. "Everything seems to be healed." He added a few words in their tongue and Smithy gave him a sour look but said nothing.

I pulled the blanket back around Smithy, thrilled at the news of his healed wounds.

"Come on, then," I said. "Let's go home."

Smithy leaned over and gave me a squeeze. "Sounds perfect."

I looked at Diancecht. "I can't thank you enough. I know that you were reluctant to do all this, but I will be forever grateful to you for it." I turned to Daghda. "And to you for supporting me in it as well, however much you were against it."

I leaned over and squeezed Finn's hand. "And to you, too Finn. For being such a good friend through it all. I couldn't have done it without you."

Diancecht just gave a nod, his sour demeanour unchanged. Finn nodded and said it was no bother at all. Daghda placed a brief, bewildering kiss on my forehead and laid his hand on Smithy's shoulder.

"Goibhniu," he said, his voice grave. "You were returned for a reason. The time has come. We must all answer this call."

Smithy looked at him, his expression unreadable. "I know," he said finally.

"Tell Anu that we are preparing now," said Daghda. "We will be ready when the battle is upon us."

"I'll tell her," said Smithy.

"Now," said Daghda. "The boat is waiting. We'll leave you two to return across the water together. Finn and I will go to Tara with Diancecht."

I took Smithy's hand and led him to the boat where it sat moored, ready. We stepped in, one at a time, cast off and headed back across the water, towards whatever would await us there.

EPILOGUE
SMITHY

Smithy glanced around the table at the people listening to Anu attentively. He could hear her words, but they just weren't that interesting. Bríd was sitting next to him, and even that didn't give him comfort. Maura eyed him curiously, as if she suspected that something wasn't right, but he didn't care. She would never voice it to anyone else. Bríd placed her hand on his leg and began to rub it. It was all he could do not to flinch. It wasn't that he didn't want her. Or her touch. He longed for it in some ways, in his heart, but his body, well, it found it difficult. It found a lot of things difficult and it was all he could do in these few days since they'd returned to this side of the water, since they crossed, since he'd come back from the dead, to hide all of this from Bríd. From everyone.

What had come back from the dead? It didn't seem like him. His limbs sometimes found themselves at odds. His hands didn't feel able to understand what he wanted. And he felt distant from everything. Even Bríd.

"Smithy," said Anu. "Are you listening?"

"Yes, of course."

"Did you hear what I said about Balor?"

He frowned, shook his head. "Sorry, wool gathering."

She sighed and gave him a concerned look. "He's returned to America to try and get approval for his energy company's expansion over there. Hopefully that will keep him busy while we can gather our resources. There's much to do. We still haven't found and retrieved all the treasures. And Lugh. He's still a problem."

"You haven't found him yet?" asked Smithy.

"No. Maura has been out with the others, checking various places. All we know is that he's here, somewhere."

"That's not much to go on," said Maura.

Bríd remained silent, following the conversation with nods. She'd been overwhelmed with all the events and all that she was required to understand, now that Anu had let her in on the full picture of who we were and the challenges before us. She'd eagerly agreed when Anu had suggested this meeting to help her understand. But he could see she was floundering and the hand placed on his leg was a way for her to gain reassurance from him. But he had nothing to give. For so many reasons. The irony of his position didn't escape him. After wanting Bríd for so long, after enduring the heartbreak and pain of her loss, he now had her, whole, intact and wanting him. And he could give her nothing. Hilarious. It would make a fine song, an air that would endure, but he wouldn't be singing it. His music was dead.

This feeling had been with him since his return from the

Otherworld. Had it become increasingly worse? It felt that way, as each day he was exposed to more parts of his old life, of who he was. His body was no longer familiar to him, as if he was managing the limbs with a remote control, or a puppet master.

He sighed and tried to concentrate once more. "When was the last time you saw Lugh?"

Anu, Maura and Finn all looked at him quizzically.

"Nothing in a long while. Not since, well, before the Gaels. Remember?" said Finn.

Smithy nodded. "Right. Just checking."

In a way he wished Daghda was here. Somehow his presence would have helped. He understood Smithy. He knew his weaknesses and would have offered quiet support. At least he thought that was true. The memories were patchy at best. All he could remember was how he felt when Daghda had parted with Smithy and Bríd before their back here. Calm, strength, confidence. Díancecht, the fecker, had given him nothing. Just a sceptical look and a nod that only told Smithy he was on his own. And that was what he felt now, more than ever. On his own. Own, though. That implied he even knew the self that he was with. And that was far from the case. He wanted to stand, to excuse himself from this little gathering, but he didn't even dare do that. Any sudden movements involving his legs especially could lead to catastrophic failure, and he couldn't risk that. Or at least, he didn't want to, not at the moment. He would leave the "when", for now, because he knew the "when" would have to come. He couldn't risk his life or anyone else's because of his body's failure. His days of being a warrior were over. His days of being anything were over. Blacksmithing, musician, everything. At least for now. How long he could safely fake it, until he could be certain the situation was permanent, he didn't know.

Bríd leaned over to him. Or Saoirse. He should really think

of her as Saoirse, because Goibhniu was gone at the moment, for all intents and purposes. "Are you okay?" she asked.

"I'm grand," he said and forced a smile. "I'm grand."

He would try to believe it and hope that eventually it would become the truth.

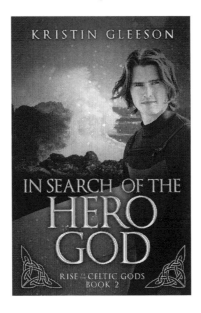

Look for the next book in the trilogy:
In Search of the Hero God
COMING IN NOVEMBER 2021
Preorder
https://books2read.com/herogod
Reviews are very much appreciated, if you can take the time.
Review link: https://books2read.com/u/mvqZnX

A NOTE ON THE MYTHS AND PRONUNCIATION

Some of the names can appear daunting to those not used to Irish or the names. And for those who like to know, I've just put a few here in case it increases the enjoyment of the novel.

Saoirse – SEER sha
    Bríd – Breed
    Aoife – EE fa
    Anu – An New/An Na (ancient, so it varies)
    Airmid – AIR med
    Cían – KEE an
    Cíara – Keer ah
    Daghda – DAHG duh
    Daragh – Da ruh
    Díarmuid – Deer mud
    Diancecht –Dee an kekt
    Eilís – I leesh
    Gearóid – Geh ROAD
    Goibhniu – Gub New (another ancient one)
    Líam – LEE um
    Sinead – Shin aid

The Myths

The myths that are explained and interwoven in this novel are from *The Book of Invasions (Leabhar Gabhala)* part of the collection of Irish myths. I have kept true to the myths, with the exception of a few interpretations and a little embellishment in the case of Bríd and Goibhniu. There is nothing in the myths that say they were together, but they are both smith gods, one female one male, so it seemed natural to link them. Bríd's fate after she married Bres is true, except for the embellishment of her rape. It isn't clear but it seemed a possible interpretation. She did give birth to three sons and died as a result of that birth.

Local myths are also interwoven. On the Kerry/Cork border you will find the Paps of Anu, breast shaped mountains that are always climbed on May 1. At their foot on the Kerry side, it is said by some that the Tuatha de Danann settled there. The site of St. Gobnait's burial and her well is also celebrated. St Gobnait was also known as a smith and there are remains of an ancient smithy there. It is my own view that it might have also been seen as a place where Goibhniu was either venerated or an ancient smith worked and invoked him there, and later became associated with the convent of religious women that was established later, led by a doubtlessly indomitable woman who came to be known as St Gobnait, a name very close to the god's and one that has no English translation in truth. (You can see my idea of her in my novel, *In Praise of the Bees*.) Some see the translation as 'Abby' but that's more than likely just an adaptation because of the 'abbess' aspect of St Gobnait's role.

ACKNOWLEDGMENTS

As usual I owe a great debt of thanks to my alpha team of readers, especially Jean, Jane, Claire and Babs and this time adding Lizzie, who gave a great fresh perspective. I also had a fantastic group of beta readers, Saorlaith, Eilín, Síleann, and Eileen who kept my Ireland real and ensured the fadas were all where they should be.

Also I want to thank my fantastic editor, Sandra, and my wonderful cover designer, Jane Dixon-Smith whose wonderful creative genius have gone a long way to help make my books a success.

And most of all, I want to thank my wonderful readers, whose support down the years has helped to make my writing such a wonderful experience.

AUTHOR'S NOTE

Originally from Philadelphia, Kristin Gleeson lives in Ireland, in the West Cork Gaeltacht, where she teaches art classes, plays harp, sings in a choir and runs two book clubs for the village library. She holds a Masters in Library Science and a Ph.D. in history and for a time was an administrator of a large archives, library and museum in America. She also served as a public librarian in America and in Ireland.

Kristin Gleeson has also published The Celtic Knot Series and The Renaissance Sojourner Series. A free e novelette prequel, *A Trick of Fate* is available free online. In addition to her novels, a biography on a First Nations Canadian woman, *Anahareo, A Wilderness Spirit*, is also available.

If you have enjoyed this book please post a review. It helps so much towards getting the book noticed.

If you go to the author website and join the mailing list to receive news of forthcoming releases, special offers and events, you'll receive an e novelette *A Treasure Beyond Worth,* a FREE prequel novelette and its ebook novel *Along the Far Shores* at www.kristingleeson.com

Music is a big part of Kristin's life and many of the books have music connected to them. Listen to the music while you read—go to www.kristingleeson.com/music and download the files. Keep checking back, as more pieces will be added to the library in the course of time.

Printed by Amazon Italia Logistica S.r.l.
Torrazza Piemonte (TO), Italy

36130794R00176